All Good Experience

The characters in this book are not intended to be those of any living persons.

To order additional copies, please contact us.
BookSurge, LLC
www.booksurge.com
1-866-308-6235
orders@booksurge.com

All Good Experience

Harry Bee

2005

All Good Experience

To my wife for all her support and understanding over the years.

Thanks To:-

Wendy - For her encouragement and proof reading and
Andy & Liam for the cover design

CHAPTER 1

O'Connells builders yard was in darkness except for some arc lights on the outside of the workshop swaying in the wind. It was raining heavily and the strong wind was driving it across the deserted yard until it battered at the sides of a raised portacabin. Inside the cabin, Steven Barkley looked across the yard and noticed there was still a light on in Seamus's office. He looked at his watch. 'Half past six, time to go.' he thought and put his papers into his briefcase. He got his coat on, put the lights out, opened the door outwards and went down the cabin steps.

Steven turned, swung the door closed and went half way back up the steps to lock it. He'd just turned the key in the lock when he heard a low growl behind him. He looked over his shoulder and there, in the dim light cast by the arc lights across the yard, was the menacing shape of Cuddles, the Doberman!

He froze with one hand on the key in the door, and the other holding his briefcase. Keeping his eye on the dog, he gently unlocked the cabin again and brought his hand to his side. The dog growled again at this movement and moved an inch closer.

'Nice boy Cuddles,' Steven croaked, but he was answered by another low growl.

He started to turn to face the dog, but another menacing growl stopped him. Steven thought desperately what he could do. He knew that because the door opened outwards, he would have to go down the steps first before he could reach the safety of the cabin. But Cuddles was making it perfectly clear that any movement would not be tolerated. Where was Seamus? 'Help!' He shouted. 'Help! Seamus help!' His cries were whipped away by the strong wind, and were lost in the vastness of the yard.

The wind was also driving the rain at him, and he was getting soaked. He risked another glance at the dog. It was still immobile, with its gaze fixed unblinkingly on Steven's back.

There was nothing for it but to try desperate measures. He carefully brought his hand up to the handle of the door again and turned it. A low growl ensued. With his heart in his mouth, he ignored it. He pulled the door open as far as it would go against his body, then, all in one movement, he went back down the steps, swung the door fully open and simultaneously swung his briefcase behind him. He felt the briefcase hit something solid and the dog yelped. He bounded up the steps and through the open door. He turned to see the hound charging up the steps towards him, jaws agape. Franticly he threw his briefcase at it. The case caught the beast in full flight causing it to lose its footing and fall off the steps. Steven grabbed the door handle and slammed the door shut.

As he stood panting, with his back to the door, Steven felt a crash, as the furious animal flung itself at it. Then it started to howl,—the most fearsome howl Steven had ever heard in his life. The door crashed again and moved on its hinges. 'Its only made of plywood,' thought Steven. 'What if he breaks in?'

There was another crash and then silence. Steven waited for a few minutes and then moved to the window and looked out. Cuddles was standing facing the cabin door. He was erect, oblivious of the wind and rain, muzzle high, and straining every sinew. He was obviously alert and ready to pounce should Steven be foolish enough to re-appear.

'You can see why they're good guard dogs,' thought Steven ruefully. 'I'd better ring for help.'

As he moved towards the telephone everything suddenly went black as the yard lights went out. 'What the....' he exclaimed. Then he heard the noise of a van starting up. 'Oh my gosh,' he thought 'Seamus is leaving!' He ran to the window and saw a van's headlights go through the big gates and then stop. Steven opened the cabin window and shouted in despair, 'Seamus, Seamus, Help!' But the wind just flung the words back into his face and he watched in despair as the gates slammed shut and the van drove off.

He grabbed the phone from its hook, but there was no dialling tone. 'On night service,' he thought miserably. 'I suppose I'll just have to spend the night here. There's no way I'm going out of that door until I can see where Cuddles is.'

'The joys of working for yourself,' he muttered as he made himself as comfortable as possible, 'Claude didn't warn me about this when I started.' .

As he followed the trim figure of Claude's secretary along the wide carpeted corridor on that bright spring day in early 1980, Steven knew he was about to take the biggest gamble of his life. 'Once I tell him about my plans,' he mused, 'there'll be no going back. He has a big mouth for a bank manager.'

The secretary gave a tap on the door and ushered Steven in to a big airy office. It was tastefully decorated in the latest pastel colours that set off the teak desk and matching conference table, surrounded by comfortable dark blue chairs. Claude Keighley-Smythe was a big man with a florid complexion gained from over imbibing at too many business lunches. He came round from behind his desk and gave Steven a perfunctory handshake. 'Now then Steven, how can I help you?' he asked as he indicated with a wave of his hand that they should sit at the conference table.

'I've decided to set up as a consultant, so I'm going to resign as Financial Director of Dugdale Engineering,' replied Steven.

Claude looked at him in astonishment 'What on earth do you want to do that for?' he said.

'I've had enough of obeying Head Office's orders, so I'm going to work for myself. I'm going to give advice to small businesses, a sort of visiting Financial Director.'

Claude pursed his lips. 'Are you sure you know what you're doing?' he warned. 'You're giving up a safe job with a good firm. What are you and your family going to live on?'

'We've got some savings, and I've done a business plan,' replied Steven, looking Claude confidently in the eye. 'We'll manage. But we'll need a bank account, so, seeing that I've dealt with you through Dugdales, I thought I'd give you the business.'

'Always happy to open a new account,' said Claude. 'We can open one now if you like. ' He got a form from a drawer in his desk and resumed his seat at the table.

'What name are you going to trade as?'

'Stemar Consultants Limited.'

'Who's going to be the shareholders?'

'My wife Margaret and I in equal shares.'

Claude looked up. 'Is that wise?'

'Why ever not?' retorted Steven

'Marriages can sometime go wrong you know. If you're on a fifty/fifty basis your wife can cause havoc by blocking everything.'

'That won't happen to us,' snapped Steven

'Fine, fine,' said Claude, hurrying on. 'Will you want an overdraft?'

'We'd better I suppose. A couple of thousand should be enough.'

'Fair enough. We'll need your personal guarantee of course.'

'What for?'

'To cover us if anything goes wrong.'

'But you know me Claude. We've dealt with each other for years.'

'I know, but I'm afraid we bankers can never be too careful,' said Claude with a condescending smile. 'Have you got a house? And has it got a mortgage?'

'Yes, but what's that got to do with it?'

'We need to make sure that you have enough assets to meet any shortfall.'

'But there's not going to be a shortfall,' Steven burst out angrily.

'How do I know? For instance, how are you going to get new clients?'

'Russell and Scott, Dugdales solicitors, have agreed to use me, and Parker Electrical, one of our sub-contractors, is thinking about it.'

'That's a good start. The Chamber of Commerce is very useful for making contacts you know. I'll have a word with the secretary if you like and get a membership form sent.'

'Thanks. It's the annual dinner soon isn't it?'

'Yee...ss,' replied Claude guardedly.

'Good. That'll be a great opportunity to meet people.'

Claude put his head down, apparently finding something very interesting to look at on the form. 'I'm afraid you won't be on our guest list this year.' He muttered

Steven looked at the bowed head in astonishment. 'Why not? You've always asked me in the past.'

Claude looked up and gave Steven another condescending smile. 'Ah yes,' he said, 'but that was as Steven Barkley, Financial Director of Dugdales. By then, you'll just be Steven Barkley, a small consultant on his own.'

Steven was stunned, and Claude, noticing his glazed look, said reluctantly, 'I suppose we might be able to fit you in this year.'

'Don't bother,' said Steven sharply.

'Well, perhaps not,' said Claude in a relieved tone. 'Right, I think that's all the paperwork done. If you and your wife could sign the forms where I've marked them, and send them back to Martin Robinson, we'll get the account opened.'

'Who's Martin Robinson?'

'Oh he's the junior assistant who deals with small business accounts like yours. Well, best of luck. Do you know who your successor is?'

'Why? Do you want to invite him to the Chamber of Commerce dinner?' Seeing from Claude's face that he had hit the mark, Steven stood up and continued 'You can keep your forms. We'll bank somewhere else, where we'll be treated as somebody's not nobody's.

He flung the papers across the table and stormed out of the room.

Steven drove home to his detached house on the outskirts of Rivingham in high dudgeon.

'What on earth's happened?' asked Margaret from the doorway of the kitchen, as Steven flung open the front door and stormed into the house.

'That pompous old fool said that we shouldn't have

equal shares because our marriage might fail.' Steven burst out, moving into the living room and throwing himself onto the settee.

'You what!' said Margaret in astonishment, following him into the room.

'And that's not all. He virtually told me that I was a nobody.'

'Surely not.' said Margaret, sitting down besides him.

'He told me that he wouldn't be inviting me to the Chamber of Commerce dinner this year, because, by then, I would be Steven Barkley a small consultant, instead of the Financial Director of Dugdales.'

'I don't believe it.'

'It's true, and it's really upset me.'

'I'm sure it has,' said Margaret putting her arms around him. 'But you're not a nobody. For a start, you're a good husband and father. You're a qualified accountant, and, from what everyone says, a clever one at that.'

'Yes all right,' said Steven, returning her embrace. 'I'm sorry. I was a fool to let him get to me like that.'

'That's better. We'll show that pompous ass that this is one couple who're going to make a success of a business *and* a marriage.'

'Yes,' agreed Steven. 'And we'll have a table at the next Chamber of Commerce dinner that's full of our clients.'

'That's the spirit.' said Margaret, 'talking of clients, a Nigel Parker rang. He wants you to ring him back.'

'Right I'll do it straight away. Let's hope it's good news.'

'What's this Nigel like?' asked Margaret. 'Have I met him?'

'As a matter of fact you have. He was one of our subcontractors who were at our table at last years Christmas do. He was the tall heavy fellow in his fifties, with a wife who was twenty years younger than he was.'

'Oh yes. I didn't really trust him. He was a bit too smooth for my liking.'

'Oh he's all right. Don't worry.'

Steven picked up the phone and dialled Nigel's number. 'Hello Nigel,' he said 'It's Steven, you wanted me.'

'Yes Steven. I've been thinking about your proposition and I've decided to take you up on it.'

'Great,' replied Steven with enthusiasm.

'There's just one thing,' mused Nigel. 'Where would you be based?'

'At home, although most of the time I'd be out at my client's offices.'

'No, no, that's not the right image. You need an office. I tell you what. We've got an empty storeroom. We could convert that. You could use our switchboard and photocopier as well. We'll charge you rent, say ten pounds a week. What do you think?'

"That's very generous.'

'That's settled then. Come round tomorrow, and my wife'll go through our books with you.'

'Right-ho. It's Commercial Street isn't it? Down by the docks.'

'That's where the office is, but we don't keep the books there. Anne works from our home in Thornfield.'

'Down on the coast?'

'That's right. Number 27 Sea View Road. You can't miss it.'

Highly delighted, Steven put the phone down and burst into the living room. 'I've got us an office to work from,' he cried.

'Marvellous,' responded Margaret. 'Tell me all about it

later. Jason wants some help with his maths homework, and Katy needs a lift to Guides.'

We're going to Helen and John's tonight' said Margaret. 'Shall we tell them that you're starting up on you're own?'

'Seeing that they're our best friends,' Steven responded, 'I think we should. You never know, John might be able to put some work my way. After all, he's bound to have lots of contacts from the garage.'

'I don't like to think of you using our friends in that way.'

'I'm not using him,' said Steven in exasperation. 'That's the way business works. Its not what you know, its who you know. Anyway, they'll think it's funny if we don't tell them, won't they?'

'I suppose so. But no touting for work.'

'OK. OK. I promise.'

After supper, Steven, puffed up with importance, said, 'We've got some news for you.'

'You're not pregnant are you Margaret?' laughed Helen.

'No. No. Nothing like that,' replied Steven, put out by Helen's flippancy. 'I'm going to set up on my own, giving financial advice to small businesses.'

'You'd better have another Glenmorangie and tell us all about it,' said John, and poured a generous measure into Steven's glass.

'Is there a demand for such a service?' queried Helen.

'I don't know,' admitted Steven. 'But I've got two clients already.' As the whisky flowed, Steven became increasingly loquacious, expounding at length about the small businessman's need for the services he could offer.

'What do you think about it Margaret?' queried Helen, when Steven eventually paused for breath.

'We've talked it over,' replied Margaret, 'and we've agreed to give it six months.'

'What happens at the end of six months?' persisted Helen.

'We'll either be divorced, or have a successful business,' laughed Margaret. 'That's right isn't it Steven?'

'Definitely,' replied Steven. As John refilled his glass, Steven fixed him with a bleary eye and said slowly, 'You see, it's not what you know, it's who you know.'

John, who'd been matching Steven's input of whisky, said deliberately, 'I quite agree.'

'So old friend,' said Steven, ignoring Margaret's thunderous looks. 'I wondered if you could put the word about for me.'

'Certainly. No problem,' said John.

'I think we'd better be going,' said Margaret curtly, and stood up.

'Oh, so soon?' said Steven.

'Its half past eleven, and you've got to work tomorrow.'

'It's all very exciting,' said Helen, 'and I think you're very brave to support him Margaret.'

'After tonight, I'm not so sure I am supporting him,' laughed Margaret.

CHAPTER 2

Well, what does it feel like to be on your own?' asked Margaret next morning.

'A bit scary,' admitted Steven, 'but once I get working it'll be all right. I'll get the bus to town and pick up my Rover.'

'Take good care of it,' warned Margaret, 'it cost us enough.'

'I know. But I think it gives the right image.'

'Hmmm,' sniffed Margaret, and started clearing the breakfast table.

As Steven proudly drove his Rover saloon onto the drive of Nigel's house overlooking the sea, he noticed, with chagrin, a new Range Rover standing by the garage. Beyond it he could see a large, sleek, speedboat gleaming in the sunshine.

Nigel greeted him at the door 'Come in, come in. I see you've got yourself a Rover.'

'Yes,' said Steven, 'its second hand, but it's a nice car. I see you've got one of the new Range Rovers.'

'Ah yes. I need that to pull the powerboat. You'll find that I'm a bit of a speed freak. You've made the right choice with the Rover. Its not too ostentatious, but it shows that you're of managerial status.'

'Thanks.'

'Now, come and meet Anne.'

Nigel ushered Steven into a large, expensively furnished sitting room. A tall slim woman uncurled herself from the settee and came towards them. She was immaculately dressed and moved with the self-confident air of a woman who is attractive, and knows it.

'Anne darling, this is Steven.'

'Pleased to meet you,' said Steven taking the proffered hand.

'So you're the man who's going to tell me how I should be keeping my books,' accused Anne, with a strong local accent which belied her expensive clothes.

'I don't know about that,' replied Steven, rather taken aback. 'I'm sure they're fine. But I understand from Nigel that you're not too happy about them yourself.'

'Oh, I'm quite happy with them. Its Nigel who wants to change them.'

'Yes,' interjected Nigel. 'I think that in the nineteen eighties we should be computerised. What's your view?'

Sensing that Anne was not very happy, Steven said soothingly, 'Computers can be of help of course, but sometimes a good manual system is all that a company needs. Look, why don't I have a glance at the books, and then we can talk about it further.'

'That's a good idea,' said Nigel, also sensing his wife's mood. 'Will you get the books darling while I make the coffee?'

'All right. But I warn you. I like my books. I know exactly what everyone owes us, who we owe, and how much we have in the bank. I'll take quite a bit of convincing that a computer can do it better.'

'Of course dear, and we won't change anything unless you agree,' said Nigel. 'Now then Steven, how do you like your coffee?'

'Could I have tea please?'

'Of course Earl Grey, China or Indian?'

Steven was stumped. 'Err, Indian'.

'Fine, with lemon or milk?'

'Milk please.'

'Right' said Nigel in a tone which gave the impression, that in *this* house, no one drank such an ordinary beverage.

Anne soon returned with the books and, after serving the drinks, Nigel withdrew.

'Right' said Steven brightly, 'lets have a look at these books.

Steven opened the books and studied them for a while. 'This is great. Do you balance the ledgers?'

'Oh yes, I have a control account in the front of each Ledger and I balance every month'

'Well done. Do you list out the balances?'

'Yes, and it takes me all day'

'I bet it does. You see, a computer system can do all of that for you automatically,' explained Steven.

'Can it? How would that work?' queried Anne.

Steven described the workings of a computerised accounts system, and as the time went on, Anne became more and more enthusiastic.

'A computer system could also give you a monthly profit and loss you know.'

'Could it? I did a night school course on accounting last year and wanted to produce some figures for us, but Nigel wasn't interested.'

Nigel poked his head round the door, 'How are you two getting on?' he queried.

'Fine' replied Anne.

Nigel looked surprised and, deciding that it was safe to do so, entered the room.

'I can see why Anne is happy with her books,' said Steven 'they're immaculate.'

Anne said, 'Steven's been telling me how a computer would help us, and I must say that I'm impressed. It would even produce a monthly profit and loss account for us. That would be good wouldn't it?'

'I suppose so,' said Nigel doubtfully. 'But what I really want it for, is to chase the debts.'

'Oh it'll do that as well,' said Anne full of enthusiasm.

'Of course we'd have to look for a programme that meets your needs,' said Steven. 'But there's quite a number of packages that would fit the bill.'

'Right then,' said Nigel. We'd better get on with it. Will you look into a suitable system for us Steven?'

'Yes, I'd be delighted to.'

'Now where shall we put it?' continued Nigel. 'It'll need a table. What about the dining room?'

'No way!' exploded Anne. 'I'm not having my dining room ruined by a dirty big computer sitting in the middle of it. No. It'll have to be set up at the office.'

'But what about security?' objected Nigel.

'Oh I'll lock everything away don't worry.'

'But we haven't any room.'

'What about that store room?'

'I've promised that to Steven,' said Nigel, with the air of a man who has played his trump card.

'Right then. I'll just have to work on that spare desk in your room.'

'But you can't do that!' cried Nigel in a horrified tone.

'Why not? I won't be there all the time. You'll still be able to have those meetings you're always in when I ring you up.'

There was a pause whilst Nigel digested this information.

'OK dear,' he said. 'You're probably right. Steven, how much is this going to cost us?'

'I would think about ten thousand pounds,' said Steven.

'As much as that?' said Nigel. 'I'm not sure we can afford it.'

'Rubbish,' interjected Anne. 'Of course we can. Anyway we can always get it on hire purchase can't we Steven?'

'Err, yes, I suppose so.'

Nigel threw Steven a murderous look. 'I still think we ought to consider it a bit more,' he said stubbornly. 'After all dear, you did say you didn't want to give up your books didn't you?'

'What's the matter?' demanded Anne. 'Don't you want me to work in your office?'

'Its not that darling. It's just that.... Well, I just want to think about it a bit more, that's all.'

'Stuff and nonsense. You go ahead and find us a suitable system Steven, and we'll decide where it's to go.'

Steven looked at Nigel who nodded wearily.

'I'll get on with it straight away. By the way, Margaret and I would like to look at that room you offered us. Would tomorrow be OK?'

'Just the job,' cried Anne. 'We'll meet you there about ten, and we can look at where I'm going to sit as well.'

Nigel was very subdued as he showed Steven out.

'Till tomorrow then,' said Steven brightly.

'Till tomorrow,' echoed Nigel in the voice of a man going to his own funeral.

That afternoon their friend, John, rang. 'Steven. You know you asked me to put the word about for you?'

'Yes.'

'Well I have done. We're members of a Garage Trade Federation, and the chap who's running it came to see me this morning. He's got an annual general meeting coming up, and he hasn't been able to get his accounts done. I told him about you and said that you'd give him a ring if you were interested. Are you?'

'Am I? Of course I am.'

'Right. His name's Alan Clark. I'll give you his telephone number.'

'Oh John that's great. Thanks very much.'

Steven dialled the number immediately.

'Alan Clark speaking,' said a soft voice.

'My name's Steven Barkley. John Keene suggested I gave you a ring.'

'Ah yes, the accountancy chappie. I've got a bit of a problem. I need some accounts doing urgently. Do you think you could help?'

'I'd have to look at the books first, but I think so.'

'Right. We'd better meet up. How about tonight at the Rivers Hotel in Dryborough at 7:30? I'll bring my wife Isobel. She does the books'

'Fine. I'll see you there then.'

That evening Steven set out for his appointment in plenty of time, but got stuck in a traffic jam on the motorway. He finally got to the hotel car park twenty minutes late. It was then that a thought struck him. He didn't even know what Alan looked like! He tried frantically to think what he knew about him. It wasn't much. Just that he would have his wife with him, and that he didn't sound very young.

There was a lounge area in the foyer with easy chairs and settees dotted around low coffee tables. Most of the seats were taken by businessmen, but almost directly in front of him sat a couple, deep in conversation. Steven strode quickly over to them 'Mr Clark?' he smiled.

The man looked up with an annoyed expression on his face. 'No' he replied curtly.

'Sorry,' said Steven and backed away.

He gazed wildly round the room and saw a small, grey

haired man sitting at a corner table with a tall, rather angular woman.

Steven hesitated, then, seeing the man giving him an encouraging look, moved quickly over to them. 'Mr Clark?' he asked again.

'Alan,' the man said softly, standing up, 'call me Alan. You must be Steven.'

'Yes. I'm terribly sorry I'm late.'

'No problem,' responded Alan. 'I'd like you to meet my wife, Isobel.'

Isobel took Steven's hand with a firm grip, and barked 'We thought you weren't coming. Did you get lost?'

'No. I got stuck in a traffic jam on the motorway.'

'We'd better get down to business,' said Alan. 'Isobel's been doing the books so I'll ask her to explain it all to you.'

Isobel produced a large brown book and said, 'I've never done any book-keeping before, so I've just used my common sense.'

Steven mentally groaned. But he needn't have worried. Isobel's system was very logical, and he was able to follow it.

'Have you any other books, such as Ledgers?' he asked.

'This is the Ledger,' responded Isobel in surprise.

'Actually, it's an analysed cash book.'

'I don't care what you call it, its a Ledger to me,' responded Isobel.

'But how do you know how much people owe you? And how much you owe your suppliers?'

'I know exactly who hasn't paid us, and as we pay everyone on the dot, we don't owe anything,' said Isobel, in a scornful tone, which brooked no contradiction.

Alan had been sitting in the corner with a quizzical

smile on his face. 'What do you think?' he asked. 'Can you have a set of accounts ready by Friday?'

'Friday! I didn't know you wanted them as soon as that.'

'The AGM's on Monday, so it doesn't give us much time.'

'I suppose not. You'll need time to get them typed up and copied. OK then. Friday. How shall I get them to you?'

'I suggest that we meet here again on Friday night.'

'Fine.'

As they came out of the hotel entrance, Alan said, 'Just one point. We haven't got any typing facilities, so we'll need them in a typed form, OK?'

Steven nodded weakly as Alan and Isobel turned away and set off for their car.

Margaret listened silently to Steven's version of the evening's events until he mentioned the deadline of Friday.

'Friday! How on earth are you going to do them by Friday? Have you done anything like this before?'

'Errr no. But I know the theory, and I'm sure we'll manage.'

'We?'

'You did work at an accountants when you left school.'

'Yes, but I was only a typist not a clerk.'

'Ah. I was coming to that.'

'What do you mean?'

'They would like the accounts typed.'

'Typed!'

'Typed.'

'And you expect me to do them!'

'I thought that if we borrowed your Dad's typewriter............,'

'Steven Barkley. You are the limit! You expect me to type out a set of accounts, on Dads battered old typewriter, when I haven't typed in twenty years. Do you know how difficult it is to type accounts, even on a good typewriter with proper tabs? How will I be able to do it on Dad's old thing?'

'You can do it,' said Steven soothingly. 'You're a very good typist.'

'Was,' retorted Margaret. 'I'm not going to do it.'

'Please' begged Steven. 'It's my first job, and it could lead to others. After all, it's a Trade Federation with a lot of members. If I do a good job for them, who knows where it will lead?'

'No!'

'Please Margaret. Please. What else could I do? Turn the job down?'

'I suppose not. But you shouldn't have agreed to get them typed.'

'I know, I know' Steven said soothingly. 'But he caught me by surprise, and there wasn't much I could do.'

'All right. I'll do it. But *you'll* have to ask Dad for the loan of his typewriter. By the way, how much are we getting paid?'

'Err. We didn't discuss a fee.'

'You what!'

'Before you start again' interjected Steven hurriedly, 'I didn't want to fix a fee before I knew how long it would take. There won't be a problem, believe me.'

'There'd better not be, and don't forget that we're looking at our new office tomorrow.'

'I haven't forgotten,' replied Steven unconvincingly

There were two girls in Parkers reception area when Steven and Margaret walked in the following morning. One of them, a small sullen looking girl, was reading a magazine, and the other, who was altogether prettier, was answering the phone. The sullen looking girl gave them a cursory glance and continued to read. The other one finished her conversation and turned to them with a bright smile.

'Can I help you?'

' I'm Steven Barkley, and this is my wife Margaret. We're here to see Nigel Parker.'

'Oh Yes. He's expecting you. Maxine here will show you to his room.'

The sullen girl closed her magazine with a sigh and stood up. She moved toward the corridor and, with a movement of her head, beckoned Steven and Margaret to follow her.

As they walked along Margaret said, 'It's a nice day isn't it?'

'Is it? I hadn't noticed,' replied Maxine in a voice which was as sullen as her face.

Steven and Margaret exchanged looks and made no further effort to engage Maxine in conversation. She led them to a door marked Managing Director, gave a perfunctory knock, opened the door, and stood back to let Steven and Margaret enter.

The room was long and fairly wide, with a desk at either end. Nigel and Anne looked up from some papers they were studying. 'Ah! there you are' said Nigel 'found us all right?'

'Yes thank you,' replied Steven. 'Can I introduce my wife Margaret?'

They shook hands and then Anne said brightly, 'I'm going to work at that desk over there,' and she pointed to the other end of the room. 'Its got a nice big top so I can spread my books out. And we can have a typist's side-piece added to take the computer screen.'

'Its going to be a bit inconvenient,' muttered Nigel. 'I thought you might like to work in the reception area with the other girls.'

'I am not one of the 'other girls',' replied Anne sharply. 'I can't stand that Maxine creature and, anyway, you were the one who was concerned about security.'

Just then Maxine entered the room with tea and coffee, plonked them down on the table, and left the room without a word.

'See what I mean?' said Anne. 'Why you continue to employ her I'll never know. Sheila's worth ten of her, yet you pay Maxine more.'

'Well, she does the invoices and things, and acts as my personal secretary,' replied Nigel defensively.

'But I'll be able to do that for you in future, won't I? It'll be just like old times.' Anne turned to Steven and Margaret. 'You see, I used to work here before we were married, but when we had our sons, I started working from home.'

'How old are your sons?' asked Margaret.

'Twelve and Fourteen. They're at boarding school, so it gets a bit lonely at home, especially as Nigel's often away on business.'

Nigel spoke up. 'Now then you two, I suppose you'd like to see the room you're going to rent. You know if you don't like it, you can turn it down, I won't be offended.'

'Let them see it first,' said Anne sharply. 'Its just next door. Come on I'll show you.'

They all trooped into the corridor and Anne flung open the door of the next room. She revealed a long narrow room, full of boxes and bits of machinery. There was dust everywhere, but the sunlight streamed in from a large window at the far end.

'How big is it?' queried Margaret.

'I think it's only about 12 by 9,' replied Nigel.

'Oh that'll be big enough,' burbled Steven happily. 'We'll only need a couple of desks and a filing cabinet. Did you say we could use your switchboard?'

'That's right,' replied Nigel. 'But you may prefer to have your own number. The telephone lines around here are in short supply, so that could be difficult.'

'Errr right' said Steven, 'and you said we could use your reception and photocopying facilities.'

'Yes, that'll be OK,' responded Nigel. 'But you'll have to take your turn if we've got a big tender going out.'

'Stop trying to put them off,' said Anne sharply. 'Anyone would think that you're trying to back out of the deal.'

'No, No. It's not that. It's just........' he tailed off weakly.

'Its just that you'd rather put *me* in here wouldn't you?'

'Well it might make more sense.'

'Rubbish. I'm going to work in your room, and that's that.'

Steven and Margaret looked at each other uncomfortably. 'If you'd rather we didn't take the room.....' said Steven.

'Look,' said Anne, 'if you're going to help me with the accounts I want you near me. This room is ideal. With a lick of paint and curtains at the window it'll soon look nice, won't it Margaret?'

Margaret nodded her head slowly. 'I suppose so,' she said. 'I've got some old dining room curtains that might just fit.'

'Right, what colour are they?' demanded Anne.

'Blue.'

'I've got a paint colour chart somewhere, so you can choose what you want. Now then, where shall we put the desks?'

'One could go against this wall here, and another one could go there,' said Steven.

'If you did that, where would you put a filing cabinet?' queried Anne.

'I see what you mean,' said Margaret. 'How about if we put the desks here, and here, and the filing cabinet there?'

'Great!' said Anne. 'I'll get some men on moving the rubbish out tomorrow.'

Back in the car Steven said, 'What do you think of that then. Are we doing the right thing?'

'Oh I think so,' Margaret replied. 'Sheila seemed nice enough, and the office is just the right size for us. I'm not so sure about that Maxine though. She's a right little madam'

'Aye she is, but with a bit of luck we won't have much to do with her.'

'I don't think anyone will if Anne has her way,' responded Margaret with a laugh. 'You do realise we're going to need desks and a filing cabinet.'

'Yes, and some chairs to sit on,' said Steven. 'Come on, we'll go to Shepherds office furnishers. I've dealt with them for years.'

That night Steven got his old textbooks out of the loft, and reminded himself of the theory of incomplete records. He and Margaret worked hard all day on Wednesday and by Thursday lunchtime things were going quite well.

'I think we'll have them finished by tomorrow morning,' announced Steven.

'Well you'd better ask Dad if you can borrow his precious typewriter,' responded Margaret. 'He's never got past the two finger stage, but that machine is his pride and joy,'

'Right. I'll ring him and see if I can get it this afternoon.'

'Of course you can borrow it,' said father-in-law Chris, 'I'll bring it round.'

'There's no need to do that,' said Steven. 'I'll collect it this afternoon.'

'No! No! Margaret will need to be shown how to set tabs and things. I'll bring it round tomorrow morning.'

When Steven gave Margaret the news she groaned. 'I love Dad dearly but I know more about that typewriter than he does. It'll take me twice as long if he's helping. Why, oh why, didn't you insist on picking the machine up?'

'I'm sorry, but what else could I do? He's doing us a favour after all.'

'OK. But you're going to have to rescue me somehow.'

The next morning Margaret's mother and father arrived with the typewriter.

'I'll just give you a hand,' said Chris.

Margaret threw Steven a despairing glance. 'It's all right Dad, I can manage.'

'No. No. You need to understand all the facilities,' responded her father, 'it won't take long.'

'Perhaps you'd like a cup of tea first?' asked Steven.

'Later,' replied Chris. 'Come on Margaret, let's get started.'

They carried the typewriter into the dining room and Steven took Margaret's mother, Kathleen, in the living room for a cup of tea and a chat.

They could hear Margaret and her father talking above the clatter of the typewriter keys and the 'ting' of the carriage return. The voices became louder and louder, until there came a scream. 'Dad. Will you leave me alone to get on with it!'

'No need to shout at me my girl. If that's your attitude, we'll go!' Chris stormed out of the dining room. 'Kathleen, we're going. You try to help people, and that's all the thanks you get.'

'Yes Chris,' said his wife, 'but you've got to remember that our Margaret was trained as a typist.'

'And I wasn't I suppose.'

'You've done very well, but you are self-taught aren't you? And Margaret did type accounts when she was younger.'

'I suppose so' sniffed Chris. 'Come on, we'll leave them to it.'

That night Alan and Isobel were waiting for Steven at the same table.

'Well, demanded Isobel. 'Were my books in order?'

'They were very good,' replied Steven. 'I'd no problem in following your system at all.'

Isobel sat back mollified, and Alan spoke up.

'Did you manage to get the accounts prepared?'

'Yes,' replied Steven, passing them over to him, 'all typed up as you requested.'

'Ah good,' said Alan, and proceeded to study the figures. After a while he said, 'does this mean we've made a profit?'

Steven looked at him in surprise. 'Of course. Didn't you know?'

'Not really. You see, I always just work on the bank figure, and at the moment we're overdrawn.'

'But that's because you are owed a thousand pounds by Robertson's. When that comes in, you'll be back in the black.'

'Well, that's a relief,' said Alan. 'I thought I was going to have to report a loss for the year.'

'Do you mean to say that you go all year without knowing if you are making a profit or not?' asked Steven. 'Don't you do management accounts?'

'I've told you,' snapped Isobel. 'I'm not an accountant. If there's money in the bank, we're OK. If there isn't, then we're in trouble.'

'Oh I entirely agree,' said Steven soothingly. 'But wouldn't the management committee like to have a regular profit report?'

'We have been asked for figures,' said Alan, 'but Isobel's so busy with her other activities, that it would have been quite a struggle to provide them.'

'Yes,' interjected Isobel. 'I'm only doing the books as a favour for Alan. I'd give them up tomorrow if we could find someone to do them.'

Alan gave Steven one of his quizzical glances, 'Would you be interested?'

Steven was taken aback. 'I hadn't really thought about it, but yes, in principal I think I would.'

'Right-ho. I'll put it to the committee on Monday. Now what about your fee for these accounts?'

'Will seventy-five pounds be OK?'

'Fine. Let me have your bill and we'll pay it on the dot,' said Alan with a twinkle in his eye. 'By the way, before you rang us, I'd talked to a firm of accountants. They told me that it would take two weeks to do the accounts and cost three hundred pounds. So thank you very much for your efforts.'

'Yes, well done,' chimed in Isobel. 'I like your style. If I have anything to do with it, you'll get the job.'

By the time he had finished telling Margaret about the nights events, Steven felt curiously deflated.

'What's the matter love?' asked Margaret.

'Oh I don't know. We did all that work. Went to all that trouble. And then I undercharged them. It's just upset me a bit that's all.'

'Never mind,' said Margaret, giving him a cuddle. 'Don't forget they 'liked your style'—that's worth something.'

'I suppose so,' said Steven cheering up. 'After all, we may be getting some more work from them.'

'Yes, I was thinking about that. Who's going to do the books for them?'

Steven looked at her with pleading eyes, 'I'd hoped you would.'

'Hmmm, I see now what people mean when they talk about putting a strain on your marriage' said Margaret with feeling.

CHAPTER 3

On Monday morning Steven presented himself at the reception desk of Dugdales solicitors, Russell and Scott, whose offices were in a large Victorian house on the outskirts of Rivingham.

Bob Russell, who was a well built, smartly dressed man in his mid forties greeted Steven warmly and then, to Steven's surprise, led the way down to the basement. He unlocked a door and led Steven into a large low room, which was warm and inviting. It had a thick carpet on the floor, and was furnished with some easy chairs and a large settee. There was a small bar in the corner, a dartboard on one wall and a full sized table tennis table down the right-hand side of the room.

'This is very nice,' commented Steven.

'Yes it is isn't it?' replied Bob. 'It's our social room. It used to be the servants quarters when this was a private house. The directors and senior staff use it after work when they want to wind down before going home. The ordinary staff can come down here in their lunch break, and we use it when we want to have a partners meeting or a private chat like now. Much more civilised than talking in an office don't you think?'

As they sank into the easy chairs, a slim young girl in her mid twenties came into the room and Bob continued 'and this is my personal assistant Jennifer, would you like some coffee?'

'Err tea please if I could,' replied Steven.

'Certainly. Tea please Jennifer, and coffee for me. I'll be

tied up most of the day but we need to have a look at that contract. Do you mind staying on a bit tonight?'

'No. Not at all,' said the girl, and blushed slightly as she left the room.

Bob leant forward in his chair and said in a confidential tone, 'Backbone of the office that girl. Don't know what I'd do without her. Now, to business. I thought I'd give you a bit of background to the firm first and then introduce you to our accounts girls. Is that OK?'

'Suits me,' said Steven.

After briefing Steven, Bob led the way up to an office on the first floor. Two women sat under a large window facing each other across a pair of desks cluttered with paper. On one side of the room was a huge safe and the rest of the wall space was taken up with filing cabinets.

'Julia,' said Bob 'this is Steven Barkley who's going to help us with the accounts.'

The older of the two women stood up. She was short and plump, with a round face framed with mousy fair hair. 'Pleased to meet you,' she said.

'And this is Flora,' continued Bob, 'Julia's invaluable assistant.' Flora took Steven's proffered hand, nodded and smiled. She was as slim as Julia was plump, with a cheerful face and her hair drawn back in a ponytail.

'Right,' said Bob. 'I'll leave you to it.'

Julia lifted a pile of files from a chair in the corner and moved it towards her desk. 'What's this all about?' she said. 'Bob told me yesterday that you were coming in, but that's all I know.'

'As I understand it,' said Steven, 'Bob wants me to prepare the management accounts and give him financial advice.'

'Does the auditor know that? He does them at the moment you know.'

'I'm not certain. I suppose so.'

'Don't be too sure,' she warned. 'What do you know about Solicitors accounts?'

'Not very much,' admitted Steven. 'I know they're governed by special rules. Something about keeping clients money in a separate bank account, and using an office account to pay your overheads.'

Julia sighed. 'I can see I'm going to have to start from scratch. Everything we do for a client is recorded in the client's ledger, with a separate account for each piece of work. Look I'll show you.'

She went to the safe and transferred a tray of large cards onto the desk. For the next two hours she explained the intricacies of solicitors accounts to Steven. 'Fascinating,' said Steven at the end of the session. 'And how do you know that everything's right?'

'The balance on the client bank account has to agree with the total of the individual balances on the cards.'

'I bet that takes some doing'

'It doesn't half.'

'When did you last do it?'

'Last month end, but we're having a bit of difficulty, aren't we Flora?'

Flora nodded her agreement. Steven said, 'I'm usually quite good at balancing, perhaps I could have a look at it.'

Julia looked doubtful 'It's in a bit of a mess.'

'That's all right.'

'I'm not so sure. I'll have to talk to Bob first.'

She rushed out of the room, leaving Steven looking bemused.

'Would you like a cup of tea?' asked Flora gently.

'Yes please,' replied Steven. 'What's up with her?'

'I'm not sure. She's a bit emotional at the moment

because her husband's lost his job. I think that's the reason she's so uptight.'

'Hmmm. Well, I suppose I'd better look at the accounts and see what happens.'

After about an hour Bob popped his head round the door. 'Fancy a spot of lunch Steven?'

'Yes please, I'm feeling rather peckish.'

'Right, we'll go to the golf club down the road.'

As they walked along Bob said, 'Well you've certainly stirred things up.'

'It seems so. But I've no idea what's gone wrong. We were talking quite happily until I offered to help with the balancing, then Julia just flipped and stormed out to see you.'

'She's convinced that you want to take over her job. I've told her it's not true, but you may have to back off a bit.'

'If that's what you want. But what about the management accounts? Do you still want me to do them?'

'Of course.'

'What about the auditor, won't he be upset?'

'Jeremy? Nothing upsets him. You've nothing to fear there.'

As Steven opened the door of the accounts office after lunch, the conversation stopped abruptly. Julia and Flora were at their desks, but leaning against one of the filing cabinets was a slim, smartly dressed man in his mid-thirties. Julia looked at the man and said meaningfully, 'this is the Mr Barkley I was telling you about.'

The man straightened up and advanced across the room with his hand outstretched, 'Hello there. I'm Jeremy Anderson the auditor.'

'Oh. Pleased to meet you,' gulped Steven.

'I think we ought to have a chat don't you?'

'Err yes, I suppose so.'

'There's a spare office down the corridor, we'll talk there.'

When they had seated themselves, Jeremy said, 'Suppose you tell me what's going on?'

'I'm not sure myself,' replied Steven. 'I've just set up on my own as a consultant, and Bob asked me help him. Unfortunately, it seems to have stirred up a hornets nest. I've upset Julia, and I have a sneaking suspicion that you haven't been told about my appointment.'

'You're quite right on both counts. But don't worry about me. I've got plenty of audit work and I was only doing the management accounts for Bob as a favour. But I am concerned about Julia. She rang me at lunchtime in tears, and begged me to come over. She's apparently terrified you're going to take her job from her.'

'I don't know what's given her that impression. All we've done is go through the books and I offered to help her to balance them.'

'Ah, there you are you see. Balancing is her work. I've never got involved with that.'

'OK then, I'll try to steer clear of the balancing.'

'Fine. Now then, I'll show you the management accounts. I've been a bit under pressure lately so they're a couple of months behind. That's probably why Bob's got you in.'.

After an hour of going through the accounts Steven had picked up the basics of the system, and they both went up to see Bob.

'Now then you old beggar,' started Jeremy. 'What are you up to? Scaring Julia half to death and dropping Steven right in it.'

Steven looked embarrassed, but Bob said with a grin, 'Oh don't mind him, that's the way he speaks to all his clients. It's a wonder he's got any left.'

'That's right,' chimed in Jeremy, 'what you see is what you get. I've no time for airs and graces.'

'I'm sorry,' said Bob. 'I should have let you know what was going on.'

'Too right you should,' responded Jeremy. 'Never mind. I'll send you the bill for the inconvenience you've caused me. I'll be off then. Best of luck Steven. If you need any help, just give me ring. Here's my card.'

Steven took the card and Jeremy breezed out of the room.

'What a character,' said Steven.

'Yes he is. But don't let his manner fool you. He's a very clever fellow, and you'd do well to cultivate him.'

'Thanks I will. Would you like me to start on the accounts straight away?'

'Yes if you can. There are one or two things happening and we need the partnerships accounts up to date.'

'Right. I'll come back next Monday. What about Julia?'

'I'll have a word with her,' promised Bob. 'Don't worry, she'll be fine.'

'I just can't understand it,' said Steven to Margaret that evening. 'I was being as nice as pie to Julia and she just blew up on me.'

'Well I must admit, you can usually get the females eating out of your hand.' commented Margaret.

'What do you mean, are you casting aspersions?' asked Steven with a laugh.

'Lets just say, you've always got on very well with your female staff, and just look at the way you got round Anne Parker.'

'OK. So what have I done wrong here?'

'It's possible I suppose, that Flora's right, and it's got nothing to do with you. But I'm not so sure.'

'Neither am I. Ah well, I'll just have to use that charm you were talking about and get her on my side.'

'Alan Clark rang earlier and asked you to give him a call.'

'Oh good, I was wondering what was happening there. I'll ring him straight away.'

'Ah! The accountancy chappie,' said the soft voice at the other end of the phone. 'How are things going?'

'Very well actually. I've just started a job which could turn out to be quite a big one.'

'Oh. So you won't be interested in doing our accounts then.'

'Oh no. I mean, I *am* interested. The job's not that big.'

'Just teasing. I'm sure you need all the work you can get. Isobel is anxious to get rid of the books as soon as she can. We're going on holiday on Friday so could I drop them off tomorrow?'

'Right-ho. Where shall I meet you?'

'I've got to see one of my members in Rivingham at half past ten, so I could drop them off at nine thirty. Have you got an office yet?'

'No. We're moving into one shortly, but I'm working from home at the moment.'

'That's OK. Just give me instructions and I'll see you at nine thirty.'

As Steven put the phone down Margaret said, 'did I hear you telling him how to get here?'

'Errr yes.'

'When is he coming?'

'Tomorrow at half past nine.'

'You what! The house is like a pigsty, and you've invited

a client here tomorrow morning. Steven Barkley, you are the limit.'

'The house looks all right to me.'

'Is he bringing his wife?'

'He didn't say.'

'I bet he is. Right, you get the Hoover out and I'll start dusting.'

'But I was going to watch the football.'

'Steven,' said Margaret with a warning in her voice.

'OK. OK. I'll get the Hoover.'

Promptly at nine thirty there was a ring on the doorbell and Steven let Alan in.

'Come into the lounge,' said Steven. 'This is my wife, Margaret.'

'Pleased to meet you,' said Alan. 'What a lovely house you have.'

'We like it,' said Margaret. 'Would you like some tea?'

'Ah yes, Steven is a tea man isn't he? A cup of tea will be fine thank you.'

'Isn't Isobel with you?' asked Steven.

'No. She's got some packing to do, and anyway she told me off for arranging to call at your house at such short notice.'

'Oh it was no problem,' lied Margaret. 'I'll just get the tea.'

'While you're doing that, perhaps Steven will give me a hand to get the books in.'

When Alan had left for his appointment, Margaret said 'What a nice man.'

'Obviously another man who can charm the ladies,' replied Steven. ''No problem' indeed, after we'd worked till eleven o'clock getting the house put straight!'

'You men just don't understand,' responded Margaret.

Steven rang Nigel. 'I need to see you and Anne about the computer.'

'I thought you were dealing with that,' responded Nigel in a grumpy tone.

'I am, but I need to ensure that we are getting a system that meets your requirements.'

'Speak English. What does that mean?'

'It means that I want to be certain that I'm giving you the right advice.'

'Well why didn't you say so in the first place?'

'Can I come round this afternoon?'

'I suppose so.'

'Will Anne be there?'

'Yes, she'll be here,' was the gloomy response.

'How's it working out?'

'Don't ask. It was the worst days work I ever did, getting you to come in.'

'What do you mean?'

'Anne's got the bit between her teeth now. She's reorganising all the office, upsetting the girls, and driving me crazy.'

'But that's not my fault.'

'No, I suppose not. But none of this would have happened if I hadn't asked you to look at Anne's books. See you this afternoon.'

At two o'clock Steven walked into the reception at Parker's to be greeted with a smile by Sheila. 'Hello again. Anne's expecting you. Can you find your own way to Nigel's office? Maxine's had to pop out.'

Anne greeted him brightly. 'Now then Steven, come and look at your new office.'

She took him into the corridor and flung open the door of the adjacent office.

Steven gasped. The storeroom had been transformed. All the rubbish had been cleared out, the windows cleaned, and a new carpet had been laid.

'Has Margaret chosen the colour scheme yet?'

'No. We didn't expect you to move so fast.'

'That's OK. I'll choose it. What colour did Margaret say the curtains were?'

'Blue I think.'

Yes. That's right. Now the carpet's burgundy, so we need something that will go with both. We'll paint it dusky pink, that'll do.'

'If you say so,' responded Steven weakly.

'Right. That's settled. Now then, about the furniture.'

'We've already ordered that,' said Steven.

'Oh. I was going to let you have two old desks that we don't need. Can't you cancel the order?'

'Not really. You see we've already paid for them.'

'Well, I suppose you can't do anything about it. Pity though, those desks would have fitted just nicely. Right, what do you want to see me about.'

'I need to discuss in detail with you and Nigel what you want from a computer system.'

'Oh Nigel can't be bothered with things like that. Anyway he's had to go out to the bank or something. I'll decide what we need.'

'Fine' said Steven. 'I'll just get some details from you. How many customer accounts will we need.......?'

On Monday, Julia showed Steven up to the spare office at Russell and Scotts. 'I'm sorry about last week,' she said. 'I got the wrong end of the stick.'

'That's OK,' replied Steven, 'these things can happen. Let's forget it shall we?'

'That's fine with me.'

'Great. I'll get started. Can I have the office bank account and the cheque stubs please?'

As Steven worked solidly through the books he began to understand the accounting system. At lunchtime Julia came in. 'Flora and I are going to get some sandwiches, would you like something?'

'I wouldn't mind a walk. I'll come with you if you don't mind.'

They got their sandwiches, and, as they ate them, they chatted about their families. Steven learnt that Julia and her husband Ken had a smallholding. However they both needed to work to make ends meet. Ken had lost his job three months ago, and since then things had been difficult. 'We bought some bullocks to fatten up just before Ken lost his job, and once we sell them we'll be OK.' explained Julia. 'We borrowed the money from the bank and they want repaying.'

'Which bank do you use?' asked Steven.

'I used the same bank that we have here, because I thought they'd be more helpful. But I'm afraid Claude Keighley-Smythe hasn't been any use at all.'

'You deal with Claude?' asked Steven.

'Yes, do you know him?'

'Know him! I should say so,' said Steven, and told them about his brush with Claude. 'My advice is to find another bank,' he concluded.

'We may do later,' responded Julia, 'but at the moment, it's quite convenient banking at the same place.'

'Flora was right about Julia,' reported Steven that night. 'It's all to do with the smallholding and the bank.'

'Maybe so,' replied Margaret, 'but why get so upset about you?'

'She probably got things out of perspective, and really did think she was going to lose her job. Anyway, everything is sweetness and light now. The old Barkley charm has worked again.'

The next day, Steven found his own way up to the spare office, and settled straight down to work. Half way through the morning he went into the accounts office and said to Julia, 'How do you arrive at the amounts to transfer from the Client account into the Office account?'

'We do a weekly list of fees to be transferred.'

'Great. Could I have the lists for the last three months?'

Julia's face darkened, 'What for?'

'I want to check them with the Office bank account.'

'Why? Don't you trust me?'

'It's nothing like that. I just want to check that I've picked up the right amounts.'

'Why? Jeremy never did.'

'I think he did.'

'Well he never told me about it. You're interfering with my side of things and I'm not having it. I'm going to see Bob.'

She charged out of the room and slammed the door behind her.

Red in the face Steven went back to his office and called Jeremy on the phone.

'Now then old sport, how're doing?' breezed Jeremy.

'Not very well. I've upset Julia again.'

'What are you doing? She's always been fine with me.'

'I know, and that's what's bothering me. Can you come over again?'

'I'm pretty busy. I can come about five if you like.'

'Yes please.'

Half an hour later Bob came into the room with a grim expression on his face.

'What on earth's going on Steven? Julia has been with us for over ten years with never a problem. Then you come in and she's in hysterics. I've had to send her home. What did you say to her?'

'Nothing, and that's what's worrying me. I only asked her for the fee transfer figures, and she blew her top.'

'There's no mystery about them. I've a copy I can let you have. It must be the way you're asking her.'

'But I'm being extra nice to her. We had lunch together yesterday, and it was all sweetness and light. You ask Flora.'

'I will. I must say Steven, this is not working out as I had expected. I'm beginning to think that we've made a big mistake.'

'I can understand that, but I'm sure we can sort it out. Jeremy's coming over at five and we could talk about it then. Now, if you could let me have those fee figures, I'll get on.'

'OK. But any more problems and we'll have to call it a day.'

For the rest of the day Steven kept his head down and only stirred from the spare office to get printouts from Flora and cups of tea from the machine.

At four thirty he rang Margaret. 'Hello love. I'm afraid something's cropped up and I might be late.'

'Why? What's happened?'

'I've upset Julia again, but I think I know what the problem is. I've got to check it out with Jeremy first, and it could take quite a while.'

At ten past five Jeremy breezed into the room. 'Now then old sport, what's this all about? What've you been doing to my favourite accounts clerk?'

'Its not what I've been doing,' replied Steven wearily, 'its what she's been doing that's the problem.'

'What do you mean?' asked Jeremy.

'I can't balance the fees paid out of the Client account, with the amounts received into the Office account. As far as I can see there's a discrepancy of fifteen hundred pounds.'

'You're joking!'

'I only wish I were. I haven't said anything to Bob yet as I need you to check it.'

They went through the figures and after a while Jeremy said. 'You're right, there's a hare away somewhere. But let's not jump to conclusions. How are you for staying back a bit?'

'I'll stay all night if needs be,' replied Steven.

'Good man. I'll give the little wifey a ring, and we'll get started.'

Just then Bob came in. 'Now then you two, working late?'

Jeremy shot Steven a warning look. 'Steven's got a couple of queries so we're staying back a bit to get them sorted out. Is that all right?'

'Certainly. I'll be downstairs playing table tennis with Jennifer for a while, so just drop the latch on the door as you leave. What shall we do about Julia?'

'Could we see you about that tomorrow morning? We

got our heads into the figures and we haven't really had time to talk about it,' lied Jeremy.

'OK. But it'll have to be first thing.'

'Fine. See you at nine.'

The two accountants worked well into the evening. Finally Jeremy threw down his pen and looked across the table at Steven. 'You were right. Who would have thought it? Julia of all people.'

'It only seems to have happened in the last three months,' said Steven.

'Yes, thank goodness.' said Jeremy with feeling.

'What do you mean?'

'Well old sport. If it'd been going on any longer, I'd have had some explaining to do. I could've been reported to the Institute, and that would've finished my practice.'

'Surely not.'

'You don't know the profession. Anyway, thanks to you, its been found early.'

'But you'd have found it at the end of the year.'

'I'm not so sure. Anyway, thanks for telling me first, and not rushing straight to Bob. I owe you one for that. We'd better pop down to see Bob and break the news to him.'

They went downstairs and tried the door of the social room. It was locked.

'They must have gone home' said Steven.

'Ye...ss,' responded Jeremy thoughtfully, then he said in a louder voice, 'I'll give him a ring after dinner. Come on, let's go home.'

'The funny thing,' said Steven to Margaret, later that night, 'is that it only started three months ago. And it's the same amount every month, five hundred pounds.'

'That's about the time her husband lost his job wasn't it?'

'Yes, that's probably got something to do with it. We'll know tomorrow morning.'

'There's one good thing. You're fatal charm wasn't at fault.'

'No thank goodness. It must have been a real shock to Julia to hear that someone else was going to look at the books. When she thought that I was just doing the Office account, she felt she was safe. Then I asked her for the fee lists, and she knew the game was up. Poor thing!'

'Yes. Poor thing. She must be in a lot of difficulty to risk everything like that.'

Bob greeted Steven and Jeremy with a grim face. 'Thanks for your phone call last night Jeremy. I had another one from Ken early this morning. Julia was rushed into hospital last night with pains in her chest and gasping for breath. She's out of danger now, and he's waiting downstairs to see us. I'll go and get him.'

Bob ushered into the room a big, heavily built man, dressed in rough clothes, and fiddling nervously with his cap. 'Sit down here Ken,' said Bob kindly. 'Can I get you anything to drink?'

'No thanks,' replied Ken in a broad dalesmans voice, and looked curiously at Steven and Jeremy.

'This is Jeremy our auditor, and Steven Barkley who's caused all the fuss.'

'It weren't 'is fault,' said Ken gruffly. 'Julia said 'e were a nice man. It's just that everythin' gorr on top of 'er. What with the bank an' ev'rythin'.'

'What about the bank?' asked Steven.

'We borrowed three thousand pounds a while back to buy some bullocks. We should've sold 'em three months ago, but the bottom's dropped out of the market, and we can't get our money back. We asked the bank to wait, but they won't. They say they'll teck the farm off us unless we pay sommat off each month.'

'And they want five hundred a month,' cried Steven.

''ow did you know that?' asked Ken puzzled.

The other three men looked at each other. 'Ken,' said Bob softly. 'I'm afraid we've got something to tell you.'

When Bob told Ken what they had discovered, he put his head in his hands. 'Ah wondered where the money was cummin' from,' he said in a low voice. 'But she allus looked after that side of things. No wonder she was in a state. What's to become of us now?'

Once again the three men looked at each other. Then Bob spoke again. 'I'm very sorry Ken, but in the circumstances we can't keep Julia on. Under the terms of our fidelity bond we would have to report this, and the insurance company would insist on us taking Julia to court.'

Ken looked up with horror on his face. 'Oh no!'

'The way round it,' continued Bob, 'is for Julia to resign on the grounds of ill health. Stress of the job etceteras. We'll treat the fifteen hundred pounds as a loan, and you can pay us back when you're on your feet.'

'Oh thank you. Thank you,' cried Ken. 'We'll pay you back, I promise.'

'I'm sure you will,' said Bob briskly. 'That's settled then. Who did you say your banker was?'

'Claude Keighley-Smythe,' interrupted Steven.

'Claude Eh! Right we'll soon sort him out. Driving my staff to a heart attack indeed. Don't you worry Ken. I think you'll find that Claude is a bit more amenable in future. If not, he'll lose our account, and a few more as well.'

'Phew,' said Jeremy when Ken had gone. 'I wouldn't want to go through that again!'

'Neither would I,' exclaimed Steven. 'You were very generous Bob.'

'I suppose so. But, if this ever came out, the Law Society would ask some very searching questions. It's a good job for all of us that we took you on Steven. Now then, we'll get an advert in the paper straight away, but I wonder if you could cover for us until we get someone?'

'Me? But I don't know enough about Solicitors accounts.'

'Now's your chance to learn. I'll ask Flora to work full time for a while and Jeremy will keep you straight won't you?'

'Delighted to old boy. It's the least I can do.'

CHAPTER 4

When Steven arrived home that evening Margaret was sitting on the living room floor, surrounded by blue curtain material, carpet samples, and colour charts.

'Hello,' said Steven. 'What are you up to?'

'I'm choosing the colour scheme for our new office of course,' replied Margaret. 'I thought this grey carpet would go well, and we could paint the walls primrose. What do you think?'

Steven gazed at her in horror. 'Didn't I tell you that Anne has already got a carpet down?'

'No you did not,' replied Margaret grimly. 'What colour is it?'

'Burgundy, and she's going to paint the walls dusky pink.'

'Burgundy! Dusky pink! I hate pink walls. I thought we were going to choose the colour scheme.'

'So did I,' agreed Steven. 'But I'm sure you'll like it when you see it.'

'Well that was a waste of an afternoon,' snapped Margaret as she started to pick up the curtains and samples, 'you might have told me.'

'I'm sorry love, it went completely out of my mind.'

'Too busy gazing into her dark brown eyes I suppose.'

'What do you mean?'

'Oh nothing. Forget it.'

'Are you jealous or something?'

'She does seem to get her own way a lot.'

Steven gently took her arm and pulled her up. 'Don't be

silly,' he murmured as he put his arms around her and gave her a kiss. 'You're the only woman who gets her own way with me. And anyway her eyes are blue not brown.'

Margaret gave him a thump, and then returned his kiss. 'All right,' she said 'I forgive you, but watch what you're doing, or she'll end up running your life like she does Nigel's.'

With the help of Flora, Steven spent the next morning working his way through the paperwork at Russell and Scotts.

It was nearly lunchtime when Bob entered the room. 'Glad to see you're settling in Steven,' he said. 'We're having a partners meeting in half an hour and I'd like you to join us. It'll be a good opportunity for you to meet the others and hear what's going on.'

'Fine,' Steven responded, 'where will it be?'

'We try to keep our meetings informal, so it'll be in the social room.'

'Social room,' sniffed Flora when Bob had left the room, 'more like love nest if you ask me.'

'What do you mean?' asked Steven.

'You've seen the way Bob and Jennifer look at each other haven't you? Well they're always working late, and finishing off down stairs in the social room.' The last two words were spat out with venom.

'But they play table tennis and unwind,' responded Steven.

'That's what *they* say. But we girls know differently.'

'Why? Has Jennifer talked about it?'

'That stuck up madam? No way. Just take it from me, we know.'

Steven decided to drop the subject and turned the conversation to fee slips.

In half an hour Bob appeared and took Steven downstairs to the social room. Standing in a group by a table were four men and Jennifer.

Bob introduced Steven to the partners. James Scott, his fellow founder of the firm, was well over six-foot tall, slimly built with a shock of dark hair. Ashley Radford, the next oldest in service, was very smartly dressed and had an upper class accent. The 'newest recruits', were Paul Chambers, who was slightly scruffily dressed and spoke with a strong local accent, and Simon Booth, who was about Stevens age and looked very pleasant.

'Lets get started shall we?' said Bob. 'Steven, please would you sit next to Jennifer.'

As they took their seats Steven noticed that there was a definite pecking order. Bob sat at the end of the table, flanked by James and Ashley, with Paul and Simon together on one side of the table, facing Jennifer and Steven.

'First, let me welcome Steven to our meeting,' said Bob. 'I don't think I need to dwell on the unfortunate happenings of last week. Suffice to say, we owe Steven a vote of thanks for the way in which he handled the affair.'

'Hear. Hear.' chimed Paul. 'If he hadn't kept his mouth shut we'd have the Law Society breathing down our necks.'

'Oh I don't think so,' commented Ashley in a rather superior tone. 'We're a very well respected firm, and with my contacts on the committee I'm sure I could have stopped it going any further.'

'Like you stopped the comments about our advert,' sneered Paul.

'That was different,' retorted Ashley. 'That advertisement was in bad taste.'

'That was a matter of opinion,' cried Paul. 'Anyway, it was agreed at a partners meeting.'

'That neither James nor I were present at,' snarled Ashley.

'That's all water under the bridge,' said Bob. 'Let's get down to today's business.'

The rest of the meeting proceeded smoothly enough, but Steven noticed that Paul made most of the comments, whilst Ashley invariably took objection to them. When James made the occasional comment, it was usually to support Ashley, whereas Simon supported Paul. Bob seemed to enjoy the cut and thrust of the arguments, and usually ended up supporting Paul's view. Jennifer concentrated on making notes and uttered not a word. Steven's contribution was limited to a few comments on the overheads, and a promise to produce management accounts for next weeks meeting.

That evening, when Flora had gone, Paul entered the room. 'There's my time sheets for today,' he said, throwing them onto the table.

'That's very efficient,' commented Steven.

'Well I use a computer you see, not like the others, who are still using quill pens.' He sniggered at his own joke. 'What did you think of our fiasco of a meeting this morning?'

'I found it very interesting,' replied Steven.

'Interesting my foot! Children's television is more interesting than that. In fact, come to think of it, James and Ashley would make a good pair of flowerpot men. They just talk rubbish all the time.' Again he sniggered at his own joke.

' I gather you've not got much time for them,' said Steven mildly.

'Not much time for them? I hate them. They're all that

I'm against in the profession. Stuffy fuddy-duddies who won't move with the times.'

'What about Bob?'

'Oh Bob's all right. He's on our side. He's just waiting for an excuse to get rid of James and Ashley, and then we'll really see some action.'

'Oh,' said Steven, nonplussed.

'Yes. And it's going to happen sooner, rather than later. That's why we need your accounts, so that we can prove that we need to make some changes.'

'But how will that help?' asked Steven.

'Well you see,' explained Paul. 'Bob, Simon and I want to move into the area of personal accident claims. It's big business in the States, but its only just getting going here. That's what the advert was about. We pushed it through when those old buffers were at a golf tournament, and they were really mad when they found out about it.'

'But didn't Jennifer's minutes show what was going on?'

'They were mysteriously late that week,' said Paul with a laugh. 'Jennifer will do anything for Bob. And I mean anything,' he said with a leer.

Just then, Bob poked his head round the door. 'Still here Steven?' he said.

'Just off,' replied Steven and, with a nod to Paul who was looking rather uncomfortable, followed Bob down the stairs.

'Getting on all right?' asked Bob as they went out of the front door.

'Yes thanks,' replied Steven. 'It'll be better when I get to know everyone. That meeting was a help this morning.'

'Ye...ss,' said Bob thoughtfully. 'As you can see, we have one or two clashes of personality, but I'm hoping to resolve them soon. Well, here's my car, goodnight.'

As Steven opened his car door, Paul suddenly materialised beside him. 'Did Bob say anything?' he hissed.

'What about?'

'You know. Jennifer.'

'No. Why should he?'

'I just wondered if he'd overheard me that's all.'

'I shouldn't think so,' said Steven. 'Anyway, he didn't say anything to me. Goodnight.'

'Goodnight,' muttered Paul, and slunk away into the darkness.

Margaret greeted him with the words, 'Your girlfriend's been on the phone.'

'Girlfriend? Who do you mean?'

'Anne Parker of course.'

'Oh her. What did she want?'

'Apparently the room is ready, and she wants you to move in tomorrow.'

'Tomorrow! I can't do that. I've got to be at Russell's.'

'I told her that, but she wouldn't take no for an answer. You'd better give her a ring at home, and see if your fatal charm has any effect.'

Steven scowled and picked up the phone in the hall.

'Ah. Steven,' cried Anne. 'Did Margaret give you the good news?'

'Yes,' replied Steven cautiously.

'Good. I thought you'd be pleased. You can move in tomorrow.'

'I'm afraid we can't do that,' said Steven, 'you see I have to be at a clients office all day tomorrow.'

'Oh! But I wanted you to see it.'

'We could come on Friday.'

'That's no good. I'll be away. No it'll have to be tomorrow. Will Margaret be free?'

'Yes I think so,' said Steven, ignoring Margaret's gesticulations.

'That's all right then, she can come to see it.'

Steven looked at the signs that Margaret was making and responded, 'I'm sorry Anne, I'm afraid Margaret hasn't got the car tomorrow.'

'That's no problem. I'll pick her up about 11:30 and we can have a girls lunch together afterwards. OK?'

'OK,' responded Steven weakly and put the phone down.

Margaret didn't say a word, but stormed out of the room and started banging pans around in the kitchen.

The children came into the hall from the living room and Jason murmured as he started to climb the stairs, 'I don't know what you've done Dad, but I wouldn't count on getting any dinner tonight.'

Katy followed him up the stairs saying, 'I think we'd better do our homework.'

Steven walked hesitatingly into the kitchen.

'What do you want?' growled Margaret.

'I'm sorry.'

'You're always sorry, but this time you've gone too far.'

'What else could I do?'

'You could have stood up to her.'

'But I did. I told her I couldn't come.'

'Yes and landed me with the job instead.'

'You'll get a free lunch out of it.'

'That's another thing. 'Girls lunch' indeed. What does she think we are? A couple of schoolgirls?'

'It'll give you a chance to get to know her better. After

all, we are going to be working in the same office. And she is our client.'

'I suppose so.'

'I'm sure so. I bet you'll have a good old chinwag. Errr, any chance of some dinner?'

'After what you've just done! No way. If you want something to eat, there's a can of beans in the cupboard. You can make yourself beans on toast.'

The next morning Steven handed Paul's time sheets to Flora. 'Paul gave me these last night. I suppose you record them on the various jobs he's done.'

'Yes that's right,' replied Flora, 'but we call them matters, not jobs. I bet he tried to get you on his side.'

'What do you mean?'

'Come off it. Ashley and he are always at each others throats, and they're forever trying to get people to take sides. I bet you any money Ashley'll collar you today.'

'Don't be silly,' responded Steven. 'I haven't been asked to take sides.'

'You will be, just wait,' said Flora with a knowing smirk.

Later in the day Steven took a cheque into Ashley to get it signed. After he had done so Ashley gave Steven a thoughtful look. 'How are the accounts coming on?' he asked in an offhand tone.

'Slowly I'm afraid,' responded Steven. 'You see, I'm concentrating on keeping the day to day activities going, so the accounts are taking a back seat at the moment.'

'But we can't have that!' cried Ashley. 'Those accounts are vital to the future of this practice.'

'Oh surely not,' replied Steven, taken aback at the vehemence of Ashley's response. 'They're only monthly figures after all.'

Ashley sighed. 'They're the half years' figures,' he said, as if to a little child. 'If they're bad, we might have to take drastic action, and if they're good, we can carry on as we are.'

'I see,' said Steven slowly.

'Do you? I hope so. I know you accountants can make the figures say anything you want, but if you produce a set of horrible results, which gives that upstart Paul an excuse to start throwing his weight about, then you'd better look out.'

'I don't know what you mean,' said Steven stiffly. 'My accounts will reflect accurately what is the true state of affairs.'

'Yes, yes, of course,' said Ashley. 'But, for the good of the firm, if you have a chance to show the figures in a good light, you'll do so won't you?'

'As I've already said. I'll table the correct figures, no matter what picture they show,' snapped Steven, and stalked out of the room.

He then went to Bob's room to get the second signature on the cheque.

'What's up with you?' asked Bob as he signed the cheque below Ashley's signature.

'Nothing,' replied Steven shortly.

'Come on. Something's biting you. Has Ashley been getting at you?'

'As a matter of fact he has. He practically asked me to cook the books to show a favourable set of figures for the half year.'

Bob sighed. 'Sit down Steven and I'll explain what is happening. Our traditional market is the business community in the area. But Paul and Simon want to move into the personal accident business. Ashley and James are against it, hence the squabbling.'

'I'd already gathered that much from Paul last night.'

'He didn't waste much time did he?' observed Bob.

'But what has it got to do with me?' asked Steven.

'We are scheduled to make a decision on the personal accident work at the next meeting. The last accounts we had showed a downturn in profitability, and if that has continued, it gives Paul more ammunition to push for us to take on the personal accident work'

'But if they show you are doing OK?' queried Steven.

'Then Ashley's hand is strengthened.'

'Hmmm. Either way, I'm going to be in the firing line.'

'I'm afraid so. But you wanted the job.'

'True. But I didn't bank on being a football.'

'Oh don't worry,' laughed Bob. 'I'll be the referee.'

'Where do Simon and James stand in all this?'

'They're like me, heartily sick of the whole business. Any way, next week we'll get it all sorted out, one way or the other.'

Steven arrived home that evening to a delicious smell of cooking. He walked into the kitchen and gave Margaret a kiss. 'That smells nice,' he said.

'It's a peace offering for last night,' replied Margaret.

'Does that mean that today's 'Girls lunch' went OK?'

'Yes it does, and I'm sorry I got upset yesterday. She's quite nice really, and only wanted to help. She apologised for rushing ahead, but pointed out that you did agree to what she suggested.'

'I agreed?'

'Yes you did. You admitted as much to me.'

'Oh. So its all my fault is it?'

'Of course. Now what vegetables do you want with your pork casserole?'

'Cauliflower and peas please. What did the room look like?'

'It was very pleasant. Not my choice of colours of course, but the curtains go quite well.'

'Where did you go for lunch?'

'We went to Cromwell Grange.'

'Very posh.'

'Yes. They had a lovely salad bar, fresh salmon and every cut of cold meat you could think of. It was lovely. Then I had profiteroles to finish with. Marvellous!'

'Beats my sandwich from the corner shop. What did you talk about?'

'Oh this and that. She's a very lonely person. They haven't got many friends, and most of those are really business acquaintances. They dote on their sons, and I get the feeling that now that they're away at school, they haven't got much in common.'

'Hmmm. You'll have to ask her to the Womens Fellowship.'

'I might just do that. Now go and get changed, and I'll serve you your peace offering.'

'Thanks. We'll get the furniture delivered as soon as we can and then we'll really be in business.'

CHAPTER 5

The next few days flew past, as Steven concentrated on keeping the books and preparing the management accounts at Russell's, whilst Margaret made the arrangements to move into their new office. Finally, the great day arrived, and Steven and Margaret sat at brand new desks in their own office.

Anne popped her head round the door. 'How're you settling in?'

'We're very comfortable thank you,' replied Margaret.

'Great. I've told Sheila to give you all the help you need. Now then, Steven, we need to get on with choosing this new computer.'

'Right,' responded Steven. 'I'll just get Margaret started on these books for the Garage Trade Association, then I'll pop in and see you and Nigel about it. By the way, where's Maxine? Is she sick or something?'

Anne's face tightened. 'She's left,' she said brusquely.

'Anything to do with what we were talking about?' asked Margaret.

'You could say that,' replied Anne. 'I just told her what I thought about her, and she walked out.'

'Well done,' said Margaret.

'Yes, I'm quite pleased with myself,' responded Anne, and left the room.

'What was that all about?' asked Steven.

'Oh just girls talk,' replied Margaret with a smile.

When Steven went into the office next door, Anne was sitting at one end of the room, typing some invoices on a top-of-the-range electric typewriter. Nigel was sitting at the other end, talking on the telephone.

He motioned to Steven to sit down in front of him, and continued his conversation. 'Yes John, I know our account is in a bit of a mess, but we're trying to do something about it. As a matter of fact I've just taken on someone to sort us out. His name's Steven Barkley, and I'll introduce you to him when you come next week. OK? We'll see you on Tuesday. Bye.'

He put the phone down and turned to face Steven. 'That was John Whittaker, the debt controller at our biggest supplier Parnell Electric's. The account's in a bit of a mess, so he's coming up next week to sort it out. Do you think you could give Anne a hand with balancing it?'

'Certainly. We'll have a look at it after we've talked about the computer.'

'Oh that. I'm very sorry Steven, but I've got to go out to the gym. Sort it out with Anne will you?'

'But surely you want to know what I'm proposing, and how much its going to cost?'

'Yes of course,' he said, as he left the office. 'Discuss your proposals with Anne, and let me have a copy.'

Steven looked across at Anne who said, 'Don't worry, he's always like that when he's got something on his mind. He'll go to the gym, and then he'll walk round the shops or something for a couple of hours until he's made his mind up what to do.'

'I didn't think the computer was worrying him that much,' said Steven.

'Oh no, its got nothing to do with that,' responded Anne. 'Now then, what system are you proposing we choose?'

'I thought this Unicorn system looked quite good. Their local agent is Shepherds, who are eager to give us a demonstration.'

'Right. We'll go tomorrow,' affirmed Anne.

'Errr, I can't do tomorrow.'

'Why not?'

'I've got an important meeting to attend for another client.'

'Can't it be put off?'

'I'm afraid not.'

'Oh very well then. How about the day after tomorrow?'

'That'll be OK.'

'Right. Make us an appointment,' ordered Anne. Now, about Parnell's account............'

That afternoon, Steven drove over to Russell's and went upstairs to see Bob. 'I've got the accounts finished,' he said, and placed the papers on Bobs desk.

'Ah good!' said Bob. 'How are they looking?'

'Overall they're not too bad. You are still making a reasonable profit, but you're 10% down on last year's figures.'

'Hmm. Can you see why?'

'I've analysed the fee income, and whilst three of you have a slight increase, both Ashley and Paul's figures are down.'

'I can explain that. Paul has been investigating the feasibility of going into the personal accident market, and Ashley is vice president of the local branch of the Law Society.'

'It still seems a lot of lost time to me.'

'I agree. It's had more effect than I thought. Can you come to the meeting tomorrow?'

'Yes. I've made arrangements to be free.'

'Good. It might be useful to have an independent witness.'

'It's not going to come to that, is it?'

'You never know,' replied Bob. 'The meeting's at eleven o'clock, so I suggest you hand out the accounts at nine. That'll give everyone time to read them before the meeting, but not too much time to start lobbying!'

Steven went back to the accounts office and started to photocopy the schedules. Ashley walked in and said, 'I see that you've completed the figures. Can I have my copy?'

'I'm afraid not,' said Steven. 'Bob told me to hand them out at nine o'clock tomorrow morning.'

'But that's preposterous,' blustered Ashley. 'I have a Law Society breakfast meeting tomorrow morning, and I won't be here until ten thirty. I want my copy now.'

'I'm sorry,' replied Steven firmly. 'But Bob's instructions were very clear. I was not to hand out the accounts until nine o'clock.'

'We'll see about that,' stormed Ashley, and strode out of the room .

At five o'clock Steven was locking the accounts in his briefcase when Paul sidled into the room. 'I hear you've completed the accounts, but we're not allowed to see them until nine tomorrow. I've got a meeting first thing, so I presume that I can have mine now.'

'I'm afraid not,' replied Steven.

'Oh well. It doesn't matter,' sneered Paul. 'You see I already know what's in them.'

'Do you?' queried Steven.

'Yes. Our profits are down by 10%, and its due to a drop in fees earned by a certain partner. Namely Ashley, with his Law Society meetings.'

'What makes you think that?' asked Steven.

'Bob told me.'

'Oh!'

'Yes. I told you he was on my side. We've been working out a strategy to dissolve the partnership and then form a new one, with Bob, Simon and myself.'

'Can you do that?'

'Oh yes. It only requires a majority vote of all the partners and 'Bob's your uncle,' or senior partner in this case,' he sniggered.

'So that's what he meant,' said Steven thoughtfully.

'What's that?'

'Oh nothing. Its just something Bob said about sorting it all out one way or the other.'

'We'll certainly do that all right,' cried Paul. 'Til tomorrow then. Goodnight.'

As he left the office, Steven met Ashley in the corridor. 'Ah! Barkley, I don't need those accounts until ten thirty after all,' he said, with a self-satisfied smirk on his face. 'You see, Bob's told me all about what's in them. Goodnight.'

Steven stood perfectly still for a moment, and then, turning on his heel, ran up the stairs to Bobs office. He gave a perfunctory knock and walked in. The room was empty.

He flung open the adjoining door to Jennifer's office.

'Where's Bob?' he cried to the startled girl.

'He's had to go out to a meeting. Is there a problem?'

'I'll say there is. He tells me not to release the accounts until tomorrow morning, and then he tells Paul and Ashley what's in them. What's he playing at?'

Jennifer looked uncomfortable, and said, 'I'm sorry, I don't know, but he never does anything without a good reason.'

'Well he'd better have one first thing tomorrow morning.'

'Oh. Didn't he tell you? He won't be in until ten thirty.'

'Damn,' said Steven, and left the room still fuming.

Promptly at eleven o'clock the next morning, Bob called the meeting to order. 'We have two items on the agenda. The management accounts for the first six months of the year, and the decision as to whether or not to go into personal accident business. I suggest we take the accounts first. Steven, would you like to guide us through them?'

Steven started to present the figures, but, when he explained that the fee income had dropped by 10%, he was interrupted by Paul, who said, 'We all know what that's down to, its Ashley and his fancy Law Society work.'

'And what about the time you waste on this mad personal accident scheme?' exploded Ashley. 'That's what's responsible for the drop.'

'I think we ought to let Steven continue,' said Bob mildly. 'Perhaps Steven, we should look at the fees analysis.'

'Certainly,' said Steven. 'If you'll turn to the back page, you will see that I've analysed the fee income by partner, and by type of work. I've also compared it with last year's results, and you can see that Bob, James and Simon all show small increases, but both Ashley and Paul show decreases of 12%.'

Paul and Ashley looked dumfounded.

'But you told me it was all down to Ashley,' squeaked Paul.

'And you told *me* it was Paul's fault,' cried Ashley.

'I think you will recall, that what I actually told each of you is that the other person's results were down by 12%. Neither of you asked about your own figures.'

'My work on PA was for the future of the practice,' said Paul.

'Who says so?' cried Ashley. 'My work with the law Society has done more for the future of the practice than your secret meetings will ever do.'

'What secret meetings?' cried Paul.

'It's common knowledge that you've been having a lot of meetings with Harry Simpson. In fact, you were there again this morning. I for one, would like to know what you were talking about.'

Paul turned red in the face. 'It's none of your business,' he replied. 'Anyway, what about your cosy breakfasts with Richard Langhorne? What are you up to?'

'That's all Law Society business, as you well know,' replied Ashley.

'Tell that to the marines,' snorted Paul.

'Gentlemen, Gentlemen,' interrupted Bob. 'Lets just calm down shall we?' 'Any more questions on the accounts? No? Then we'll proceed to the next item on the agenda. The decision on whether or not to move into personal accident work.'

There followed a heated debate on the merits and demerits of personal accident work. Paul argued passionately for the scheme, and Ashley violently opposed it. Bob, James and Simon kept quiet for the most part, although Bob made some telling comments, which, to Stevens eye, only seemed to fuel the argument.

Finally Bob called a halt.

'Right gentlemen, you've all had your say. It's time to vote.'

'All those in favour raise their hands.' Paul and Simon put their hands in the air.

'All those against.' Ashley and James raised their hands.

'So its down to you Bob,' said Paul triumphantly.

'Ye..es' said Bob thoughtfully. 'I'm going to abstain.'

'You can't do that,' cried Paul and Ashley in horror.

'Oh yes I can,' said Bob. 'You see, I've come to the conclusion that this partnership has become unworkable.'

'I agree,' interrupted Paul. 'I suggest that we dissolve the partnership, and set up a new one with those partners that can work together.' He sat back with a self-satisfied smirk on his face.

'I agree as well,' said Ashley. 'I think it is time that those of us who think and work in a truly professional manner, should regroup and let the riffraff paddle their own canoe.'

Paul's smirk disappeared, to be replaced by a puzzled frown.

'Right' said Bob. 'I'm glad that we all seem to be thinking along the same lines. Have you anything to say James?'

'Only that I'm sorry that it's come to this,' replied James. 'Are you absolutely sure you want to dissolve the partnership Ashley?'

'Positive,' replied Ashley fiercely.

'Have you anything to add Simon?' asked Bob.

Simon shook his head.

'Right then. All in favour of dissolving the partnership raise their hands.'

All five hands were raised.

'Steven, you are a witness that the vote was unanimous. We don't want anyone saying afterwards, that Jennifer didn't minute the proceedings correctly, do we?'

Paul shuffled uneasily in his seat.

'Gentlemen. That concludes the meeting of the old partnership. If Ashley and Paul could leave the room, the rest of us can get on with the business of the new partnership.'

'What did you say?' cried Paul.

'James, Simon and I formed a new partnership last night, to carry on the business of the old one.'

'But you told me that the new partnership would be with James and I,' interjected Ashley.

'No it wasn't, it was to be with Simon and I,' cried Paul, glaring across the table at Ashley.

'It was neither,' said Bob quietly. 'You both heard what you wanted to hear. I told you, Ashley, that there would be three partners, and that two of them would be James and I. And I told you, Paul, that it would be Simon and I. Neither of you asked who the third party was to be.'

'You've tricked us,' cried Paul.

'Yes you have,' Ashley agreed. 'You won't get away with it. I'll report you to the Law Society.'

'What about?' asked Bob. 'Steven is witness to the fact that we unanimously agreed to dissolve the partnership, and James, Simon and I wish to form a new one. What's wrong with that?'

'It was based on false information,' said Ashley.

'No it wasn't. All the information was in the accounts.'

'But we didn't have time to read them,' cried Paul.

'That was your own fault.' responded Bob. 'They were available at nine o'clock, but you were too busy scheming with your crony, and you Ashley, were too busy having breakfast with your Society friends. The other two got theirs on time, and had ample time to digest them, didn't you?'

Both James and Simon nodded.

'Aren't you going to say anything James?' begged Ashley.

'I gave you the chance to back down, but you didn't take it,' responded James.

'And what about you Simon?' cried Paul. 'I thought we were mates.'

Simon looked uncomfortable and then said, ' I'm sorry Paul, I just got fed up with all the bickering and back biting, and decided that it was time to call a halt.'

'That's just what it is, 'time to call a halt," said Bob. 'I saw the landlord this morning, and he's agreed to transfer the lease to the new partnership. I'd be grateful, gentlemen, if you would leave the premises. James, would you escort Paul to clear his desk, and Simon, would you do the same with Ashley.'

'You haven't heard the last of this,' snarled Ashley. 'I'll sue.'

'Go ahead,' said Bob mildly. 'I think you'll find you haven't got a leg to stand on.'

'But what am I going to do?' asked Paul.

'Go and join Harry Simpson, if he'll have you. That's what you were planning to do wasn't it?'

Paul gasped, and slumped back in his chair.

Bob stood up to signify that the talking was over, and reluctantly Paul and Ashley left the room, followed by James and Simon.

Steven sat back in his chair and looked at Bob in awe. 'That was some coup,' he said. 'How long have you been planning that?'

'I've been thinking about it for quite a while,' admitted Bob. 'I was sick and tired of all the feuding, and last week Simon and James told me that they'd had enough as well. It was very hard for each of them to break with their friends, but last week's meeting convinced them that it was time to make the change.'

'Well, I'd better get back to my accounts,' said Steven. 'Wait until Flora hears this! For once I'll be telling her something!'

CHAPTER 6

Steven and Margaret were working in their office the next day, when Sheila rang through.

'There's a Mr Clark, from the Garage Trade Federation, in reception to see you,' she said. 'Shall I bring him along?'

'Alan Clark? Here?' cried Steven.

'Yes, in reception,' replied Sheila patiently.

'Tell him we'll be along in a minute,' said Steven, then, turning to Margaret, he said, 'Alan Clark's here! Did you know he was coming? '

'Oh yes. He said he had some invoices he wanted to drop in, so I invited him over.'

'You might have told me.'

'I forgot. You go and scrounge another chair, and I'll get him.'

Steven knocked on the door of Nigel's office and rushed in.

'Can I borrow a chair?' he gasped.

'Certainly,' replied Nigel. 'Has yours broken already?'

'No. We've got an unexpected visitor.'

'Anyone I know?'

'No. It's just another client,' said Steven impatiently. 'Can I take this chair? Thanks.'

Without waiting for a reply, Steven rushed out of the room with the chair in front of him and collided with Alan, who was just passing the door with Margaret.

'Oooff!' exclaimed Alan, as the chair caught him in the midriff.

'Steven!' cried Margaret.

'Oh I'm sorry,' said Steven.

'So you should be,' said Margaret. 'Are you all right Alan?'

'I will be, when I get my breath back,' gasped Alan.

'Here, let me help you,' said Margaret, and, putting her arm around him, guided him into their office.

'Put the chair down there Steven,' commanded Margaret, and helped Alan to sit down on it.

'I'm terribly sorry,' said Steven.

'So you should be,' snapped Margaret.

'I must admit. It wasn't the welcome I was expecting,' said Alan with a wry smile, 'but there's no harm done.'

'I bet you could do with a cup of coffee.' said Margaret.

'That would be very welcome,' replied Alan with feeling.

'I thought so,' said Margaret. 'Steven, you get the coffee, whilst Alan shows me the invoices.'

'Me?' asked Steven.

'Well I think its the least you can do, don't you Alan?' said Margaret.

'Absolutely,' said Alan with a grin. 'And a chocolate biscuit would come in fine.'

'I'm not sure we can run to that,' laughed Margaret. 'But if Steven uses his charm on Sheila, she might have some hidden away.'

'Right-ho,' said Steven, and left the office.

'I was just saying to Margaret' said Alan, when Steven returned, 'we've a governors meeting next month, and I wondered if you could do some of those management accounts you talked about.'

'Of course,' replied Steven. 'Would you like me to come along and present them?'

'That might be a good idea,' said Alan thoughtfully. 'It'll

give the governors a chance to meet you, and you a chance to meet them!'

'That's what I thought,' said Steven.

'OK' said Alan standing up. 'I'll have a word with the chairman, and if he's agreeable, you can come along with me.'

'Thanks,' said Steven.

'Thank you! It's a load off my mind to have the accounts done for me. And to get a cuddle from Margaret was almost worth having the breath knocked out of me!'

'Almost?' enquired Margaret.

'Lets say, well worth it,' replied Alan, smiling as he left the room.

'What a nice man,' said Margaret with feeling.

'Yes he is, isn't he,' replied Steven. 'And he's no fool. He knew that I wanted to go to the meeting to widen my contacts.'

'Talking about contacts,' said Margaret. 'When are you going to get us some more clients?'

'Oh there's plenty of work to come,' replied Steven. 'A lot of people said they would use me.'

'Well where are they?' demanded Margaret. 'The phone hasn't exactly been red hot with offers has it?'

'I'll ring some people I used to deal with in Scarthorpe,' promised Steven. 'I'll soon get some more business, you'll see.'

'We can't afford to wait, so you'd better get on with it.'

'OK, OK,' said Steven. 'I'll start first thing tomorrow morning.'

'Why can't you do it today?'

'Because I'm going with Anne to look at Shepherds computer this afternoon,' retorted Steven.

'Oh yes. And whilst you're there, you'd better get another chair and a typewriter.'

'What do we want a typewriter for?'

'If you're going to produce management accounts, I presume you'll want them typing?'

'Well yes, of course. But I thought.......'

'Don't think,' interrupted Margaret. 'I'm not going to borrow Dad's typewriter again. If you want to have typed accounts, you'll have to get me a new typewriter. Understood?'

'Understood,' replied Steven.

When they returned from the computer demonstration, Anne walked into Margaret's office carrying a small case, followed by Steven carrying a new chair.

'Here we are,' said Steven. 'One new chair as ordered.'

'Great,' said Margaret. 'What about the typewriter?'

Anne placed the small case on the table.

'What's this?' asked Margaret.

'It's a portable typewriter,' replied Steven proudly.

'Don't blame me,' cried Anne as she left the room. 'He wouldn't take my advice, so I'll leave you to it.'

Margaret carefully opened the cover and looked at the small typewriter nestling in its case.

'Isn't it dinky?' burbled Steven. 'And I got it at a good price.'

'I've no doubt,' said Margaret. 'How am I going to do accounts on that?'

'The salesman said it has all the tabs. And you would be able to take it home to work on during school holidays.'

'I'm sorry Steven, it just won't do. Look at how small the keys are. I'll get my fingers all tangled up.'

'I'm sure you won't. Just give it a try ' pleaded Steven.

'No. You're not going to get round me. What did Anne suggest?'

'Oh she wanted us to get the same model as her. But that would cost three hundred pounds. We can't afford that!'

'That's true. But I'm sorry Steven, this is too small. It's almost like a kiddie's toy.'

'That's what Anne said.'

'Well she was right there! Come on, we'll have to return it, and get something more suitable.'

Anne was talking to Sheila in reception. 'Taking it back then?' she asked with a smile.

'Yes' replied Margaret. 'And this time we won't be buying a toy!'

The next morning, Steven got out his file of contacts, and started ringing. His first call was to a supplier to whom he had often given work when he was at Dugdales.

'Can I speak to George Bullington please?'

'Who shall I say is calling?'

'Steven Barkley.'

'From which firm?'

'Stemar Consultants,' replied Steven, trying to sound important.

'Hold the line please.'

There was a pause, then the girl said, 'What firm did you say you were from?'

'Stemar Consultants, but I used to be with Dugdale Engineering.'

There was another pause. 'I'm afraid Mr Bullington's in a meeting, could you call later?'

'How much later?'

'I'm afraid Mr Bullington'll be tied up all day. Would you like to speak to his secretary?'

'No. No. I'll call back tomorrow.'

After about an hour of this type of call, Steven's spirits started to sink. Then, at last, he got a bite!

'Could I speak to John Reynolds please.'

'Who shall I say is calling?'

'Steven Barkley.'

'From which firm?'

'Stemar Consultants, but I used to work for Dugdale Engineering.'

'Hold the line please.'

John Reynolds came on the phone. 'Hello Steven. How're you doing.'

'Quite well actually. As you know, I've set up on my own as a consultant, and I wondered if I could come and talk to you about the services I offer.'

'Of course you can. Let's see now. How about next Tuesday? I'd like you to meet my son who's taking over much of the business now. Come about 12:30 and we can have a spot of lunch.'

'That's fine,' said Steven gratefully, '12:30 next Tuesday. I'll be there!'

Steven put the phone down with a cry of delight.

Margaret turned in her chair. 'Whatever's the matter?'

'John Reynolds has agreed to see me.'

'Who's he?'

'Just one of the biggest engineers in Scarthorpe, that's who. Not only that, but he wants me to meet his son. He must want me to help him.'

'H'mmm we'll see. One Swallow doesn't make a Summer'

'All right then,' retorted Steven. 'I'll get some more,' and he resumed his telephoning.

Two hours later he was still at it. 'Could I speak to George Calder please?'

'Speaking,' a rough Yorkshire voice boomed. 'Is that Steven?'

'Yes it is,' replied Steven, with relief that someone had recognised him.

'How are you doing?' boomed George. 'I hear you've set up on your own.'

'Yes I have,' said Steven. 'And I wondered if I could come and see you about it?'

'Yes fine. When?'

'I wondered about next Tuesday, say about 10:00?'

' Yes that should be OK. Have you ever been to our place?'

'No.'

'Well it's a bit difficult to find, but I'll send you a map. Give us your address.'

Steven gave him the address, confirmed the appointment, and put the phone down.

'I've got another one' he said to Margaret.

'You don't sound as excited about this one,' she responded.

'He's only a small subcontractor. Still, he's a nice enough fellow.'

'Well, you said you wanted to help the small business man, didn't you?' said Margaret.

'They don't come much smaller than George' replied Steven with feeling.

The phone rang and Margaret answered it.

'Is Steven Barkley there?' said a male voice she didn't recognise.

'Yes, who's speaking please?'

'Its Bill Jones from Rivingham Cleaning.'

'Hello,' said Steven, 'can I help you?'

'Jeremy Anderson gave me your name. We're having

some computer problems and we wondered if you could help us.'

'Certainly' replied Steven excitedly, 'when do you want me to come round?'

'As soon as you like, how about ten o'clock tomorrow morning?'

'Fine,' replied Steven and put the phone down. This is my lucky day,' he cried and gave Margaret a kiss.

'What's that for?' gasped Margaret.

'To celebrate,' cried Steven. 'That Bill Jones wants me to look at his computer tomorrow. Three new clients in one morning. Not bad going.'

'But they've only agreed to let you see them,' protested Margaret. 'That doesn't mean to say that they'll give you work.'

'Oh they will,' said Steven. 'Just you wait and see.'

At ten o'clock the next morning, Steven was sitting in the front room of the large Victorian house which had been converted into the offices of Rivingham Cleaning. He only had to wait for a few minutes before Bill bounded into the room.

'Hello Steven,' he greeted. 'Nice to meet you. Come on upstairs.'

Bill leapt up the stairs two at a time, and strode along the landing. He flung open the door to the front room, and turned to see Steven puffing to the top of the stairs.

'Come on Steven. Hurry up. We haven't got all day!' he cried, and walked swiftly into the room.

Steven completed the journey as fast as he could, and entered the large office which was furnished with two desks, two or three filing cabinets and some chairs. At one of the desks sat a beautiful young woman.

'Steven,' said Bill, waving his hand towards the vision in the corner. 'I'd like you to meet my personal assistant, Fiona Sinclair.'

'Pleased to meet you,' panted Steven breathlessly, as he advanced across the room with his hand outstretched.

As Fiona rose gracefully from her desk to return the proffered handshake, Steven could see that she was, indeed, lovely. She wore a well-tailored suit which fitted her exactly, and emphasised the curves of her slim figure. She had a pretty elfin face, framed by perfectly coiffeured blonde hair.

Fiona returned Steven's greeting with a perfunctory shake of his hand, and a smile that was not reflected in her eyes.

'Fiona love,' said Bill. 'Could you ask Jean to come up? And organise a cup of tea for Steven, and a coffee for me please.'

'Certainly,' she said, and walked elegantly out of the room.

'You can put your eyes back in their sockets,' said Bill, 'and you can stop panting.'

'That was from rushing up the stairs after you,' protested Steven.

'I know that, but I'm not sure Fiona did,' responded Bill with a smile.

'What can I help you with?' said Steven, anxious to start to create a good impression.

'You can start by sorting out the computer. Jean'll be up in a minute. She's a good lass, but not the brightest of girls. Once she's grasped something, she's great. It's just that she needs plenty of guidance which the computer people couldn't, or wouldn't, give.'

There was a knock on the door, and a tall angular girl, of about twenty, came in carrying two cups. She was wearing a blouse, cardigan and skirt, and a mop of mousy brown hair surmounted her plain face. Her plainness was emphasised by the elegance of Fiona, who followed her into the room.

'Ah Jean,' cried Bill. 'I'd like you to meet Steven Barkley, who's going to have a look at the computer with you.'

'Pleased to meet you I'm sure,' said Jean, in a strong local accent. ' I hope you're better than the last lot. I couldn't understand a word they were saying.'

'I'm sure Steven will be an improvement on them,' said Bill, in an embarrassed tone.

'Well it wouldn't take much,' sniffed Jean.

'How much experience have you had with computers Steven?' asked Fiona coolly from her desk.

'I've worked with them for years on the accounts side,' replied Steven.

'But do you program them, or maintain them?'

'No,' replied Steven, 'I leave that to the experts.'

'So what *can* you do for us?' continued Fiona.

'I don't know yet,' replied Steven. 'Let me look at the system first, and then I'll tell you what I can do. If I can't help you, I'll say so.'

'Can't be fairer than that, can you?' interrupted Bill.

Fiona didn't reply, but her scornful look showed that she did not think much of Steven's ability.

'Right, we'd better get on with it,' said Steven.

'But what will you do?' asked Jean, in a belligerent tone, taking her cue from Fiona.

'We'll start by you showing me the computer, and the manuals,' replied Steven.

'Good idea,' agreed Bill. 'Jean, will you take Steven down to the office, and Fiona and I'll join you in a minute.'

'I'd like some time on my own first, if you don't mind,' said Steven.

'I bet you would,' muttered Fiona. 'That'll increase your fee.'

'I won't charge for the initial consultation,' said Steven stiffly, and stood up.

'Well in that case we can't lose,' said Bill to Fiona, 'can we?'

'I suppose not,' said Fiona grudgingly, and started to look at the papers on her desk.

In the downstairs office Jean pointed to the corner, where a machine stood, covered by a dustsheet.

'Is that it?' gasped Steven.

'That's it,' confirmed Jean.

'But don't you use it at all?'

'I got all the names and addresses in to it, but when it came to posting, I got completely lost.'

'Have you got the manuals?' Steven asked.

'Oh yes they're over there,' Jean replied, and pointed to a line of books gathering dust on the shelf. 'I tried to read them, but they're double Dutch to me.'

'OK,' said Steven, 'lets make a start shall we? 'You boot the machine up, and I'll get the manuals down.'

'There you are, talking jargon just like the others. What do you mean, 'boot the machine up'?'

'I'm sorry,' laughed Steven, 'it means start the machine up. It comes from the early days, when people used to give computers a kick when they wouldn't start. Amazingly it sometimes worked.'

'I've felt like doing that plenty of times,' said Jean with feeling.

'Lets hope we don't get to that point this morning' said Steven with a grin.

They had just got the machine started when Bill and Fiona came in. 'How long do you think you'll be?' asked Bill.

'Oh! A couple of hours at least,' replied Steven.

'As long as that?' said Bill. 'Fiona and I have got to go out shortly to visit some sites. We won't be back until about three o'clock.'

'That's fine' said Steven. 'It'll give me plenty of time to find out what makes this beast tick.'

'Right,' said Bill 'see you later then.' He left the room with Fiona, who had not said a word.

'I seem to have blotted my copy book with Fiona,' commented Steven.

'The ice maiden?' queried Jean. 'I wouldn't worry about her. She's just peeved because we're not using her boy friend.'

'Boy friend?'

'That's right. Paul they call him. She brought him in last week, but to be honest he was as bad as the first lot. Knew a lot about computers, but nothing about accounts.'

'Well, we'd better show them what we can do then.'

'We?'

'Yes. We. I can't do it on my own. I need your help, just as much as you need mine. If we pool our knowledge, we can probably get this thing working.'

'No one's ever put it that way before. The first problem is the posting of the purchases. You see every site sends in a weekly return.................'

It was half past three before Bill and Fiona came back. 'Sorry we're a bit late — got held up by some road works on the A1,' said Bill. 'How are things going?'

'Great,' enthused Jean. 'Steven has set up a dummy company so that we can try things out before putting them on the main system. He's explained things so well, that even I can understand them.'

Steven looked abashed at this fulsome praise. Bill was

obviously surprised, and Fiona's face was a picture. There was a slight pause, and then Bill said, 'I must say Steven, that's the first time I've heard Jean say something good about the computer. You're a miracle worker!'

'Thanks,' said Steven. 'There's a long way to go yet, but it looks like quite a good system.'

'So it should,' sniffed Fiona, 'the money it cost.'

'Now we've gone through all that,' said Bill sharply. 'If Steven can get this computer working, we'll carry on with it. If not, we'll talk to Paul.'

Jean gave Steven a look that said, 'I told you so,' and turned back to the computer.

'Come on Steven,' said Bill, 'we'll go up to my office and discuss your fee.'

When they got upstairs, Bill apologised for Fiona's behaviour. 'Part of the problem is that she's got hooked up with Paul, and it looks as if she's practically promised him the job. She's very efficient, and will make a good second in command. But she's not the boss. I am. And I want you to do it, so that's that.'

'That's fine with me,' said Steven. 'How long has she been your assistant?'

'Only a couple of weeks. She was the best supervisor we had, and as things have been a bit hectic lately I brought her in to help out.'

'Have you agreed what her duties are, and the level of her responsibility?'

'No I haven't,' said Bill slowly. 'What you're getting at?'

'Well, she's a bit young, and is obviously trying to find her feet. If you don't tell her how far she can go, and then knock her down in front of the staff, like you've just done over the computer, she'll soon loose all credibility.'

'You're right,' agreed Bill. 'I'll get her up here when

you've gone, and we'll sort it out. Now then, about your fee. '

'I charge ten pounds per hour,' said Steven.

'That's a bit steep.'

'It's the going rate for a qualified accountant, you ask Jeremy.'

'OK, if you say so, I accept. When can you start?'

'I'm quite busy at the moment. Could I start a week on Monday?'

'Fair enough.'

'Fine. I'll take the manuals home with me, so that I can familiarise myself with the system.'

CHAPTER 7

Bob asked Steven to attend the interview for Julia's replacement at Russell's. 'There's only one applicant who's had any experience of Solicitors accounts,' explained Bob, 'so I thought we would just interview her. OK?'

'Fine,' said Steven. 'What's her name?'

'She's called Barbara Latimer. She hasn't worked for some time, but she has good experience. I'll get Jennifer to bring her up.'

Jennifer ushered into the room a smart, medium built, woman, with a rounded figure, pretty face and thick black shiny hair. The interview went very well. Barbara answered all the questions intelligently, and without hesitation, until Bob asked, 'Why do you want to come back to work?'

Barbara paused, and a shadow came over her face. 'My husband has just been diagnosed as having Multiple Sclerosis,' she said in a low voice. 'He's only 36 like me, and we have two small children. It seems so unfair. I'm having difficulty coming to terms with it, and I thought that if I came back to work, it would help me to cope.'

There was silence for a moment, and then Bob said gently, 'Who'll take care of the children?'

'We've worked that out,' replied Barbara. 'Tom, my husband, will have to give up work soon anyway. So he can be in when the children come home from school, and my mother-in law has offered to help out.'

After a few more questions, Bob brought the interview to a close, and asked Jennifer to show Barbara out.

'Well, what do you think?' Bob asked.

'I liked her,' replied Steven. 'The only problem could be her family situation.'

'I agree. It's obviously hit her hard. As I understand it, MS takes a long time to develop, so I should think she'll have time to work out how to manage. Anyway, I think she's worth giving a chance, I'll write and offer her the job. That'll mean you'll be dropping back to just doing the accounts, but I don't suppose you'll mind that.'

'No. That'll be fine,' lied Steven, and thought ruefully about the nice steady earner he'd just seen disappear. 'Still,' he thought briskly, 'I've got some new jobs to go to. One door closes, and another opens'.

The following Tuesday, Steven donned his best suit, picked up his shiny new briefcase, and drove to Scarthorpe. He followed George Calder's instructions, and found himself driving down dingy roads, with old foundry walls on either side covered in old tattered hoardings. At every junction there was a run down pub, waiting in vain to slake the thirst of the foundry workers, who had long since been made redundant.

Finally, Steven turned into a side street, and drove through some big double doors into a yard. There were bits of machinery and piping lying all over the place. A battered old van was parked in the far corner, next to a wooden-boarded, two-story, building. There was a set of rickety wooden steps leading up to a door on the first storey, and a grimy sign, with the word OFFICE on it, pointed up the stairs.

Steven parked his Rover next to the van, got out his briefcase, and climbed the stairs. He opened the door, and peered into a long, narrow, dimly lit room. An old fashioned, high drawing desk ran along the full length of the left-hand wall. A little wizened old man was perched on a stool in front of it, writing in a bound ledger.

On the right of the room were filing cabinets, and a cluttered desk, at which sat Steven's prospective client.

George's voice boomed out. 'Hello Steven. Come in. Come in. You found us all right then?'

'Yes,' said Steven. 'Your instructions were excellent.'

'Fine, fine' said George. 'I'd like you to meet Percy.' The little man slipped off the stool, and scurried towards Steven, almost bent double, like a hunchback.

'Pleased to meet you I'm sure,' he said, giving Steven a limp handshake.

'Percy here keeps my books,' said George, 'and tries to keep me straight. That's right isn't it Percy?'

'Yes. Yes. That's right George,' simpered the little man, who appeared to be at least 80 years old.

George was dressed in an old jumper and jeans, whilst Percy wore a battered old suit. As he gazed round the room, which looked as if it hadn't been dusted or swept for 20 years, Steven felt completely out of place in his best suit and executive brief case.

'Have a pew,' commanded George, putting a battered old office chair down in front of his desk 'Would you like a cup of coffee?'

'Err, tea if you've got it,' Steven replied.

'That's no problem,' said Percy, 'That's what I drink.'

Steven gingerly sat himself down on the proffered chair. As Percy busied himself making refreshments, Steven noticed a cartoon pinned to the wall just above George's head. It was of a scruffy man, with his pockets turned out to show he had no money, with the caption, 'I always quote the lowest prices.'

'Thank you for seeing me,' said Steven.

'Not at all,' replied George, 'what are you doing now a days?'

'I'm helping small businesses with financial advice and computers.'

'Well I hope you can help me, but I doubt it.'

'Try me,' said Steven confidently.

'I've got about a dozen fitters working for me,' said George. 'They go all round the country fitting pipework for large engineering companies, such as Dugdales and Reynolds. We've got plenty of work, but we don't seem to be able to make it pay.'

'What you need is a costing system which shows how you've done on each job,' stated Steven confidently. 'Then you'll be able to identify where you are losing money.'

'I'm not sure we can afford computers and such like,' said George.

'Oh you don't need anything like that,' said Steven. 'A simple manual system will do it.'

'What do you think Percy?' said George, looking across at the little man who had been listening to everything that had been said, whilst ostensibly working on his books.

'I think it's a good idea,' he replied. 'You know what I think. We pay the men far too much, and quote too low a price. Just like the man in the cartoon I gave you.'

'Yes. Yes.' said George wearily. 'OK we'll give it a go. Mind you, we can't afford to pay fancy fees. How much will you charge?'

Steven looked round the room and thought about the prospect of the job at Reynolds. If he combined it with this one, he could quote a reduced fee.

'One hundred and fifty pounds plus any expenses,' he blurted out.

'That's a lot, ' responded George. 'What do you think Percy?'

'It does seem a bit high,' the little man commented. ' But it'll be worth it I'm sure.'

'OK then. If Percy says so, we'll do it. When can you start.'

'Next Tuesday if you like.'

'Fine. We'll see you then.'

The contrast between Reynolds' premises and George's place couldn't have been greater. The yard was spacious and clean, and on the left-hand side was a two storey, modern, office block. Along the right hand wall were neat rows of racks, containing steel bars, and opposite him were the entrances to two huge workshops.

A line of gleaming cars, including a Jaguar and an Aston Martin sports car, were parked in front of the offices. Steven pulled into one of the slots marked 'Visitors' and got out of his car. As he pushed open the swing door into the plush reception area, Steven was glad this time that he was wearing his best suit, and was carrying his shiny new brief case.

After a short wait, he was ushered into the Boardroom. The walls of the room were panelled with light oak. In the centre was a large oak board table, surrounded by a dozen chairs, standing on a plush maroon carpet.

Steven was studying some portraits on the wall of previous directors, when the door opened and John Reynolds and a young man of about thirty walked in.

'Hello Steven,' said John, 'nice to see you again. Let me introduce you to my son Alan. We'll go and get a spot of lunch,' he continued, 'and you can bring us up to date with what you are doing, and how things are at Dugdales.'

' We'll go in my car,' said John when they got outside, and directed Steven into the front seat of the Jaguar.

'Its a good job we're not going in my car,' laughed Alan,

proudly pointing to the Aston Martin, 'we'd have had quite a squeeze.'

'Aye,' responded his father fondly. 'You should have brought your Rover two litre today, then you could have taken us.'

'What car are you driving?' Alan asked Steven.

'The Rover 1600 over there,' responded Steven.

'They are a bit under powered aren't they?' said Alan.

'It's good enough for me,' replied Steven tersely.

'I suppose that's all that matters,' sneered Alan. He spent the rest of the journey giving his opinion on cars, making it very clear that he didn't think much of second hand Rover 1600's.

By the time they arrived at an expensive looking country hotel, Steven was starting to have misgivings. As they walked into the bar, he wondered nervously if he had enough money in his wallet to buy the meal.

'What are you having?' he proffered .

'Put your money away,' said John, 'we have an account here, and anyway we invited you for lunch.'

'Thank you very much,' responded Steven gratefully.

During the superb lunch, John listened patiently to Steven's sales pitch, whilst Alan looked bored stiff.

'That's all very interesting,' said John, 'but I wanted to talk to you about Dugdales. Do you think the new Managing Director will be able to turn it round?'

Alan at last looked interested, and Steven realised that the purpose of the lunch, was not to discuss giving him work, but to find out about Dugdales.

'I've no doubt he will,' he replied, 'but I'm afraid I've lost touch.'

'But surely you know if they've got any good prospects in the pipeline?' demanded Alan.

'So that you can pinch them?' thought Steven, but said

out loud, 'I'm afraid not, I didn't get involved in the sales side.'

Alan slumped back in his seat and assumed his bored expression. There was an uncomfortable pause, which Steven broke by saying, 'I reckon Rivingham have a good chance of beating Scarthorpe on Saturday.'

'Rivingham,' cried Alan. 'You don't support that tin pot team do you? They've never won a trophy have they?'

John joined in. 'Alan was a professional footballer you know. Till he gave it up last season to come into the business.'

'You?' said Steven in disbelief. 'Who did you play for?'

'Aire Valley Rovers,' mumbled Alan .

'Now who's talking about tin pot teams,' cried Steven. 'They've never been out of the fourth division have they? What position did you play?

' I was the goalkeeper,' replied Alan.

'The goalkeeper eh! Weren't Aire Valley bottom of the league last year?'

'Yes'

'And how many goals did you let in?'

'None of your business,' muttered Alan.

'I think we'll skip coffee if you don't mind,' said John. 'Got a lot on this afternoon. Need to get back.'

'Suits me,' said Steven. 'I need to get back to see my team playing in the First Division.'

The journey back to Reynolds premises was conducted in near silence. Steven collected his briefcase from the opulent boardroom, and made his escape as quickly as possible.

'I've blown it,' Steven said to Margaret when he got home. 'I shouldn't have gone for Alan like that. But he just got on my wick. First he rubbished my car, and then he knocked the Rivers.'

'And that was unforgivable,' smiled Margaret.

Steven smiled back. 'Of course! But I still shouldn't have lost my rag. Reynolds are very influential. I'll never get any work in Scarthorpe.'

'But you have some work, 'said Margaret. 'You've got George's job.'

'I know, but that won't bring in much. Besides, I was hoping to work with a big company, and establish my reputation as a top-notch consultant.'

'You are a top notch consultant,' said Margaret, 'and perhaps you are being reminded, that you are supposed to be helping small business people like George, and not rich parasites like Alan.

'Steven, when are you going to help me with balancing our supplier Parnell's account?' demanded Anne the next morning, 'John Whittaker's coming tomorrow you know.'

'Just coming,' replied Steven and joined her in her office. As soon as he did so, Nigel left the office muttering, 'Got to go and see a customer. Bye.'

After looking at the figures for a while, Steven said, 'there does seem to be a lot of differences. I can't understand it. Your books are usually so accurate.'

Anne looked at Steven thoughtfully for a moment, and then said, 'The problem isn't my books. It's Nigel.'

'What do you mean?'

'Parnell's are our biggest supplier, so Nigel has taken personal control of the account. He pulls all of the invoices out of the post for checking, and he decides how much we'll pay. I only get to write up what he gives me.'

'But why are there so many missing invoices?'

'Nigel has them in a file somewhere, and only releases them when he's sure they're correct.'

'Where's the file?'

'You'd better ask Nigel.'

'I will,' said Steven. 'How does he expect the books to be right if he holds back invoices?'

'Have you finished?' Nigel asked as he came into the room later in the morning.

'No. We're having problems tracing some missing invoices,' replied Steven. 'Have you got any?'

'Well I've got a few in here,' responded Nigel. From a drawer in his desk he pulled out a fat file, bulging with bits of paper.

'A few!' cried Steven. 'There seems to be a whole year's there. Can I have them please?'

'Why?'

'So that I can balance the account of course.'

'I'm not so sure about that.'

'Look, do you want me to be present tomorrow or not?'

'Of course I do.'

'Well I'm not going to sit there like a stuffed dummy. You either let me do a proper reconciliation, or I'm not coming to the meeting.'

'All right. All right. Keep your hair on.' said Nigel, and, walking across the room, plonked the file on Anne's desk. He then turned to leave.

'Where are you going?' asked Steven.

'I've got to go to the gym,' replied Nigel.

'But aren't you going to help us sort this out?'

'Oh it's all there. I'll look at it with you in the morning, before John comes.' said Nigel and shot out of the door before Steven could utter another word.

'Well done,' murmured Anne.

'What do you mean?' asked Steven.

'I've being trying for years to get that file out of him, and you've done it in one week!'

'I see. Well, we'd better take advantage of it, before he changes his mind and comes back for it.'

'Oh he won't do that,' said Anne. 'He's gone for the day now. Whenever he has a problem he runs away and hides for a while.'

Steven looked at her in astonishment.

'Don't look at me like that,' laughed Anne. 'I know my husband. He'll go off for a while, and then tomorrow morning, he'll be ready to face John. You'll see.'

The next morning Steven was in bright and early, but Nigel had beaten him to it. 'How did the reconciliation go?' he asked.

'Pretty good,' replied Steven. 'There are just one or two outstanding queries I need your help on.'

'Certainly,' replied Nigel. 'Fire away.'

Steven produced a bulky file and they spent the next hour going through the reconciliation. When they had finished, Nigel said, 'You've set it out very well Steven. John will be impressed. When he comes, I'll introduce you, and then I'll let you go through the figures with him.'

'OK But no rushing off to the gym.'

'Whatever do you mean? Of course I'll stay here.'

'As long as you do,' said Steven.

When John arrived, Steven was surprised to find that he was a tall lean American, in his late thirties, with a crew cut.

'Howdy,' drawled John. 'Nice to meet yuh.'

'Likewise,' replied Steven. 'You're an American.'

'How did you guess?' chuckled John wryly.

'Err yes. Well,' stumbled Steven, trying to retrieve the

situation. 'Its just that I'd assumed that you were English, that's all.'

'Nope. I'm all-American, but don't let that bother you.'

'Of course it doesn't bother us,' interrupted Nigel, giving Steven a glare. 'Now how about some coffee?'

'Tea for me,' replied John. 'I can't stand the stuff you British call coffee.'

'I'm a tea drinker too,' interjected Steven, in an effort to establish some common ground.

'Yes,' sneered Nigel, 'but only Indian.'

'That's the kind I like best as well,' said John. 'Can't stand this scented stuff like Earl Grey, can you?'

'No,' replied Steven.

Nigel stood up abruptly and left the room saying, 'I'll organise the drinks.'

John relaxed into his chair, and chuckled again. 'I always like taking the Ess Aitch one Tee out of Nigel. So, you're the Accountant who's going to sort him out are you?'

'I'm going to try to.'

'The best of luck. I've been trying to get his billings sorted out for over a year.'

'We've managed to balance everything,' said Steven, 'would you like to see it?

'Would I ever,' replied John, leaning forward eagerly.

Steven produced his reconciliation, and the two of them were well in to it when Nigel returned with the drinks.

'Oh! I see you've started without me,' he muttered.

'Yep,' responded John, 'and I must say, Steven's done a fine job with these figures. For once I can see the make up of the balance according to your ledger, so we can now start to get things sorted out. Park your ass Nigel, whilst Steven and I get this thing agreed.'

With a grunt Nigel sat down in his chair, and watched

across the desk as Steven and John carried on with the reconciliation.

Finally John said, 'that's everything agreed. Now then, let's have a look at these old outstanding bills. What about this big one that's six month old?'

'Which one's that?' asked Nigel.

'Invoice 4579 for some switchgear.' responded John.

'Ah yes,' said Nigel. 'That was for the job at Webster's. There was some faulty gear and we had to replace it all. I'm waiting for a credit note.'

'We've sent you one haven't we?' asked John.

'Yes, here it is,' said Steven triumphantly. 'It came through in July.'

'I must have been on holiday when it came in,' growled Nigel.

'If we set it against the main invoice, that means that we can clear the balance of two thousand three hundred pounds,' continued Steven.

'Fine,' responded John. 'What about this one? Invoice 5723 for six thousand pounds in June.'

'That was another query,' interrupted Nigel, 'and we definitely haven't had a credit note for that.'

'What was wrong?' asked John.

Nigel looked at his file. 'There were three fuse boxes missing,' he said.

'What was their value?' John asked.

Nigel consulted his file again. 'A hundred and four pounds,' he replied.

John gasped. 'Are you telling me, that you've held up a six thousand pound invoice, waiting for a credit for a measly one hundred pounds?'

'It's the only way to get credits out of you,' muttered Nigel.

'When did you ask for a credit note?' queried John.

Nigel shuffled in his chair. 'Seeing that we had this meeting coming up, I thought that I'd raise it today.'

John snorted in derision.

Steven hastily interrupted. 'How about if we knock the one hundred and four pounds off the six thousand, and pay you the balance next week. That'll give you time to raise the credit note, and keep the books straight.'

'Yeah. I guess that'll be OK' said John. 'Are there anymore like that Nigel?'

'There are one or two,' responded Nigel smoothly. 'But first I'd like a word with Steven. Will you excuse us a minute?'

'Surely,' responded John. Nigel with a jerk of his head beckoned Steven to follow him out of the room.

'In here,' growled Nigel, and strode into Steven's office. ' Now then, what do you think you are playing at?'

'What do you mean?' asked Steven.

'Have you got six thousand pounds in your pocket?'

'Errr..... No.'

'Well neither have I. You had no right to make offers of payment. Your job was to sort out the account, and leave the negotiating to me.'

'I'm sorry,' said Steven. 'I was only trying to help'.

'Well you haven't. You've made things worse. If you hadn't set everything out so clearly, and opened your big mouth about credit notes, I'd have been able to plead ignorance and delay payment for another couple of months. Now I'm caught.'

'I'm sorry,' said Steven again. 'What can I do?'

'Nothing. You've done enough harm. Now get in your car and go home. I'll tell John that you've had an urgent message that your wife's sick or something. I'll see you tomorrow.' He turned on his heels, and walked quickly out of the room, leaving Steven open mouthed with amazement.

Margaret greeted him with astonishment. 'What are you doing home so early?'

'Nigel's kicked me out,' responded Steven.

'What on earth for?'

'For doing my job too well,' said Steven bitterly, and related the events of the morning with hardly a pause for breath.

'Well I suppose Nigel had a point,' said Margaret thoughtfully. 'It was his money you were giving away.'

'Yes, but he had no right to kick me out like that'.

'I agree. That was unforgivable. What are you going to do now?'

'I don't know. I suppose I'll just have to go in tomorrow and apologise.'

'You'll do no such thing, at least, not until he has apologised first, for sending you home like a naughty schoolboy.'

'That's exactly what it felt like,' cried Steven.

'I know, I saw your face when you came in. It was just like when Jason was sent home for putting a frog down Angela Simpson's dress. All full of righteous indignation and fear!'

'All right. There's no need to remind me I'm just like a big kid.'

'Well sometimes you are. But then, so is Nigel. It'll all get sorted out tomorrow—you'll see. By the way there's a message for you to ring Alan Clark.'

'Thanks,' said Steven. 'I might as well do it now, then I'll go over to Russell's and see how Barbara is getting on.'

'Hello Steven,' said Alan mildly, when he answered the phone. 'I thought you weren't due home until later.'

'I wasn't,' replied Steven miserably. 'But I've just had an argument with a client and been sent home.'

'Oh dear, nothing serious I hope.'

'I don't know. Margaret thinks it will all blow over, but I'm not so sure.'

'Well I hope it does. Anyway, I've got some good news for you. The Chairman has agreed to you attending the next meeting of the Governors.'

'Oh that *is* good news. Thank you very much for arranging it.'

'Not at all. There's only one difficulty. It's in two weeks time, and he'd like some management figures circulating before the meeting.'

'That's not a problem, I'll get on with them straight away.'

'You look more cheerful,' said Margaret when Steven got home from Russell's.

'Yes I am. Barbara's doing a terrific job. She's got all her ledgers balanced, and she's sorted out quite a few queries. She was quite complimentary about the way I'd kept things going, and it's really cheered me up.'

'I bet it did. Nothing like a bit of flattery from a pretty girl is there?'

'It wasn't flattery. It's just that we got on very well.'

'Hmmm' said Margaret.

CHAPTER 8

The next morning, Steven went straight into his office at Parkers, and started working on Garage Trade Association's accounts. After about half an hour Nigel came in.

'Ah there you are Steven,' he said gruffly. 'I'm sorry I blew my top yesterday. We'll say no more about it shall we?'

Steven looked at him in astonishment. 'Err, right. If that's what you want. It's fine by me.'

'That's what I want,' affirmed Nigel and walked out of the room.

Steven sat for a moment, and then rang Margaret. 'Do you know what Nigel's just done?' he burst out.

'He's apologised,' Margaret responded calmly.

'How did you know that?' gasped Steven.

'Because I had a word with Anne yesterday afternoon while you were out, and she was furious! I guessed she'd do something about it!'

'I see,' said Steven weakly.

'So, did you apologise as well?

'No. I was so taken aback.'

'Well I think you should do so, don't you?'

'Yes. I'll do it now, and thanks.'

'Don't thank me, thank Anne.'

'I will.'

Steven knocked on the door of Nigel's office and went in. Nigel glanced up with a frown from some sheets of paper he was looking at with Anne.

'I just thought I ought to apologise about yesterday,' said Steven. 'I realise I was out of order, and it won't happen again.'

'Too right it won't,' growled Nigel.

'Is there anything I can do to make amends?' asked Steven.

'There is as a matter of fact,' snarled Nigel. 'Seeing that you're so good at sorting figures out. You can have a look at this list of people who owe us money, and see where we can get the six thousand pounds you promised John next week.' He flung the papers down on the desk and stood up. 'I'm going to the gym,' he announced, and strode out of the room.

'He goes to the gym an awful lot doesn't he?' remarked Steven.

'I've told you, its his way when he has a problem,' said Anne 'and we really do have a problem.'

'How's that?'

'We haven't got the money to pay Parnell's next week, and they're threatening to stop supplying us.'

'Right, we'd better have a look at that list of debtors.'

'What? Oh you mean the people who owe us money. Here it is. There are lots of them, and its difficult to know where to start.'

'You start with the biggest accounts,' said Steven. 'And you break them down into who pays you quickly, and who messes you about. You ring the quick payers first, and gently twist their arms, and then you start on the others, and threaten action. Come on I'll show you how it's done.'

They worked hard all day, analysing figures, and phoning customers. Nigel popped in and out, and finally sat silently at his desk, looking at some catalogues. At four o'clock Anne put the phone down with a big smile on her face. 'We've done it! That was Johnson's. They'll put a cheque for fifteen hundred in the post on Friday. Steven you're a genius!'

'Just experience that's all,' muttered Steven.

'John Whittaker seems to think you're one as well,' said Nigel. 'He threatened to close their account with us if I didn't keep you on. Seems like he was right.'

Jean greeted Steven eagerly when he arrived at Rivingham Cleaning the next morning. 'I've got all the opening balances loaded like you showed me,' she enthused 'So we can get on with the postings now.'

'Well done,' replied Steven, equally enthusiastic. 'I've read through the manual, and I'm pretty certain how to do the postings, but we'll try it in the dummy company first shall we?'

'Oh yes, that was a great idea of yours. You are clever.'

'I don't know about that,' muttered Steven.

'Oh but you are. I was just telling my boy friend about you last night, and he would like to meet you.'

'What on earth for?'

'He's thinking of changing his job, and he would like some advice'

'I'm not a recruitment specialist you know.'

'But you know such a lot about business and computers and things. I'm sure you could help him. Please say that you will.'

'Well, I'm a bit busy at the moment, perhaps later on'

'Great. I'll tell him that you'll see him next week.'

'More like the week after,' said Steven.

'OK. The week after next it is then.'

'Now, about these postings,' said Steven.

They worked hard all morning, and soon Jean was posting the invoices with great confidence. Just after twelve o'clock Fiona came into the office.

'Hello Steven,' she said pleasantly, 'I thought I might find you here. Do you fancy a spot of lunch?'

'Err,' spluttered Steven, taken aback by Fiona's invitation.

Jean said swiftly, 'We were going to have a sandwich, and work through, weren't we Steven?'

'Were we? Yes, that's right' said Steven, regaining his composure.

'Shame,' said Fiona. 'I wouldn't want to interfere with Jean's plans. I just wanted to show my appreciation for what you said to Bill. It's really helped our relationship.'

'Has it?' gulped Steven.

'Oh yes. We've cleared the air, and we both know where we stand.'

'Good. I'm pleased to hear it.'

'So, as I say, I owe you one.'

'Think nothing of it,' replied Steven, and Fiona walked gracefully out of the room.

Jean gave a snort of derision. 'Cleared the air. Both know were we stand. More like where we lie down if you ask me.'

'What do you mean?'

'She's a man-eater that one. Good job I saved you from that lunch, otherwise she'd have got her claws into you.'

'I'm perfectly capable of looking after myself thank you. What did she mean? 'Jean's plans.''

'I've no idea,' responded Jean tersely. 'Would you like some sandwiches? I've made them specially.'

'That's very nice of you.'

'It's the least I can do,' simpered Jean. 'I'll put the kettle on.'

When Steven told Margaret that night about the

conversation, she looked at him thoughtfully, 'And do you fancy the lovely Fiona?'

'Of course not, whatever gave you that idea?'

'Oh just the way you looked when you described her.'

'Don't be silly, she's very attractive, that's all. You know what they say 'When a man stops looking, he's ready to turn up his clogs"

'Well as long as it's just looking.'

Steven found the route to the premises of Calder Engineering just as depressing the next day as it was when he first visited George. He climbed the rickety staircase and entered the gloomy room once more. There was no sign of George, but Percy scuttled across the floor to greet him.

'I'm sorry, but George isn't here. He's had to go round to see Alan Reynolds about a new contract. He asked me to show you the books, and he'll talk to us both when he gets back. Now, would you like a cup of tea?'

Percy scurried round making the tea, whilst Steven perched at the long desk and studied the books. They were immaculately written up, in neat, copperplate handwriting, and balanced off each month.

'These are beautifully kept books,' said Steven admiringly. 'It's a shame that the picture they show doesn't match their quality.'

'Yes' said Percy. 'I've been wanting to talk to you about that. I'm an old man, and I haven't got any children. I've got some money put by, and I thought about lending it to George until he got back on his feet. What do you think?'

'I think it's very good of you. Why do you want to do it?'

'I'm a Methodist lay preacher, and I like to practice

what I preach. I like George, and I'd love to get him out of the clutches of that Claude Keighley-Smythe.'

'Claude Keighley-Smythe? The bank manager?'

'That's him. I hope I haven't said anything out of turn.'

'No, you haven't said anything out of turn. I don't like him either. But why do you bank in Rivingham instead of Scarthorpe?'

'When we did work for Dugdales, you always paid us on the nail. And sometimes, when we had problems, you paid us early. We found that, if we banked at the same branch as you did, we could get the cheques cleared quicker. That's why George agreed to see you. As a thank you for helping us out in the past.'

'I see,' said Steven slowly. 'But looking at these figures, he can't really afford me can he?'

'No,' said Percy. 'But George is like that, he'll pay everyone before himself. The men get twice as much as him, and many a time he's gone without wages just to make sure they get paid.'

'And you?' asked Steven.

Percy looked down. 'I haven't been paid for two months, but then, I haven't got a family to keep.'

There was a sound of footsteps on the stairs, and Percy said fiercely, 'George doesn't know that, and don't you tell him.'

George burst into the room before Steven could reply. 'Now then Steven. How are you getting on? Sorry I wasn't here when you came.'

'Oh, we're getting on like a house on fire,' said Steven. 'Percy keeps a lovely set of books.'

'Yes he does doesn't he,' said George fondly. 'I don't know what I'd do without him.'

'How did you get on at Reynolds?' interrupted Percy. 'Did they pay you?'

'No. But they promised me a cheque by the end of the week, and they want to place a large order with us.'

'That's good,' said Steven.

'Ye..ss' said George, 'but there's a slight snag. Alan Reynolds wants me to put a central heating system in at his home.'

'What's wrong with that?' asked Steven.

'He doesn't want to pay for it. That's right isn't it?' asked Percy.

'That's right,' said George glumly.

'But that's outrageous,' exclaimed Steven. 'Does his father know about this?'

'I shouldn't think so,' said George despondently. 'But it makes no difference. Alan is running the show now, and it's him I've got to deal with.'

'What are you going to do?'

'I've not got much choice have I? I desperately need the work, and Alan knows it.'

'Well make sure you include it in the price,' said Steven.

'The price has already been fixed,' said George tersely. 'Now then, about this costing system.'

The three of them discussed in detail how Percy's books could be adapted to give information on each of the jobs. Finally, Steven said, 'I've got all the information I need now. I'd like to go home and write it all down. I'll come back next week if you like, and we can start to implement it.'

'If you think that's necessary,' said George doubtfully. 'Can't we just start it now?'

'No' said Steven. 'I need to make sure that the system is going to work, before I ask Percy to start changing his books . And besides, I think you are going to need a cash flow forecast if you get this big job. Otherwise it'll bust you.'

'You're right. But it seems like a lot of work,' persisted George. 'We can't afford to pay much more you know.'

'Don't worry about that,' said Steven. 'I quoted a fixed fee didn't I? No more arguments. How does next Friday suit you?'

After the long drive home, Steven wearily told Margaret all about the day's events. 'As soon as I saw the position I should have walked out of the door,' he concluded, 'but I couldn't. They're such nice people, and they need all the help they can get.'

'I understand,' said Margaret. 'We'll just have to put it down to experience, shan't we?'

'Yes,' said Steven. 'Like we used to say when we were articled clerks, it's all good experience!'

'Ah, there you are,' cried Anne, flinging open the door to Steven and Margaret's office the next morning. 'We thought you'd walked out on us.'

'Oh, we wouldn't do that, would we Steven?' said Margaret

'No of course not,' replied Steven, 'I've just been busy with some new clients.'

'As long as you don't forget your original clients in the process' continued Anne.

'No way,' said Steven. 'What's happening about the computer?'

'Its coming tomorrow, and I'll need you here to help me,' replied Anne.

'No problem,' said Steven. 'I was planning on spending the rest of the week here anyway. I'll pop in and see you when we've got things organised. OK?'

'OK,' replied Anne pleasantly, and went back to her own office.

The rest of the week was spent setting up the computer at Parkers, working on the management accounts for Garage Trade, and taking frequent phone calls from Jean at Rivingham Cleaning.

'That girl seems to have a lot of problems,' said Margaret on Friday.

'She's only young,' said Steven, 'and she hasn't worked with computers before. I'll give her a ring, and ask her to keep all her queries together. Then I'll pop across later this afternoon to sort them out.'

'Hmmm,' said Margaret, 'perhaps that's what she wants.'

'What do you mean?' asked Steven.

'Oh nothing.'

'I'm so glad you've come,' cried Jean, later that afternoon. 'I've put all my queries together as you suggested, and I've asked the girl on the switchboard to hold any calls. So we won't be interrupted.'

'Fine,' said Steven. 'Lets get on with it then.'

'I'll just make a cup of tea first,' said Jean. 'I've bought us some apple turnovers. Do you like them?'

'Yes.'

'Good, I won't be a minute.'

As Jean left the room, Bill poked his head round the door. 'How are things going?' he enquired.

'All right. I think,' replied Steven cautiously.

'She seems to be making a lot of phone calls,' Bill continued.

'Yes she does. That's why I've come over, to see if we can get things sorted out.'

'Fine. Can I have a word with you when you've finished?'

'Certainly.'

Jean soon arrived back, and handed Steven his tea and apple turnover.

'Now then,' said Steven. 'What about these queries?'

'Oh there's no rush, let's finish these turnovers first. They're a bit difficult to eat aren't they?'

'Yes they are,' mumbled Steven, his mouth full of gooey cream cake. He was just manoeuvring to eat a particularly large piece of the sticky cake, when Fiona walked in.

'Sorry to interrupt the tea party,' she said sardonically. 'But could I have a cheque please Jean?'

Jean sullenly got the chequebook from her desk, and made out the cheque. Whilst she did so, Fiona watched with amusement, as Steven finished eating his apple turnover, getting cream all over the lower part of his face in the process. 'I don't know about computer training,' she said with a smirk. 'I think some training in eating cream cakes is called for.'

Steven blushed, and stood up. 'I'd better wash these sticky fingers' he said and rushed out of the room.

When Steven returned, Fiona had gone. 'Right' he said tersely, ' lets get these queries sorted out'

'You're mad at me,' said Jean, looking contrite.

'No. No. It's just that Bill wants to see me, and I need to get on.'

'That's all right then. I couldn't bear it if you were cross with me. Now, I have some problems with these invoices here..............'

When they had sorted all the queries, Steven went upstairs to see Bill. As he came into the room, Fiona stood up from her desk. 'I'm going home now,' she announced and gave Steven a smirk as she left the room.

'I hear you've been having cream cakes with Jean,' said Bill grimly.

'Yes I have,' replied Steven, surprised at Bill's stern tone. 'There's nothing wrong with that is there? The girl had bought them, and it seemed churlish to refuse.'

'She's not a girl, she's a young woman.'

'I know that, but you know what I mean.'

'But you don't know what I mean. She's a queer girl that one. She gets crushes on people. My ex-partner, Jim, had the devil's own job trying to get rid of her. At the Christmas party, he foolishly gave her a kiss, and that was that. She'd do things like staying back at night when she knew he was working late. She'd park her car next to his, so that they walked back to them together. To be honest I think that was part of the reason he wanted to sell up.'

'Surely not.'

'Well, it caused trouble with his wife, especially when Jean started ringing him at home. She came in here one morning and she really gave Jean an earful. After that, Jean cooled down, but it was always there in the background.'

Steven sat back in amazement. 'Phew. Thanks for warning me.'

'Don't thank me, thank Fiona. She was the one who saw the look in Jean's eye, and decided you needed protecting!'

When Steven got downstairs, Jean stood up from her desk. 'Is your car in the car park?' she asked.

'Ye...es,' replied Steven.

'Good. I'll just put my coat on, and we can walk round together.'

'Actually, Bill wants to see me about a few things,' said Steven. 'I've just come down to get my briefcase.' He grabbed his case and shot back upstairs.

Bill looked up in astonishment as Steven burst into the room. ' She was waiting to walk me to the car,' cried Steven wildly.

'OK. OK. Just calm down,' said Bill. 'I'll just sign these letters, and then we'll both go out together.'

After about ten minutes they came downstairs, to find Jean standing there with her coat on.

'Still here Jean?' asked Bill. 'I thought you'd have left ages ago.'

'I stayed back, in case Steven needed anything,' replied Jean.

'No, I don't need anything,' responded Steven, 'I'll see you next Thursday afternoon. And I'd be grateful if you could put all your queries to one side till then. Saves on the phone bills you know. And besides,' he laughed, 'my wife wants to know who this Jean is who's always ringing me.'

'Oh right,' said Jean, crestfallen. 'I'll be going then.'

'Yes, I think you'd better,' said Bill. 'Goodnight'

'I was talking to Alex Campbell after church,' said Steven, over Sunday lunch.

'What did he have to say?' responded Margaret.

'He's getting behind with his invoicing, so I suggested that he gets a computer.'

'Steven, you didn't.'

'Of course I did, what's wrong with that?'

'I thought we agreed that you wouldn't ask our friends for work.'

'There's no need to worry. It'll be a doddle. You'll see.'

'No. I don't want to see. Tell him you can't help him.'

'Don't be silly. I've already said I'll call round tomorrow.'

'Cancel it.'

'I can't. This is not like you Margaret. You're being completely irrational. We're not having any problems at Parkers are we? And I've sorted out Rivingham Cleaning haven't I.?'

'I suppose so.'

'Well, there you are then.'

'You'd better be right. If I lose Mary Campbell as a friend, I'll never forgive you.'

'It'll be all right. I've told you, it's a piece of cake.'

On Monday morning, Steven pushed back a huge double door to create a gap for him to enter the premises of Campbell & Co. He found that he was standing in a large, flag-stoned, area, with high racking to his right and a huge stack of cardboard cartons in front of him. On the left was an office, through which he could see Mary and Alex Campbell sitting at their desks. Alex looked up and waved for Steven to come in.

'Hello Steven,' said Mary. 'Alex says you're going to solve all our problems with a computer.'

'Oh, I don't know about that,' replied Steven.

'Well that's the impression Alex gave me yesterday. You really sold him on it.'

'Don't take any notice of her,' interrupted Alex. ' She's just trying to wind you up. Though I must say, what you said yesterday really did interest me.'

'Great,' said Steven, thankful that Margaret wasn't there. 'But you do realise that I need to see your systems first before I can recommend anything.'

'Of course,' said Alex. 'To be honest, we've had computer salesmen round before, but since our invoicing is rather specialised, we haven't felt like trusting them with our business. But with you—well, that's different.'

'Thank you for the compliment,' said Steven, even more pleased that Margaret wasn't around, 'Can you tell me a bit about your business then.'

'Certainly,' said Alex, ' would you like a cup of coffee?'

'Steven takes tea,' said Mary, 'don't you Steven?'

'Yes, that's right,' replied Steven.

'I'll make it,' said Mary. 'I'm supposed to be an equal partner, but somehow, when it comes to making tea, some of us are more equal than others.' She smiled sarcastically at Alex and left the office.

'Don't mind her,' said Alex with a laugh. 'She's just getting her daily dig in. Now then, what do you know about our business?'

'Not much,' admitted Steven. 'Beyond knowing that you're a wholesaler of sorts.'

'That's a pretty fair description of us. We are officially engineering wholesalers. What that means, is that we supply the various works and shipyards in the area with consumables they use every day. For instance, do you see that large stack of cartons over there? Well they're cleaning rags. We sell boxes and boxes of them every week. But we also sell specialised stuff, like gaskets, and that's what takes the time.'

'Yes,' chimed in Mary, as she came back into the office. 'Each gasket has to have its full description typed out, both on the confirmation order to the customer, and then to our supplier. It takes ages.'

'Hmmm' said Steven, 'Can I have a look at some examples please?'

For the next two hours, Steven spent time going through the invoicing procedure with Mary and Alex.

Finally Alex said, 'Well, what do you think?'

'It's a bit more complicated than I thought,' admitted Steven.

'I told you so,' said Mary in triumph.

'Yes. Yes.' Said Alex testily, 'but can you solve it Steven?'

'I could try.'

'Good man, how long will it take you? You see, it's our year end next month, and I'd like to buy the computer before then for tax purposes.'

'That should be all right.'

'Good, let us know how you get on. About the church meeting tomorrow night....'

That evening, Steven poured through his computer brochures. As time went on, he became more and more uneasy.

'Are you having problems with Campbell's computer?' asked Margaret.

'Not really,' lied Steven.

'Why are you looking so worried then?'

'It's just that their invoicing system is a bit special that's all.'

"It's a doddle' you said. 'Piece of cake' you said. I've warned you, if this system doesn't work, you'll be in serious trouble.'

'It'll work. It's just a matter of finding the right computer that'll match the specification,' said Steven, and turned his attention back to the brochures. Half an hour later, he cried out in triumph. 'I've got it. Look, Bingham Computers do an invoicing programme which has unlimited description fields.'

'What does that mean?'

'It means that Mary can type in as big a description as she wants, and the computer can cope with it.'

'Are you sure?'

'Well that's what it says here. I'll give them a ring tomorrow, and see if they have got a local supplier. There you are. I told you I could do it!'

'Let's see it working first.'

♦

CHAPTER 9

At the office the following morning, Steven rang Bingham Computers and was told that the local stockist was Bernard Lacy, of Dacre Colliery.

'Where on earth is Dacre Colliery?' asked Mary.

'It's a pit village on the way to Durham I think. I'll give them a ring, and get directions on how to find it.'

A female voice, with a Durham accent, said, 'Dacre Electrical.'

'Hello,' said Steven. 'I'd like to come and see a demonstration of your invoicing system please.'

'You what?'

'I'd like to see your invoicing system.'

'What for?'

'To see if it will work for my client.'

'Pardon?'

'That is Bernard Lacy's isn't it?'

'Yes.'

'And you do sell computers?'

'Oh. Its computers you're on about. Why didn't you say so? It's the boss you want. Just wait a minute.' Steven winced, as the voice bawled out, 'Bernard, can you pick your phone up? There's a bloke on about computers.'

'Hello, Bernard Lacy here. Can I help you?'

'I hope so,' said Steven. 'I'm wanting to see a demonstration of the Bingham Computer, and I'm told that you're the local stockist.'

'That's right, when would you like to come?'

'As soon as possible please. How about tomorrow afternoon?'

'I'm afraid not, tomorrow's half day closing. Can you come in the morning?'

'Right-ho. Tomorrow it is. Can you give me directions on how to find you?'

After receiving his instructions, Steven put the phone down. He turned round to see Margaret looking at him quizzically. 'Why are you looking at me like that?' He asked.

'They didn't sound very professional.'

'It'll be all right,' said Steven. 'A lot of these computer people share premises with other firms, until they get properly started. It'll be OK.'

'It had better be.'

Further conversation was stopped when Nigel walked into the room. 'Steven' he said, 'my overdraft is up for renewal, and the bank want a twelve months cash flow forecast. Just put one together for me will you?' He then turned to walk out of the room.

'Hang on a minute,' protested Steven. 'I can't produce it out of thin air you know.'

'What do you mean?'

'To start with, I need a sales forecast. Then we need to estimate the costs associated with that forecast, and go through the overheads.'

'Anne'll give you all that.'

'With due respect Nigel, you're the only one who can give me the sales figure.'

'Oh. OK. A million pounds. Will that do you?'

'No it won't. If you want me to put my name to a forecast, I'll want a detailed breakdown of how you intend to get that million.'

'All right. No need to get on your high horse,' sneered Nigel. 'I'll give you a breakdown on Thursday.'

When Nigel had left the room, Steven said to Margaret, 'We'd better get these management figures for Garage Trade finished today. It looks as if I'm going to be busy.'

Later in the morning, Anne popped her head round the door. 'Nigel tells me you're going to do a cash flow forecast for us.'

'I will if I get all the information.'

'That's what I called in about. I'm ready to start if you are.'

'I've got some management figures to do today for another client. Can I see you tomorrow afternoon?'

'What's wrong with tomorrow morning?'

'I'm going to a computer demonstration.'

'My. My. You are busy. So when do you think you could fit us in?'

'As I said, tomorrow afternoon,' said Steven, ignoring the sarcasm in Anne's voice.

'Then that'll have to do,' said Anne, and flounced out of the office.

Steven and Margaret looked at each other. 'Oh! Oh!' Said Margaret. 'You'd better watch it, or we'll be losing a client, and our office.'

'You're right. I'll pop in later, and ask her to start putting some information together for tomorrow. That'll keep her quiet.'

The road into Dacre Colliery ran downhill between rows of grimy bay-windowed Victorian terraced houses, punctuated by side streets of smaller flat houses. In the middle of the village, was a row of scruffy shops. As instructed, Steven walked along the row, looking in vain for a computer shop. He reached the end, and retraced his steps, this time looking up at the signs above the shops.

Finally he came to one that proudly proclaimed that it was the premise of Dacre Electrical Supplies. Steven pushed open the door and walked in.

The large, faintly lit, shop was full of household electrical goods scattered haphazardly around the premises. Out of the gloom came a small wiry woman of about forty, wearing an overall coat.

'No reps without an appointment,' she said sharply.

'I have an appointment,' replied Steven, equally sharply, 'with a Mister Bernard Lacy.'

'Oh. You must be the computer bloke. Sorry about that. You see, you're early, and Bernard asked specifically not to be disturbed this morning. I'll go and tell him you're here.'

A few minutes later she led Steven to the back of the shop, and indicated that he should go through the open door into a small cubby-hole of an office. In keeping with the rest of the premises, it was poorly lit and untidy. The walls were covered in shelving on which various files and papers were scattered. Cardboard boxes littered the floor, and a large desk against the wall was covered by bits of computer. A man was bent over the desk, and as he straightened up to greet Steven he seemed to fill the room with his bulk.

'Hello,' he said, 'Bernard Lacy. Sorry about the mess. Would you like a cup of tea?

'Yes please,' said Steven, and winced as Bernard bawled out, 'Two teas please Doris, and I'm not to be disturbed.'

Bernard lifted a cardboard box off a battered dining chair, and invited Steven to sit on it. 'I won't be long,' he said. 'I've just got the printer to connect, and we'll be ready to start.'

The demonstration went surprisingly well. Steven explained the invoicing problem at Campbell's, and, between them, Bernard and he were able to work out how the computer could cope with it.

'That all seems very good,' said Steven. 'Could you demonstrate it at my clients premises?'

'It's a bit difficult to leave the shop,' said Bernard. 'Why don't you demonstrate it?'

'Me?'

'Yes why not? I tell you what I'll do. If the demonstration goes all right, and I get and order, I'll give you 10% commission.'

'But I'm an independent adviser. I can't take commission.'

'Who's to know? It's what I do with the other consultants. They recommend me, and I accept an invoice for installation. That way everyone's happy.'

'I'm not so sure.'

'You haven't been in this game long have you?'

'No.'

'I tell you, everyone does it. You think about it, and give me a ring.'

Steven was going to continue protesting, but Doris appeared at the door.

'I thought I told you not to interrupt us,' said Bernard testily.

'I know you did, but there's an official here from the employment office, and he wants to see your wages records. He's most insistent, and says he has the right to see them.'

'More bureaucracy,' growled Bernard as he left the room. 'I'll soon get rid of him.'

'Don't bother,' said Steven, 'I've seen all I want anyway.'

'You'll give me a ring about the demonstration?'

'Yes,' promised Steven and left the shop, passing as he did so, a grim looking young man.

'I don't like it,' said Margaret over lunch.

'Neither do I,' responded Steven. 'But it's the only computer I can find that has the extended description facility.'

'Well, you know my view, you should never have taken the job on in the first place.'

'That's not very helpful.'

'It's not meant to be. You got yourself into this. Now you can get yourself out of it!'

'Margaret. Please. I need your advice.'

'My advice is that you go and see Alex, tell him the whole story and admit that you've failed.'

'You're right Margaret. I'll go and see him straight away.'

'Don't forget you're going to see Anne this afternoon.'

'Oh, I won't be long. Give her my apologies, and tell her I'll be in later will you.'

'Steven, you're the limit.'

'I know. But you love me really don't you?' laughed Steven, giving her a quick kiss.

Both Alex and Mary were at their desks when Steven arrived at Campbell's.

'Hello Steven,' greeted Alex. 'How did the demonstration go?'

'The demonstration went quite well,' replied Steven, 'but I'm afraid there's a couple of snags.' He gave them a description of Bernard and his premises and concluded with Bernard's offer of commission.

'What's wrong with that?' asked Alex. 'My business is built on commission.'

'Yes, but I'm supposed to be giving you independent

advice. If I take commission from a dealer, I'm compromising my position.'

'Steven,' said Alex kindly, 'listen to me. Is there any other computer that can do the job?'

'Not that I can find.'

'Have you told us everything about the deal?'

'Yes.'

'Well there you are then. Take the commission, and show us the computer as soon as you like.'

'And we appreciate your honesty,' chimed in Mary.

'Well if you say so,' said Steven doubtfully.

'We do' said Alex. 'We'll see you next Monday at your office. Two o'clock suit you? '

'Fine.'

'Well?' asked Margaret when Steven got back to the office. 'Did you tell them you couldn't get them a computer?'

'Not exactly,' admitted Steven.

'What do you mean?' asked Margaret.

'I did what you said,' continued Steven. 'I told them everything, but they still want to see a demonstration.'

Anne, bursting into the room, interrupted their conversation. 'Are you coming to see me or not?' she demanded. 'I've been waiting an hour already.'

'Sorry Anne,' muttered Steven. 'I got tied up.'

'So I hear. You've got to learn—Steven—that other people have important things to do as well. If you keep clients waiting you'll soon loose them. Come on, let's get started.'

Giving Margaret a wry smile, Steven meekly followed Anne out of the room.

Nigel was waiting in reception when Steven arrived early on Thursday morning. 'Come into my room,' he commanded, 'and I'll go through those sales figures with you.'

'You're early,' said Steven.

'I've been here since six o'clock,' replied Nigel. 'Working on your damned figures.'

With a flourish, Nigel turned over the front cover of a flip chart, to reveal a sheet of figures which had the amount of one million pounds written at the bottom.

'There you are,' he said. 'Will that do you.'

'Very impressive,' replied Steven. 'Can you explain what it means?'

'Well it's obvious isn't it? That's how we're going to achieve the million pound turnover you asked for.'

'What I meant was, can we go through which orders you have on the books now, and which ones are just promises.'

'Is that necessary? I thought that all you wanted was a breakdown of the million.'

'Yes, but I need to know how certain it is, so that I can work out various 'what ifs'.'

'What ifs?'

'Yes. What happens if you don't achieve your turnover, or if you exceed it.'

'Oh I see. Right-ho then, here we go. The first one is the order for Dugdales which we are half way through. The next...............'

When Nigel had finished, he sat down with the air of a conjurer who had just produced a rabbit out of the hat. Steven quickly did some calculations, and looked up with a worried expression. 'You've only got 20% of the turnover on the books at the moment. The rest of it depends on winning those orders you've listed.'

'I know that. But that's contracting. You always have to

assume that you're going to get another contract, otherwise you'd not sleep at night.'

'I agree, but the problem is that the forecast is heavily dependent on getting that job in Scotland for McBrides.'

'Oh we'll get that. Old Jock McBride is a personal friend. He'll make sure we get it.'

'But what if you don't?'

'Steven! I asked you to do a cash flow, not teach me how to run my business. You asked for a breakdown of the million pounds and you've got it. Now just get on with it will you. I'm going out.'

Steven started to work on the figures in the office, and was joined by Margaret. Later on Anne came in. 'Isn't Nigel here?' she asked in surprise.

'No, he left about an hour ago.'

'What did you say to him?'

'Nothing. I just asked him to go through the sales figures with me.'

'Ah! That explains it. He hates having to go into detail about anything.'

'Well you've got nothing to worry about if you get that order from McBrides.'

'McBrides? Who are they?'

'They're a big Scottish outfit, based in Glasgow.'

'Oh yes. I remember. We got an invitation to tender from them last week. It'll be a big job if we can get it.'

'You're telling me. Still, with Nigel's connections with Jock McBride you should be in with a chance.'

'Jock McBride?'

'You know, the Chairman. He's a friend of Nigel's.'

'Whatever gave you that idea? I've never heard of the man, and, if he'd been a friend of Nigel's, I would have done, believe you me!' With a laugh, Anne turned on her heels and left the office, leaving Steven gazing after her, open-mouthed.

'What's the matter?' asked Margaret.

'He lied to me,' replied Steven in a dazed tone. 'How can I work for someone who lies to me?'

'You're not working for him, you're his consultant,' said Margaret thoughtfully. 'I think there's a subtle difference. As far as Nigel's concerned, you're still an outsider. And, in a way, you've confirmed that, by querying his forecast.'

'But that's my job,' protested Steven.

'I know that. But you're going to have to get used to the fact, that from now on, you will always be on the outside looking in. No matter how well you get on with your clients, you'll never be their employee.'

'But I want to be part of the team.'

'I know you do. And you will be. But always as the bought in player, who will be sacked when the job is done.'

'I hadn't thought of it like that.'

'I'm afraid that's the way it's going to be.'

'Hmmm. I think you're right. Still, it also means that I have the right to walk away when I want to. Doesn't it?'

'Yes'

'Well that's what I'll do when Nigel gets on my nerves too much.'

'We'll still need an office,' warned Margaret.

'True. But we'll meet that problem when we come to it. Right, I'd better get over to Rivingham Cleaning and then I'll call on Barbara at Russell's.'

'I thought you weren't going out till this afternoon.'

'I wasn't, but I need a break from Parkers. I'd promised Jean that I would see her today and I haven't heard from Russell's for a while.'

Jean greeted him with dismay. 'You're early. I wasn't expecting you till this afternoon.'

'I know, but I've had to rearrange my schedule. Have you got any queries?'

'Yes, they're in the file over there. But I'm not ready.'

Steven picked up the file. 'This looks ready to me.'

'It's not that. It's just........ I'm not ready that's all,' she concluded lamely. 'Shall I make you a cup of tea, and nip to the shop for some cakes?'

'No thank you. I haven't got much time, so I'd rather get on. What's this query here about?'

Steven swiftly sorted out Jean's problems and said, 'I'll be off then. I'll come back next week to do the month end, and this time, I'll stay a bit longer.'

'Fine,' said Jean, 'I'll be ready for you next time.'

Barbara was also surprised to see him. 'Hello' she said warily, 'I wasn't expecting you.'

'I was passing, so I thought I'd drop in. How're you getting on?'

'Very well.'

'Good. When will you be ready for me to do the monthly figures.'

Barbara looked uncomfortable. 'Hasn't Bob told you?'

'Told me what?'

'I've already produced the figures for this month. You see, your working papers were so well set out, that I was able to follow them. I gave Bob the figures yesterday.'

'Oh.' Said Steven nonplussed.

'I hope you don't mind.'

'No. No. Of course not.'

'Bob's ever so pleased.'

'I bet he is,' thought Steven and said, 'I'll just pop up to see him.'

As Steven ran upstairs his mind was in a whirl. He tapped on Bob's door and burst in. He pulled up short when he saw Jennifer and Bob breaking free from an embrace.

'Don't you ever knock?' cried Bob angrily and red faced. Jennifer, also red faced, turned and ran through the adjoining door to her office.

'I'm sorry,' stammered Steven.

'What do you want?' snapped Bob.

'It was about the monthly figures.'

'Oh those. Judging by your action in barging in here, I presume that you know that Barbara's doing them now.'

'Yes, and she's using my working papers.'

'I wasn't aware that they were your property. We paid you for the work didn't we?'

'Yes,' said Steven reluctantly.

'And the papers were on a file in the accounts office?'

'True.'

'Well there you are then. I was going to suggest that you popped in on a quarterly basis to check them over. But in view of your attitude.....' Bob stopped.

'My attitude?'

'Yes. Barging in here as if you owned the place. I think, in the circumstances, we should call it a day don't you?'

'If you say so' said Steven. 'And don't worry. I'll keep my mouth shut. Not that I would be telling the staff anything they didn't already know.'

'What do you mean?' asked Bob, his face going red again.

'Ask them what they call the social room,' snarled Steven. As he turned and left, he caught a glimpse in the next office, of a white faced Jennifer, standing with her hand to her mouth.

'That's the first client I've lost,' Steven said miserably to Margaret when he returned to the office.

'It seems to me, that you'll always be working yourself out of a job,' replied Margaret.

'I suppose so,' sighed Steven, 'but I've lost it because of my clumsiness, not my skill.'

'Nonsense. You've lost it, because you set up a good system that an untrained girl could follow. The fact that you charged into Bob's office has got nothing to do with it.'

'I think it's got everything to do with it,' said Steven ruefully.

'You're probably right,' admitted Margaret. 'But I'm not sure it's all over yet. Sometimes when things are brought out into the open, it can have all sorts of repercussions.'

'But its not out in the open. I won't tell anyone.'

'I know you won't. But you told them that the staff knows, and that's what Jennifer was looking so upset about. I bet they're doing some hard talking this afternoon and it won't be about work.'

CHAPTER 10

The next day Steven took the familiar road to Calder Engineering, and was greeted glumly by George. 'Hello Steven,' he said. 'Come in.'

'Whatever's the matter?' asked Steven.

'I've just been talking to Claude Keighley-Smythe about a loan. We need to buy the materials for the Reynolds job, but he won't budge without a cash flow.'

'Well that won't take long. Where's Percy?'

'He's off sick. He's got a dickey heart you know, and the doctor's told him to have some time off, and avoid stress.' George gave a hollow laugh. 'Avoid stress. In this place. You know he hasn't paid himself for two months?'

'Yes'

'I thought so. He's been keeping a lot from me. Trying to shield me I suppose. He had a bash at doing some costing figures like you showed him, and they don't look good.'

'Let's have a look at them.'

'You're right,' said Steven, after they'd spent the next hour pouring over Percy's neat copperplate figures. 'They don't look good.'

'If we could just get on with this Reynolds job, everything will be all right.'

'Are you sure? Let's have a look at your costings.'

'They're only rough,' said George apologetically, and pulled out a battered file from his desk drawer.

'Something doesn't seem right,' said Steven as he poured over the pencil figures. He whipped out a sheet of paper started writing figures down. After ten minutes he said, 'There it is! Look. There's an addition error in your materials. You've overestimated by ten thousand pounds.'

'Is that good or bad?'

'Good. It means you've got ten thousand up your sleeve. For once George, you've quoted a decent price!'

George's face lit up. 'You mean we'll have enough money to cover Alan's central heating, and still make a profit?'

'Looks like it.'

'Great. Wait till I tell Percy.' He picked up the phone and in excited tones told Percy what they had discovered. He put the phone down and looked at Steven. 'Well that'll have cheered him up. Now about this cash flow.'

'We'll get on with it straight away, and I'll come with you to see Claude if you'd like me to.'

'Would you? That'd be great. I'll give him a ring now and make an appointment.'

The rest of the day was spent in preparing the cash flow forecast. At five o'clock Steven picked up all the hand-written sheets of paper and said, 'Right. I'll take this back with me, and get it typed up, ready for our meeting with Claude next week.'

'Thanks Steven. I don't know how to thank you.'

'Oh don't worry about that. Just get that costing system working, so that you control the job, instead of it running you.'

'OK. OK. As soon as Percy gets back, we'll get on with it.'

'See that you do. I'll just ring Margaret and tell her I'll be late.'

'What a nightmare of a journey,' groaned Steven as he slumped into his armchair. 'It took me three-quarters of an hour just to get out of Scarthorpe. Then there were roadworks at Wetherby, and worse ones on the A19. I turned off in the end, and came through the villages. Funny thing, I'm sure I saw Nigel's Range Rover parked outside a house in Netherton.'

'What's wrong with that?' asked Margaret.

'Oh nothing. It's just that Anne said he was going up to Scotland on business today, and wouldn't be back till late.'

'You were probably mistaken. There's loads of Range Rovers around, especially in the country areas.'

'Yes you're probably right.'

'By the way,' said Margaret casually. 'Your girl friend rang.'

'Girl friend?'

'Yes Jean. Something about meeting you for a drink.'

'You're having me on.'

'I'm not. She said you promised to meet her and her boyfriend sometime after work.'

'Oh that,' groaned Steven. 'She wants me to advise him on his future.'

'Does she. You didn't tell me about it.'

'I'd hoped she'd forgotten about it, but I was wrong. I'll give her a ring next week and arrange something. Did you ring Bernard Lacey about the computer for Alex?'

'Yes, against my better judgement. He'll see you at ten o'clock on Monday morning.'

First thing Monday morning Steven rang Jean, and arranged to meet her, and her boyfriend, straight after work on Thursday. He then drove to Dacre Colliery.

'Bernard's had to go out,' said Doris. 'He'll be back about eleven, but he's left the computer running for you in the back room. Would you like a cup of tea?'

'Yes please,' replied Steven, and went through into the

little cubby-hole. He sat at the computer and started to input information.

'Here's your tea,' said Doris. 'How're you getting on?'

'Quite well thank you.'

'Funny things computers. Don't understand them myself. Bernard does all the books on them. Says they're the thing of the future, and that eventually they'll control all our lives.'

'He's probably right.'

'Do you think so?' said Doris, then she gave a little chuckle. 'Mind you, it didn't help him with that inspector from the low pay unit.'

'Didn't it?'

'No. You see he couldn't hide the fact that he only pays us one pound fifty an hour, and the minimum rate is one pound seventy-five.'

'So I suppose that'll mean that you'll be getting a rise.'

'From Bernard? You must be joking! He says he can't afford to pay us any more money. So he's increased the rate, but he's reduced our hours, so we still get the same wages. The old skinflint.'

'How did the inspector get on to Bernard?'

A crafty look came over Doris's face and she dropped her voice. 'One of the other girls is going out with a lad who works in the office at the unit. So he knew what to do you see.'

'You mean, that inspector was her boy friend?'

Doris nodded her head in agreement. 'We didn't want to get Bernard into trouble. He's a good bloke really. Just a bit tight fisted. So we thought we'd give him a fright. Lot of good it did us.' She looked anxiously at Steven. 'You won't tell him will you?'

'I won't tell him,' Steven assured her, and turned back to his computer.

Later in the morning, Bernard came bustling in. 'Now then,' he said, 'how's it going?'

'Quite well,' replied Steven. 'I've been through the stock and sales and they seem OK. But what about wages, is there a program for them?'

'Oh yes,' replied Bernard. 'I use it myself. I'll do ours now if you like, and you can see how easy it is.' Steven moved over and Bernard started to operate the computer. Suddenly he stopped. 'Oh I forgot, I've got to change everyone's wages. Still, it'll be a good demonstration of the capabilities of the program.'

'Why are you changing the wages?' asked Steven innocently.

Bernard gave a chuckle and closed the door. 'The girls tried to trick me into giving them a rise.'

'How's that?'

'Well, you remember that young man who was in the shop last time you came. Said he was an inspector from the low pay unit?'

'Yes'

'He was no more an inspector than you or I. I saw through him straight away. I let him go through the motions, but later on, I made some enquiries. He's just a clerk, Joyce's boy friend I think. What the girls didn't know, was that I wanted to cut down on the opening hours anyway, and this gave me the opportunity. I've increase their rate, but I've reduced their hours. So they get what they want, at no extra cost to me, and I save on the overheads. Neat Eh!'

'Very neat,' agreed Steven.

Bernard looked anxiously at him. 'Don't tell the girls will you? I wouldn't want them to think that I'm a skinflint.'

'I won't tell them' promised Steven.

Back at the office, Steven finished off the cash flow and took it into Nigel. 'As you can see,' he explained, 'the figures show an increase in the overdraft for about two months and then a steady decrease. It starts to drop when the contract from McBrides starts to pay its way. I've done another set of figures to show what happens if you don't get that contract, and I'm afraid it's a pretty bad picture.'

He put the revised figures in front of Nigel, but he pushed them away. 'Steven,' he snarled, 'I've already told you, we're going to get that contract. I can't give the bank manager a set of figures that show that we're going bust, he'd close us down tomorrow.'

'I understand that,' said Steven impatiently. 'But its no good putting you're head in the sand. There's too much riding on that contract, and you need to be out there, selling, in case it doesn't come off.'

'Steven, I've told you before. Stop trying to tell me how to run my own business. Give your figures to Anne, and she'll type them up.'

'But I'll need to add some notes, so that Claude will know the basis of the figures.'

'I'll do all that. Thank you for your efforts, but that's all I need from you at the moment.'

'When's Claude coming?'

'On Friday, but I won't be needing you.'

'Fair enough, if that's the way you want it.'

'That's the way I want it.'

Steven stormed back into his room.

'What's the matter?' asked Margaret.

'That stupid ass Nigel won't listen to sense,' shouted Steven.

'Shhh. Keep your voice down. He'll hear you.'

'I don't care,' responded Steven. 'The whole world can

hear as far as I am concerned. Unless something happens pretty soon, he's going to go bust. And he won't do anything to avoid it.'

'All right. All right. Calm down. Lets pack up and go home, and you can tell me all about it in private.'

'That's a good idea. Come on, lets go home, before I do something I'll regret.'

By the time they had got to their house, Steven had calmed down, but his voice soon started to rise again, as he explained the situation to Margaret. 'There is no doubt about it,' he cried. 'Unless he gets some more work soon, Nigel will be in serious trouble.'

'Don't you think he knows that?' asked Margaret.

Something in her tone made Steven look at her. 'What do you mean?'

'Well it strikes me that Nigel already knows that he's in trouble, but having you smashing him in the face with it, is not helping.'

'But what am I supposed to do?'

'Talk to Anne. If anyone can get him to do something, Anne can.'

'You're right, I'll try to see her tomorrow on her own.'

The next morning Anne came in to Steven's room with the typed cash flow. 'Nigel suggested that you check this over and sign it,' she said pleasantly.

'Sign it?'

'Well you prepared it didn't you?'

'Yes, but based on Nigel's figures.'

'Stop splitting hairs Steven.'

'I'm not splitting hairs. Sit down for a minute will you? I want to have a word with you.'

Anne sat down and Steven showed her the second set of figures.

'Hmmm,' said Anne, 'I can see now why Nigel didn't come in till late last night.'

'What do you mean?'

'As I've told you before, when Nigel has a problem, his first instinct is to run away. That's what he did last night.'

'But what are we going to do about it?'

'The first thing is to keep the bank happy. You check this typed one over, and I'll talk to Nigel.'

'But I'm not going to sign it.'

'Steven, we need you to sign it. We've given you a start. Now it's your turn to pay us back.'

There was a long pause, as Steven digested this comment. 'OK,' he said, 'I'll sign. But only if I can say that it's based on Nigel's sales figures.'

'Fair enough.'

'It's Thursday,' groaned Steven at breakfast.

'What's wrong with Thursday?' asked Margaret.

'I've got to go and see that dreadful girl at Rivingham Cleaning, and then meet her boy friend.'

'Oh yes. Perhaps you shouldn't lead the girls on if you don't want them to be interested in you.'

'I don't lead them on.'

'Well this one seems very keen.'

'Don't be so ridiculous, Margaret. I'm going to the office.'

That afternoon, Jean greeted Steven with enthusiasm. She was wearing a straight, tight, black skirt, with a slit up the side, and a thin white blouse. The top three buttons of the blouse were undone, and Steven could see the swell of her breasts over the top of a skimpy lace bra. 'Hello Steven,' she said. 'I've got most of the postings done, and I've held all the queries, just like you told me to.'

'That's very good,' gulped Steven. 'Lets have a look at the queries.'

'They're on the desk in the corner. You have a look at them, and I'll make you a nice cup of tea.'

Steven sat down at the desk and studied the papers until Jean came back with a tray. 'I hope you like chocolate cake,' said Jean, sitting down besides Steven and handing him a piece. 'I made it myself.'

'As a matter of fact, I do,' mumbled Steven, uncomfortably aware that Jean was sitting very close to him. 'Shall we get on with the queries?'

'Oh there's no rush. Bill and the ice maiden have gone swanning off somewhere, so we won't be interrupted.'

'But I have to get the monthly figures done this afternoon,' said Steven, trying to avoid gazing down Jean's blouse, 'so we'd better get started.'

'Oh all right. But you have remembered that you're meeting Tom tonight?'

'Tom?'

'My boy friend.'

'Oh! Yes. We're seeing him straight after work aren't we?'

'That's right.'

'OK. Now lets get these queries sorted out.'

As they sorted through the papers, Jean leant closer and closer. Steven tried to move away, but was boxed in, by the desk, the wall, and Jean. He was desperately trying to think of a way out of his predicament, when Bill and Fiona came into the office.

'Hmmm, very cosy,' remarked Fiona, and carried on upstairs.

'Ah Bill,' gasped Steven. 'I wonder if we could have a word about these queries? Can you let me out Jean?'

Jean reluctantly moved over, and Steven crossed the room to Bill holding one of the invoices. 'I think we'll look at it in my office,' said Bill, and ran up the stairs with Steven trailing behind him.

'What do you think you're playing at?' Bill demanded.

'What do you mean?' countered Steven.

'I mean sitting there, with Jean practically on your lap. I thought I warned you about her.'

'You did, but what could I do?'

'You could move to another desk or something.'

'I was just going to when you came in.'

There was a snort of derision from Fiona at the other desk.

Steven rounded on her fiercely 'I was,' he shouted.

'Oh yes,' responded Fiona, 'and what about this meal you're having tonight?'

'Meal?'

'Don't come the innocent with me. I heard her booking a table for two at the Crown.'

'Oh that. We're meeting her boy friend there for a drink. But I'm not staying for a meal. She must be staying on with her boyfriend.'

'If you say so.'

'I do say so. I am not a bit interested in Jean. I just want to get the job done.'

'OK. OK.' Said Bill. 'But you've got to admit, its looks a bit black. Especially going out with her tonight.'

'I told you. It's with her boy friend, and it's only a drink. Now can I get on with my work please?'

Steven stormed out of the room and down the stairs. Jean looked up in alarm as he burst into the room. 'Right Jean, get those invoices put into the computer. I'm going to find a spare desk to sit at.'

'But Bill said this corner desk was for you.'

'Did he? I'm sorry but I don't like corner desks. A touch of claustrophobia.'

'Oh you poor thing. I thought you were getting rather uncomfortable when we were looking at the queries. I tell you what, you can have my desk. Is that all right?'

Jean's desk was beside the window, in full view of the door, and not hemmed-in in any way. 'That would be fine,' said Steven, 'I'm very grateful.'

'Not at all. Anything for you.'

Late in the afternoon Steven took the figures up to Bill. 'There you are' he said. 'One set of sales figures broken down by site. By next week, we'll be able to do a profit and loss on each site, and then for the whole company.'

'That's great,' cried Bill, 'isn't it Fiona?'

'I suppose so,' replied Fiona.

'And it's all down to Jean,' continued Steven.

There was a snigger from Fiona.

'I wish you'd stop doing that Fiona,' said Steven. 'I know what you're thinking, but she does a damn good job on the computer.'

'That puts us in a bit of a quandary,' said Bill. 'You see, after this afternoon's episode, we've decided to sack her.'

'What?'

'We can't have her chasing everything in trousers can we?'

'But surely it doesn't warrant the sack.'

'Fiona thinks so.'

'Look,' said Steven. 'I'll have a word with her tonight. See if I can get her to see sense.'

'OK. But any more incidents like this afternoon and she's out.'

After work, Jean and Steven walked over to the Crown. The lounge was empty apart from a nondescript young man sitting in the corner. He raised his hand in greeting, and Jean introduced them to each other. 'Would you like a whisky Steven?' she asked, when the pleasantries were over.

'Oh no, its too early for that,' responded Steven. 'I'll have a pint lager shandy please.'

'What about you Tom?' she asked.

'I'll just have a half of beer,' replied Tom. 'I've got to go to work soon.'

Steven sat down opposite Tom. 'Nice girl you've got there,' he said.

'I wish I did have her,' responded Tom glumly. 'I've asked her to marry me, but she won't accept. She says I'm boring and have no ambition. That's why I agreed to see you.'

Jean came back with the drinks, and sat down beside Steven. 'Now then,' she said, 'how are you two getting on?'

'Fine,' replied Steven. 'Where do you work Tom?'

'At the naval storage depot down the road.'

'This far inland?'

'Yes. Apparently it was set up during the war. We supply spare parts for ships all over the world.'

'Interesting, and what do you do?'

'I'm a clerk in the despatch department.'

'But they want to promote you, don't they.' interrupted Jean.

'Yes' responded Tom dispiritedly.

There was a pause. 'Go on. Tell Steven about it,' urged Jean.

With a sigh, Tom said, 'They're going to computerise the

whole operation, and they want me to be the representative on the working party from the despatch department.'

'That's good isn't it?' beamed Jean.

'It does sound a good opportunity,' said Steven. 'Why don't you want to do it Tom?'

Tom looked even more unhappy. 'Because I'll have to go to Portsmouth for six months on a course.'

'And he doesn't want to leave me,' said Jean impatiently. 'But I think it's too good an opportunity to miss. Don't you Steven?'

'Tom,' said Steven, ignoring Jean, 'Why don't you tell me more about the project? Then we can look at your options.'

As Tom explained all about the new system, he became transformed from a downtrodden clerk, to an animated young man.

When he had finished, Steven looked at him thoughtfully and said, 'I can see why they've chosen you for the job, you're a computer buff aren't you?'

'Oh yes, he's got his own computer at home, and he's always playing with it,' said Jean.

Steven turned to her and said, 'Jean, with due respect, I'm here to talk to Tom, not you. Please let him answer for himself.'

Jean's jaw dropped in amazement, then she sat back in her seat with a hurt expression on her face.

Tom looked equally startled, but said, 'You're right. When I get in front of a computer screen, all else goes out of my mind, and I can be there for hours.'

'Well then,' said Steven, 'I don't see what you are hesitating for. Computers are going to be the biggest thing to hit the world since the invention of the wheel, and you've got the chance to be in at the ground floor. It's a once in a lifetime opportunity, and you'd be a fool to turn it down.'

'But what about Jean?'

'What about her? If she's daft enough to let a good prospect like you slip through her fingers, then she doesn't deserve you. Right I'm off. I've got a wife and kids waiting for me.'

'But I thought......,' said Jean, her face a picture.

'You thought I'd stay and have a cosy little dinner with you tonight? Grow up Jean. Stop chasing men who are old enough to be your father, and settle down with someone your own age. See you next week. Best of luck Tom.'

Tom jumped up from his seat, and shook Steven's hand. 'Thank you,' he said. 'Thank you very much.'

'Not at all,' said Steven, 'I just hope it works out all right for you.'

Jean didn't move, but sat slumped in her chair with a look of utter shock on her face. Steven gave her a wave and left the pub. When he got out side he found he was shaking. "Phew," he thought, "if that doesn't do the trick, nothing will."

CHAPTER 11

Margaret met Steven in the hall. 'Come through into the kitchen,' she said softly as she led the way, 'the kids are watching Tele in the front room.'

'What's the matter?' asked Steven.

'George Calder's rung. Percy died earlier today.'

'Percy? Dead?'

'I'm afraid so. George wants you to ring him.'

'Of course. Poor Percy. George said he had a dickey heart. He'll be devastated.'

'Yes, he sounded pretty upset. Here's his home telephone number.'

'I'll ring him straight away,' said Steven. When George answered he said, 'I'm sorry to hear about Percy, what happened?'

'He had a heart attack this morning. Fortunately his niece, Carol, had called in to see him, so he wasn't alone. She called the ambulance straight away, but there was nothing they could do.'

'Bit of a shock for her.'

'Yes it was. She was very close to Percy. Took him to church every Sunday, and generally looked after him. She's taken it remarkably well. Says it's the way Percy would have wanted to go, and that he's at rest now.'

'I can understand that. But how do you feel? You've had a shock as well.'

'You're right. It's hit me quite a bit. I relied on Percy such a lot. Not just for the accounts, but for advice and support.' There was a catch in his voice. 'I'll miss him. You know, I'm not a churchgoer but to me Percy was a real Christian.'

'He was that,' agreed Steven.

'The funeral's next Tuesday,' continued George, 'which clashes with our appointment with Claude. Could you go on your own? You know all the figures, and I couldn't face Claude at this point.'

'I could get him to change the appointment.'

'To be frank Steven, I don't think he'll give us anything. And I'd like to know sooner rather than later. With Percy going, I'm not sure what I'm going to do now. I might just pack it all in, and go back on the tools.'

'I can understand how you feel. But you're still in shock. At least wait until I've seen Claude before you make any decisions.'

'OK Steven. I'll give you a ring on Tuesday night.'

Steven put the phone down and looked at Margaret. 'He has taken it badly. Let's hope Claude sees sense, otherwise George'll close down.'

'Will that be such a bad thing? After all, you said that he was struggling.'

'I know, but with the Reynolds job he could get back on his feet.'

'For how long?'

'Margaret,' said Steven, raising his voice, 'stop being negative.'

'No need to shout.'

'I'm sorry. It's been a long day. I liked Percy a lot. He was so keen to see George succeed. It seems such a shame that his death'll cause George to give up.'

Claude Keighley-Smythe was sitting in reception when Steven and Margaret walked in the next morning.

'Good morning Claude,' said Steven. 'I'd like you to meet my wife Margaret.'

'Hello,' said Margaret. 'I've heard a lot about you.'

'All good I hope,' replied Claude jovially.

'Not exactly,' responded Margaret.

'Oh,' said Claude, rather nonplussed.

There was an embarrassed pause.

'You're seeing Nigel this morning,' said Steven, desperate to break the silence.

'Yes that's right. You're not joining us I gather.'

'No.'

'Quite right. I always prefer to talk to the man who runs the business, rather than the manipulator of figures.'

Steven flushed. 'On that front, I'm afraid George Calder can't make the meeting next Tuesday, so he's asked me to come on my own.'

'That's all right, in his case I hardly think it matters, do you?'

Nigel appeared and said, 'Sorry to keep you waiting Claude. I understand you know Steven.'

'Oh yes.'

Something in his tone made Nigel look sharply at him, and then at Steven and Margaret. 'I hope you haven't been upsetting Claude,' he said with a half laugh. 'We can't go upsetting the bank manager, can we?'

'Some people don't seem to have your business acumen,' said Claude. 'Shall we go to your office?'

'Certainly,' said Nigel, and, throwing Steven a murderous look, ushered Claude down the corridor.

'Oh. Oh.' Said Steven, as they made their way to their own office. 'That was not a very diplomatic thing to say to Claude.'

'Well he deserves it,' said Margaret.

'I agree, but it still wasn't diplomatic. Never mind,

let's get on with Garage Trade's figures. I've got to get the computer from Dacre later on. I'm seeing Alex and Mary on Monday, so I need to practice over the weekend.

'Where do you propose to do that?'

'I thought in the dining room.'

'You what! We've got John and Helen coming tomorrow night.'

'I know. I'll put it all away for then. I promise.'

'You'd better.'

At five o'clock on Saturday evening, Margaret stormed into the living room where Steven was watching the football results with Jason and Katy. 'Steven,' she screamed, 'there are bits of computer all over the dining room, and John and Helen are due at seven.'

'I'll soon put them away love. Just let me see the report of the Rivers match first.'

'Steven!'

'OK. OK. Keep your hair on.'

'I'm fed up. You've spent all day on that damned computer. We've got company coming in two hours, and you haven't lifted a finger to help. The dining room's a mess, this room's a tip, and all you can do is watch Tele.' She marched over to the television and switched it off, to a chorus of 'Mam!' from the youngsters.

'And you two can get your rooms tidied up.'

'But Mam,' said Jason.

'No buts. Just do it.'

'Come on Jason,' said Katy. 'We'd better do what she says. When she's in this mood, there's no talking to her.'

'You little madam,' cried Margaret raising her hand, 'I've a good mind to.......' She didn't finish her sentence as the two youngsters scurried out of the room.

'Margaret,' said Steven, appalled, 'whatever's got into you?'

'It's just everything. All we seem to do now-a-days is work, work, work. You expect me to come into the office every day, have a meal on the table when you come in, and then spend all night listening to your moans about your clients. Now you're working all weekend. I tell you Steven, I'm sick of it. I wish we'd never started.'

Steven stood up and put his arms around Margaret who burst into tears and sobbed on his shoulder.

'I'm sorry love,' he said. 'I hadn't realised it was getting to you so much.'

'No. You're too busy sorting out your girl friends problems' to worry about me.'

'Margaret, that's unfair.'

'Is it? How do I know what you're getting up to with Ann when you say you are working late? And what about that Jean, and Fiona.'

'Margaret, Margaret. They are not my girl friends. I'm not interested in any one else but you.

'How do I know that?'

Steven kissed her tenderly, 'Margaret, without you, my life wouldn't be worth living.'

'Honestly?'

'Honestly. Now come on, dry your tears. I'll get the dining room tidied up, and vacuum in here. You get the dinner on.'

'OK. But no more work. Especially when John and Helen are here.'

'No more work. I'll take the computer down to the office, and tomorrow we'll have a run out after church, how's that?'

'That'll be lovely. I'll go and apologise to the kids. It's not their fault.'

'I suppose not. But they could help a bit more about the house, instead of just waiting to be fed.'

'Look who's talking.'

'OK. Point taken.'

Whilst Margaret was in the kitchen, putting the finishing touches to the dinner, John said, 'How's business Steven?'

'Quite good actually,' replied Steven. 'But the trouble is, all we talk about is work. We just can't get away from it.'

'Yes, Margaret was telling me about it the other day,' said Helen. She dropped her voice, 'she got quite upset actually.'

'Did she? Well, we've just had a good chat, and sorted things out. So, if it's all the same to you, we'll give work a rest tonight.'

'Good,' said Helen 'and, if you don't mind me saying so, about time too.'

Steven flushed and said quietly, 'OK Helen. I know what you're saying. I just didn't realise how much things were getting on top of her. It'll be different from now on.'

On Monday morning Steven was setting up the Bingham computer, when Anne popped her head round the door. 'Morning Steven,' she said. 'No Margaret today?'

'No. We've decided that she'll only come in when she's definitely needed.'

'Good idea. I don't know how she manages with a job and two teenage children at home. She's been looking a bit peaky lately.'

'It seems like everybody's noticed but me,' said Steven bitterly.

'Oh that's usually the way with men. How about if I take her out for a girls lunch again? Might cheer her up.'

'That's very good of you.'

'That's all right. I've got a lot of time for Margaret. You're very lucky Steven. Don't let your marriage get like ours.'

'What's the matter with our marriage?' asked Nigel from behind her.

'Well if you don't know, I don't,' replied Anne tartly, and flounced back to her office.

'I'd better go and see what that was all about,' said Nigel gloomily. 'By the way Steven, Claude has given us the extra overdraft, thanks to your figures.'

'You did tell him they were based on your sales forecasts, didn't you?'

'Of course I did. Your precious professional position was made quite clear. Honestly Steven, anyone would think that you didn't trust me.' Without waiting for a response he continued, 'He needs regular monthly figures and he's left me a form. Have a look at it with Anne will you?'

'I can't do it today I'm afraid. I've got a computer demonstration.'

'Well tomorrow morning then.'

'I'm going to see Claude for another client.'

'Steven, you're going to have to get your priorities right.'

'Yes, I know. How about tomorrow afternoon?'

'I suppose that'll have to do. I'll tell Anne.'

Alex and Mary Campbell arrived promptly at two o'clock, and were shown in by Sheila.

'Hello Steven,' said Alex, 'nice place you've got here. Where's Margaret?'

'It'll be quite crowded in here with three of us and a computer, so I've given her the day off.'

'Quite right too,' chimed in Mary. 'Margaret hasn't been herself lately. You men just take us for granted. I finally put my foot down and told Alex that either we got a cleaner, or I would just have to work part time.'

'Yes, I remember,' said Alex with feeling. 'We had an almighty row, which ended up with me giving in as usual.'

'Hmmm,' said Steven. 'We'll get on with the demonstration shall we?'

They all gathered round the computer, and Steven showed them the way it produced invoices. He also showed them how the computer was able to post the invoice to the sales ledger, and update the stock at the same time.

'That's fantastic,' said Alex, 'isn't it Mary?'

'Steven certainly makes it look easy, but I'm not so sure I can manage it.'

'OK.' Said Steven, 'I'll move over, and you drive it.'

'You make it sound like driving a car,' laughed Mary nervously.

'It is. When you first learn to drive a car, everything's new to you, and you think you'll never get the hang of it. But with practice, it becomes second nature. That's what happens with computers.'

'If you say so,' said Mary doubtfully.

'Trust me,' pleaded Steven.

'Oh I do,' replied Mary.

'Come on,' said Alex, 'give it a try.'

Mary reluctantly took her place at the computer, and Steven took her slowly and carefully through the steps needed to create an invoice. At the end he said 'Now then, press 'P' to print.'

Mary did so, and gave a squeal of delight when the printer came to life and produced an invoice.

'Well done,' cried Alex. 'Now then Steven, show Mary how to update the ledgers and stock.'

Under Steven's guidance, Mary soon did so.

'There love,' said Alex,' that'll save you a lot of time won't it?'

'I suppose so,' said Mary, 'but how do I know which buttons to press?'

'Oh I'll train you,' said Steven.

'But what happens when you're not there?'

'Well, you'll have the manual,' said Steven, lifting up a fat book from the table and handing it to Mary.

'But I can't understand this,' cried Mary, leafing through the book. 'You'll have to have something simpler for an idiot like me.'

'But you're not an idiot,' replied Steven.

'I am when it comes to computers,' retorted Mary. 'No Steven. If you want me to use that thing, you'll have to write me a simpler set of instructions.'

'You're caught there,' chuckled Alex. 'And I must say, I agree with Mary. Unless you can write an idiots guide the deal's off.'

'OK.' Said Steven. 'I'll write a simpler guide. But can you see how the computer will make things easier for you?'

'Oh yes,' said Alex. 'But lets see how much it's going to cost first.'

'OK. I'll let you have a price by the end of the week.'

'Well, Claude was wrong,' mused Steven, as he waited for his appointment with the bank manager. 'We have survived, and our marriage hasn't broken up.' At this last thought, his stomach gave a lurch. 'Was his marriage all right? What about the comments from Helen and Mary? And what about that outburst last Saturday?'

The arrival of Claude, stopped any further musings. 'Sorry to keep you waiting Steven, come through to my office. It's a long time since you were here.'

'Yes it is,' responded Steven.

'I understand from Nigel that you're so busy that you couldn't spare the time to come in to our meeting on Friday. You know, you really ought to get your priorities right Steven. Surely you'd have been better off giving time to Nigel, than a tin pot firm like Calder Engineering. Still, we managed quite well without you. Nigel has a good grasp of his business, and is really going places.'

'Did he show you his sales forecast?'

'Oh yes. Very impressive. That McBrides contract will take him into another league altogether.'

'If he gets it.'

'Of course he'll get it. With his contacts at the highest level he's sure to pull it off. You know Steven, in banking we have to learn who's genuine, and who's pulling the wool over our eyes. Though I say it myself, I'm a pretty good judge of character. If Nigel says he'll get the contract, he will. Which brings us to George Calder.'

'What about him?'

'Well he's a no-hoper if ever I saw one.'

'What do you mean?'

'Just look at him compared with Nigel. He drives a battered old van. His clothes probably came off a market stall. He lives in a council house. Need I go on?'

'But the figures......'

'What about the figures? Pie in the sky if you ask me.'

'But he's just got a big contract with Reynolds. It'll be the making of him.'

'Look. I'm sorry to disillusion you, but my experience of George Calder is that he couldn't make a profit selling bananas to monkeys.'

'That's unfair.'

'Have you seen his latest accounts?'

'Yes, but he's changing things.'

'Like what?'

'He's putting in a new costing system, so that he can keep track of his jobs.'

'And who's going to keep the system working? That Percy fellow?'

'Percy's dead,' said Steven in a low voice. 'George is at the funeral today.'

'Oh. I'm sorry to hear that. But it makes the situation worse. If Percy isn't there to keep the books straight, then George doesn't stand a chance. I'm sorry Steven. Unless George can come up with some security, I can't extend the overdraft. '

'But we only want five thousand pounds. What about a floating debenture? '

'On what? A broken down van, some old equipment, and a yard full of scrap? Come on Steven.'

'A personal guarantee.'

'We already hold that to cover his existing overdraft. Not that it's much good, seeing that he has no savings, and nothing to sell. You won't believe this Steven, but I went out on a limb for him last time, and I can't risk any more of the bank's money. In fact, in the light of Percy's death, I may have to call in the two thousand we've already lent.'

'Don't do that! At least give him a chance. I tell you, this Reynolds job is a good one. I've seen the figures and for once he's put in a good price.'

'OK. On you're assurances Steven, I'll leave the existing

limit on. But I'll need to see an improvement over the next six months. Otherwise, I'll have to close him down.'

Steven went back to the office absolutely miserable. 'How am I going to tell George?' he wailed to Margaret. 'Not only did I fail to get him a loan, I nearly lost him his existing overdraft.'

'It's not your fault,' comforted Margaret. 'I'm afraid in this case Claude is probably right.'

'You what!'

'Don't raise your voice like that. All I said was, that with Percy dying, and George's past history, I can understand why Claude turned you down.'

'Thanks a lot,' said Steven bitterly. 'That's really helped. I'd better go and see what figures Anne's got for me. At least she supports her husband.'

'Steven!'

'I'm sorry. I shouldn't have said that.'

'No you shouldn't,' said Margaret. 'You can go and see your ever-efficient Anne. I'm going home,' and she stormed out of the office.

'Trouble?' asked Anne, as Steven walked into her office.

'These walls are very thin aren't they?' said Steven

'Only when you shout. Did I hear my name mentioned?'

'Errm. Yes.'

'Well?'

'I don't know how to put this, but I think she's a bit jealous.'

'You're kidding.'

'I'm not.'

Anne gave an incredulous laugh. 'What have you been saying?'

'Nothing. I just said that you supported your husband, and she flipped her lid.'

'You said that?'

'Yes.'

'And you implied, I suppose, that she didn't support you.'

'I suppose so. Yes.'

'No wonder she flipped. Go home straight away.'

'But we've got to get these figures sorted.'

'Steven. Your marriage is more important than these figures. You and Margaret have something precious, don't throw it away like Nigel and I did. Now go and apologise to Margaret.'

'She'll get over it. It's just the time of the month. I'll talk to her tonight.'

'Talk to her now Steven, or you'll regret it.'

'No. We'll do the figures first.'

'On your head be it.'

Nigel came in at five o'clock just as they were finishing the figures.

'How's it going?' he asked. 'Have you got those figures for my friendly bank manager?'

'Yes,' replied Steven, 'we've just finished.'

'Good, lets have a look at them.'

'Shouldn't you be getting off Steven?' asked Anne.

'What's the matter?' sneered Nigel. 'Frightened to keep the little wife waiting?'

'Nigel!' barked Anne.

'It's all right Anne,' said Steven, 'It won't take long.'

'Suit yourself,' said Anne, 'but I'm going home.'

As they went through the forecast, Nigel took a perverse pleasure in querying every figure. After an hour Steven said 'Right. That's it. I'm off home.'

'But we haven't gone through the overhead figures yet,' protested Nigel.

'Look,' replied Steven, 'it's been a long day, and I'm tired. You go through them and I'll answer any queries on Thursday. OK?'

'No it's not OK,' snapped Nigel. 'I want to give these figures to Claude tomorrow.'

'Well give him them then,' responded Steven equally sharply. 'They're as much use as the sales figures you gave him last week, and he was happy enough with them.'

'What are you getting at?'

'I'm getting at the fact that you lied to me about McBrides. Personal friend indeed. You've never met the man.'

'What makes you think that?'

'Because Anne had never heard of him.'

'Anne doesn't know everything.'

'No, I've gathered that.'

'What do you mean?'

'Nothing. I'm going home before I say something I regret.'

Without giving Nigel time to respond Steven went straight out to his car, and drove off.

CHAPTER 12

When Steven arrived home, the house was in darkness, and Margaret's car was missing. 'That's funny,' he thought, 'I can't remember Margaret saying she was going out.' Then he remembered their last words, and went cold all over. He let himself in, but there was no clue as to the whereabouts of Margaret and the kids. Neither was there a dinner for him, so he raided the freezer and put a Marks & Spencer meal in the microwave. It had just 'pinged', when the phone rang. Thinking it was Margaret he demanded, 'Where are you?'

'At home,' replied the broad Yorkshire voice of George Calder, 'Where did you expect me to be?'

'Oh its you George,' responded Steven. 'I thought you were some one else.'

'I gathered that,' said George. 'What's up? Anyone would think it was you who'd been to a funeral, not me.'

'I'm sorry,' said Steven, 'my mind was on other things. How did the funeral go?'

'As well as these things do. I suppose. But how did you get on with Claude?'

'Not very well I'm afraid. He won't give you an extra loan, and in fact, at one stage, was talking about withdrawing the two thousand you already have.'

'You what?'

'You heard. I managed to talk him out of that one, but they'll be keeping a tight reign on you from now on.'

'Well, I suppose I can hardly blame him. What with my past history, and Percy dying an' all.'

'That's just what Margaret said.'

'She's obviously got good sense that one, just like another female I was talking to today.'

'Who was that?'

'Percy's niece Carol. You know, the one who found him.'

'Oh yes. What was she saying?'

'Apparently, Percy was quite well off, and as Carol's his only surviving relative, most of his money's coming to her. She's a spinster, and works as a bookkeeper for a local builder. But she says she's always wanted to work for herself. Percy's told her all about me, and she wants to become a partner in my business.'

'Good heavens.'

'Yes it's a shock isn't it?'

'Does she know what she's getting into?'

'Oh yes. Percy hasn't pulled any punches. She knows all about my low prices, and says that things'll have to change.'

'And what do you think about it?'

'It's either that, or close down altogether. If Claude won't lend me any more money, I can't see that I've got much option.'

'You'd better think long and hard about it George. Partnerships can often run into trouble, and working with a woman makes it twice as hard.'

'You're managing.'

'Yes, but we're married,' responded Steven, wondering desperately where Margaret was. 'What does you're wife think about it?'

'She left me five years ago,' replied George tersely.

'Oh. I'm sorry. I didn't know.'

'That's alright. Water under the bridge. But I agree.

It'll need a lot of thinking about. For her sake as much as mine. Why don't you come down and talk to both of us next week? I'd value your advice, and Carol has heard all about you.'

'If you really want me to, I could come next Tuesday.'

'Great, next Tuesday it is then.'

Steven had just settled down to eat his meal, when the phone rang again.

This time he just said 'Hello?'

'Hello, is that Steven?' said an excited female voice.

'Yes. Who's that?'

'Its Jean from Rivingham. I've got some marvellous news.'

Steven mentally groaned, and said, 'Jean, I'm rather tied up at the moment.'

'Oh it's all right, I won't keep you. I just wanted you to know that Tom and I have got engaged.'

'You what?'

'Tom and I have got engaged,' she repeated, 'and we've got you to thank for it.'

'What do you mean?'

'The other night, after your talk, Tom and I had a meal together. I persuaded him to apply for the promotion, and he agreed to do so on the condition that we got engaged. He's been accepted for the job, so we got engaged tonight. I wanted you to be the first to know. You're so clever. I knew that if anyone could talk Tom round, you could. We're having an engagement party next Saturday at the Crown and we'd love you to come, with your wife of course.'

'That's very nice of you,' replied Steven still in shock, 'I'll talk to Margaret and let you know.'

'Right-ho. I'll see you on Thursday as usual. Bye.'

Steven picked listlessly at his lukewarm meal, and

thought ruefully about the way he seemed to be able to sort out other peoples problems, but not his own. Why oh why did he have to say such a stupid thing to Margaret? After his meal, he poured himself a lager and slumped in front of the television to await the return of his family.

By half past nine he was starting to feel uneasy. By ten o'clock his imagination was working overtime. Where were they? Had there been an accident? Had Margaret walked out on him? After all, he had said some silly things, and you did hear about people just up and leaving. He thought about ringing his in-laws, but decided to give it another half an hour before making such an embarrassing phone call.

At twenty past ten he heard a car on the drive. He got to the front door just as Katy burst in, followed closely by Jason and Margaret.

'Where've you been?' cried Steven.

'We've been to see that new James Bond film,' Katy blurted out excitedly, 'It was great, You should have been there.'

'Yes,' chimed in Jason, as they moved down the hall into the living room, 'You should have seen the space fight at the end. It was fantastic.'

'Then we stopped off for some fish and chips,' continued Katy. 'We've had a smashing time.'

'Pity you couldn't make it,' said Margaret from the rear.

'But I didn't know anything about it,' protested Steven.

'I promised the kids a treat after I got annoyed with them at the weekend. I'm sure I told you, but perhaps you were too tied up with your clients problems to take any notice.'

'Now don't start that,' replied Steven, his voice rising.

'Please don't start to fight again,' cried Katy. 'We've had a lovely night, please don't spoil it Dad.'

Steven opened his mouth to continue the argument, but one look at Katy's pleading face, stopped him. 'Sorry,' he said, 'I was just worried about where you were. Come on, we'll have a cup of something, and you can tell me all about it. Mind you, you'll have a job to get up for school in the morning.'

'But it's half term tomorrow,' said Jason, 'didn't you know?'

'I'd forgotten,' admitted Steven. 'Now then, who's for tea, and who's for cocoa?'

After the children had gone to bed, Steven looked across at Margaret and said quietly, 'Why didn't you leave me a note?'

'Because I was mad at you,' replied Margaret calmly.

'So I was right. You were trying to teach me a lesson.'

'Of course.'

'Had you told me about the treat?'

'No. But we waited till half past five. If you'd come home at the normal time you could have come with us.'

'But Nigel wanted to go through the figures with me.'

'Exactly. Your precious clients are more important than we are. You didn't even remember that it was half term. We usually have some days out before winter sets in. But not this time. You're too busy giving advice to all and sundry to spare time for your own family.'

'That's not true.'

'All right then, what are you doing for the rest of the week?'

'Well I'm going to the Garage Trade Federation's governors meeting tomorrow, Rivingham on Thursday, and I have to see Campbell's on Friday with a quote.'

'See? No time for us at all.'

'Margaret! I'm trying to build up a business here.'

'Well you can do it without me. I'm going to bed.'

Steven poured himself a stiff whisky and slouched despondently in his armchair. He sat for over an hour going over and over things in his mind. He finally went to bed to find Margaret asleep, with her back turned towards him.

Alan Clark had arranged to pick Steven up at 7:30, and arrived at the house at 7:20. Steven was still getting his shoes and tie on, so Alan waited for him in the car.

'The meeting's at the Post House at Mainforth at 9:30,' Alan said when they finally set off. 'It'll only take us an hour and a half, but I always like to allow plenty of time in case I get held up. Not like some people I know,' he said, glancing sideways at Steven.

'Alright. Alright,' said Steven sharply, 'I was ready at 7:30 wasn't I?'

'It was a joke,' protested Alan. 'What's the matter with you this morning?'

'I'm sorry, I had a bad night.'

'Well you'd better not speak to the governors like that.'

'I won't. I promise. Who's going to be at the meeting?'

'There's four Governors. The Chairman is Charles Jefferson who runs a large group of garages in the Leeds area. He'll try to catch you out by asking awkward questions, but just give him back as good as he gives you, and you'll be all right. Frank Cobbert runs a small garage in Ryemouth, and has just joined us to represent the small single garages. Then there's Robin Richmond, who's chairman of a group of garages in the Halifax area, and finally there's Edward Braithwaite from Braithwaite's of Rivingham. He's the official treasurer, but all he does is sign the cheques.

'Sounds quite a high powered group of people.'

'Oh they are. But very practical, and down to earth.

You'll have no problems with them, as long as you don't get ratty that is.'

'I'm sorry. Things are just getting on top of me at the moment.'

'Do you want to talk about it?'

'Not now thank you, tell me more about the federation.'

For the rest of the journey Alan briefed Steven about Garage Trade Federation and they arrived at the hotel promptly at 9:00. Alan led the way to a small committee room that was already occupied by a very tall slim man, who was impeccably dressed in a dark pinstriped suit.

'Robin,' said Alan, 'I'd like you to meet Steven Barkley who has been doing the books for us.'

'Pleased to meet you,' drawled Robin. He then turned to Alan said, 'I came early because I wanted to have a word with you about that training course you ran last week. Some of my staff were not too happy about it.'

Whilst Alan and Robin talked about the contents of the course, Steven looked aimlessly out of the window, feeling like a spare part. The door burst open and a wiry, medium built man bounded into the room. 'Hello Alan. Hello Robin,' he chimed. Turning to Steven he said 'You must be Steven Barkley. I'm Edward Braithwaite. Welcome to our committee.'

'Pleased to meet you,' said Steven, 'You're the treasurer I believe.'

'That's right. And I can tell you, it's a relief to have a proper accountant looking after the books. Not that Isobel didn't do a good job,' he added, looking swiftly across at Alan, 'but you know what I mean.'

'I think so,' replied Steven with a smile.

The door opened once more, and a thickset, broad

shouldered man walked into the room. This time Alan broke off his conversation with Robin, and crossed the room to meet the newcomer. 'Charles,' he said ' I'd like you to meet Steven Barkley.'

'Ah, the accountant,' barked Charles in a gruff Yorkshire voice. 'Have you got all your figures ready?'

'I think so,' replied Steven.

'Think so? For the money we're paying you, you'd better do more than think. Now then Alan, have you got the agenda?'

As Charles turned away to talk to Alan, Edward murmured in Steven's ear 'Don't worry about him, his bark's worse than his bite.'

The last person to arrive was a small fair-haired man who was introduced to Steven as Frank Cobbert. He appeared slightly nervous, but was greeted kindly by all the other members of the committee.

Charles called the meeting to order, and everyone took their places, with Steven sitting next to Alan. They worked their way down the agenda until they came to the financial figures.

'Edward,' said Charles, 'do you want to speak on this?'

'Only to say that I'm very pleased that Steven is doing the books, and am looking forward to his explanation of the figures he's sent us.'

'Fair enough. Steven, would you like to take us through the accounts?'

'I'd be happy to,' said Steven. 'I've prepared the accounts on an accruals basis as opposed to a cash basis........'

'Talk in plain English man,' interrupted Charles. 'What's all this about accruals and cash basis?'

Steven flushed and said, ' It's to give you a more accurate picture. You see, on an accruals basis, you allocate the income and expenditure to the period it relates to, as opposed to when it's actually paid. For instance, you don't pay your annual insurance policy until June. But I've allowed for three months of the estimated bill in this quarter's figures. We call that accruing. If I hadn't done that, there would have been no amount shown against insurance, and you would appear to have been making more profit than you are.'

'I understand,' growled Charles, 'carry on.'

Steven went through the rest of the figures without interruption. When he had finished, Edward said 'I propose as Treasurer that we accept the accounts.'

'I second that,' said Charles. 'All in favour?' Everyone raised their hands. 'And I think we add our thanks to Steven,' Charles continued, 'for his clear explanation of the situation.'

The rest of the agenda was swiftly dealt with and they came to any other business. 'Robin has something he wishes to raise,' said Charles.

'Thank you,' drawled Robin. 'As you may know, we have a branch in Rochdale, which is a member of the Lancashire section of the Federation. It appears that they're having one or two staff problems and, to cut a long story short, they wondered if we would consider a merger. I've brought their latest accounts with me and details of their membership.'

'Right,' said Charles. 'What I suggest is that Robin gives us some more background over lunch, whilst Steven casts his eye over the accounts. Then we can take a decision this afternoon.'

They all agreed, and the accounts were passed over to Steven who spent most of the lunch break analysing them. Whilst he did this, Robin expounded at length the benefits that would ensue from a merger.

'You mentioned staff problems,' said Alan, interrupting Robin's flow, 'what are they?'

'Oh it's just that they're considering moving premises, and some of the staff are not too happy about it.'

'Where are they based now?'

'They rent part of our premises, but we need more space. We're finding that business is booming over there Charles, how are things with you?' The conversation moved naturally on to the subject of the current market for cars, and the subject of the merger was dropped.

After lunch Charles restarted the meeting. 'Well,' he said, 'you've all heard what Robin has had to say, and I, for one, am inclined to proceed with a merger.' With the exception of Steven, all the others nodded their heads.

Charles looked hard at him, and growled, 'You don't seem to be in agreement with the rest of us Steven.'

'I'm afraid not.' Steven replied, flushing slightly under Charles' hard piercing glare.

'Explain yourself,' snapped Charles.

'It's the accounts,' replied Steven firmly. 'If you merge with the Lancashire section, you'll be taking a financial risk.'

'But they've got money in the bank,' interrupted Robin.

'Yes they have. But if you look at the note at the bottom of page four, you'll see that they have a capital commitment of eighty thousand pounds for a new member's centre. I can't see from the accounts how they are going to finance it. They certainly haven't got enough in the bank to cover it. And, unless they have a terrific increase in sales, they won't be able to finance it out of profits.'

'But their sales are doing very well,' objected Robin.

'So why do they want a merger?' asked Steven. 'I think

they've over-reached themselves, and have got cold feet. It makes sense to them to join with us, and hope that our combined income will generate enough money to pay for the centre. But, as I said before, from our point of view, it's a risk.'

'So you're saying we shouldn't go ahead?' asked Alan.

'No. I'm not saying that.'

'Well what are you saying man,' snapped Charles.

'I'm saying that we shouldn't merge, but offer to take over their membership. If we can join their membership with ours, we can spread the costs, and become more profitable.'

'But what about their centre?' asked Robin.

'Has it started yet?' asked Steven.

'Actually. No. There's a problem with the planners, so there's been a delay.'

'Well there's the answer. We offer to take over the membership. They cancel the contract, and wind up their section. With a bit of luck, there'll be enough in the kitty to settle any damages that the builder may claim.'

Charles looked at Steven thoughtfully. 'Hmmm. You might have a point there. What do the rest of you think?'

'I think we should go ahead,' said Robin. 'The new centre will be an asset, and Richard is very confident that, with our combined membership, we'll make a bomb.'

'Who's Richard?' asked Charles.

Robin looked uncomfortable. 'My brother-in-law.'

'You haven't mentioned him before What's he got to do with it?' asked Charles, fixing Robin with his piercing stare.

Robin squirmed in his seat. 'He's chairman of the Lancashire section.'

A gasp went round the room.

'You mean to tell us that you knew all about the centre, but you didn't mention it?' asked Charles incredulously.

'I did mention that they were moving premises,' said Robin lamely.

'Yes. But you didn't say they were buying some new ones,' said Charles. 'I think, Robin, that you'd better consider your position on this committee. In the meantime, you can go back to your brother-in-law and put to him Steven's suggestion that we take over the membership. If there is no more business, we'll close the meeting.'

In the car going home, Alan said, 'You handled that very well.'

'It's just part of my training,' replied Steven modestly. 'Any accountant will tell you that you learn more from the notes to the accounts, than the accounts themselves.'

'Well it's certainly taught me a lesson. And I can tell you that the rest of them were most impressed.'

'Good,' said Steven. Then he thought about Margaret's comment, and a frown came over his face.

'What's the matter?' asked Alan.

'Oh its just something Margaret said.'

'What was that?'

'Just about being able to sort out other peoples problems, but not my own.'

'That's what Isobel says to me.'

'Does she?'

'Oh yes. My job's very like yours you know, only I come at it from the people angle, whilst you come at it from the accounts. Come on, get it off your chest. You'll feel better.'

Steven poured his heart out all the way back home. As they approached Rivingham, Alan said, 'If I was you, I'd take Margaret out tonight for a meal and get it sorted out.

The longer you leave it, the worse it'll be. And I'd also take a break.'

'I can't do that, I've got commitments.'

'Change them. Most people are very understanding, and those that aren't, are not worth bothering about.'

'Hmmm. I'll think about it.'

'Do more than think,' warned Alan as he dropped Steven off.

When Steven got into the house, Margaret was in the kitchen, and the children were in the front room watching the television. He popped his head round the living room door and said brightly, 'Hi.' Jason raised his hand in greeting, and Katy responded with 'Hi.' But neither of them took their eyes off the television.

Chastened, Steven made his way to the kitchen. Margaret was at the sink with her back to him. 'Hello love,' he said tentatively.

Margaret looked round and in a dull voice said, 'Hello,' then turned back to the sink.

'Is that all the welcome I get?' he asked, raising his voice slightly.

'What do you expect?' asked Margaret.

'Well, I expect a little bit of interest when I come in. The kids just ignore me, and you, you.....' words failed him.

Margaret stopped what she was doing, and turned to face him. 'It's your own fault. You're not interested in us, so why should we be interested in you?'

'Now don't start that again. I came in to apologise, and all you do is throw it back in my face.'

'You should have apologised last night.'

'I was going to, but you'd gone to sleep.'

'Huh! You could have wakened me.'

'Oh yes, and what good would that have done?'

'It would have got it sorted out, instead of leaving me all day to brood about it.'

'I'm sorry,' said Steven, moving closer to Margaret. 'Truly I am. How about if I take you out to dinner tonight? Then we can talk things over.'

'But I'm half way through preparing the meal.'

'The kids'll eat it. Or you can put it in the freezer. What do you say?' he moved even closer. 'Please.'

'Oh. All right. I'll give Mam and Dad a ring and see if they'll baby sit.'

Steven grabbed her round the waist and kissed her. Margaret only just returned his kiss and pushed him away. 'It'll take more than a quick kiss and a dinner to sort this out,' she warned.

'I know,' sighed Steven, 'but I'm willing to try if you are.'

'Of course I am,' she replied, and gave him a peck on the cheek.

Over dinner Margaret gradually thawed. 'The problem,' she said eventually, 'is that you have changed your attitude to work. You used to say that you worked to live, but now you live to work. You never stop.'

'You're right,' agreed Steven. 'It's because there's such a lot resting on my shoulders. I've got to find the work, and then I have to physically do it. If I get a lot of work, I can't cope. Then I upset the clients, and you of course. If I start running short, I panic, and rush out to get some more work. Then I can't cope again. It's a vicious circle.'

'You're just going to have to ease off and get some help.'

'I'd love to, but we can't afford any help at the moment. We do need a break though. How would you like to go away for the weekend? I'll see Alex and Mary first thing on

Friday, and I'll be free by lunchtime. Where would you like to go?'

'The kids were just saying that we haven't been to Ryemouth for a while. How about going there?'

'Suits me. You can ring up tomorrow morning and book us in at the Royal.'

'We can't afford that.'

'Yes we can. If we can't afford an assistant, at least we can afford a holiday. You deserve it for putting up with me.'

'True,' responded Margaret, and an impish smile crossed her face. 'I think we'll skip the sweet and have an early night. OK with you?'

'OK!'

CHAPTER 13

The next morning Steven and Margaret were in their office when Anne looked round the door. 'Hello you two,' she said. 'How are things?'

'Fine,' responded Steven, and Margaret nodded her head in agreement.

'Good. I'm pleased about that. Margaret, I wondered if you'd like to come out for lunch with me tomorrow?'

'I'd love to,' replied Margaret, 'but we're going away for the weekend.'

'My. My. Things have changed. How've you managed to get him to do that?'

'Feminine wiles,' smiled Margaret.

'You'll have to tell me more about them,' smiled Anne back. 'How about next Tuesday?'

'Lovely,'

'Excellent,' responded Anne. 'By the way Steven, those figures you did for Nigel were just what Claude needed. He was very pleased.'

When Anne left the room Steven gave Margaret an accusing look, 'I thought you were jealous of Anne,' he hissed.

Margaret laughed softly, 'Whatever gave you that idea?'

'But you said.......'

'Steven,' she said, turning back to her work, 'when will you ever learn about women?'

'Never,' responded Steven gloomily, as he picked up the phone to ring Campbell's. Mary answered the phone. 'Hello Steven how are you doing?'

'Great. That's what I'm phoning about. We're going away for the weekend, and I wondered if I could see you first thing on Friday morning with the quote for the computer.'

'Oh that can wait until Monday.'

'But Alex said that he wanted it quickly.'

'I know that, but a weekend won't make much difference. Come and see us on Monday morning. 10:30, and I'll have the kettle on.'

'If you're sure Alex won't mind.'

'I won't let him mind. Remember I'm a 50% partner.'

'Oh yes. Of course. I didn't mean to imply......'

'That I didn't count?'

'Yes. I mean, no.'

'All right, calm down,' laughed Mary, 'I'm only winding you up. Alex is sitting right opposite me and nodding his agreement, aren't you Alex? There you are, no problem. You go away and enjoy yourselves, and I'll see if I can get this miserable skinflint of a husband to take *me* away for a change.'

'Oh dear,' said Steven, as he put the phone down. 'I hope I haven't started something between Alex and Mary.'

'Oh don't worry about them,' said Margaret. 'I warned Mary yesterday morning that you might have to put them off.'

'Yesterday morning?'

'Yes.'

'But how did you know I was going to suggest it.'

'Feminine intuition, Steven, feminine intuition.'

That afternoon Jean greeted Steven with a big beam. 'I've got a gateau in the fridge for when Bill and Fiona get back so we can celebrate my engagement.'

'Oh yes, your engagement. I'm terribly sorry Jean. We're

going away for the weekend so we won't be able to come to your party.'

'That's a shame, but don't worry. We'll remember you when we toast absent friends.'

'Thanks,' replied Steven.

'That's OK. Now, I've got a couple of queries on the journals. I've put them on your desk by the window. Shall we start?'

They'd worked solidly for over an hour when Bill and Fiona came in.

'I'll just go and put the kettle on,' cried Jean and bustled out of the room.

'I hear we're having gateau,' said Steven, 'but this time you'll be joining us.'

'That's right,' replied Bill. 'There's been quite a transformation in our little Jean, and apparently we owe it all to you.'

'Quite a little miracle worker aren't you?' said Fiona sardonically.

'I do my best,' laughed Steven.

'You'll have to talk to Bill's wife,' continued Fiona.

'What about?'

'Nothing,' said Bill sharply, giving Fiona a glare. 'Ah, here's Jean with her cake.'

They sat down in a circle in the office, and shared a happy time, laughing at each other's efforts to eat the gateau decorously. Even Fiona joined in the fun. After the tea break, Fiona and Bill went upstairs, while Steven and Jean completed the monthly accounts.

When Steven walked into Bill's office with the figures, he could see that Bill and Fiona had been having an argument. He decided to ignore it, and said, 'There you are—Profit and Loss accounts for each of the sites, and one for the whole company.'

'Thanks,' said Bill gloomily. 'Does it tell us how much we're worth?'

'No,' said Steven in surprise. 'You'd need a Balance Sheet for that.'

'Could you do one?'

'It'll take a bit of work, but yes, yes I can, but why do you want it?'

Bill looked at Fiona and gave a sigh. 'It's all a bit embarrassing. My wife thinks I'm having an affair with Fiona, and is threatening to divorce me. She's going to sue for half the business. We haven't got that kind of money, so we're going to have to sell the company.'

Steven looked from one to the other dumbfounded.

'And before you ask,' said Fiona icily, ' there is nothing going on between us.' She stood up and walked out of the room. As she passed Steven he saw that she had tears in her eyes.

'She's upset,' he observed.

'Can you blame her? She's done nothing wrong, and now she could lose her job.'

'How come?'

'Come on Steven. Wake up. The alternative to selling out, is for her to go. That's what Estelle wants, but I've refused. If she can't trust me, then we might as well get a divorce.'

'What's brought all this on?'

'I suppose it's my own fault. Do you talk a lot at home about the business?' Steven nodded his agreement. 'Well so do I,' continued Bill. 'And lately I've been singing Fiona's praises. Last week the car broke down, and we had to spend the night in a hotel. Nothing happened. I swear. We had single rooms and everything, but Estelle won't believe it. She says it's the last straw, and either Fiona goes, or she does.'

'Has Estelle met Fiona?'

'Of course.'

'Hmmm. I can see the problem.'

'Now don't you start.'

'Well you've got to admit, she's very attractive.'

Bill sighed. 'Yes, she is very attractive. But I've never laid a finger on her.'

'But you've wanted to?'

Bill paused. 'Yes, I've fancied her, what man wouldn't? But she's never given me any encouragement.'

'Don't you think Estelle knows that? That's why she wants her out of the road, before something does happen.'

Bill sighed again. 'You're probably right. But what am I going to do?'

'I'm sorry Bill, but I don't think I can help. You could reorganise things, I suppose, so that you're not working so closely together. But whether that will be enough for Estelle or not I don't know. The only other advice I can give you, is do nothing in a hurry, and get your car serviced.'

Friday morning was bright and sunny, and the Barkley's thoroughly enjoyed their drive to Ryemouth through the beautiful autumn countryside. As they dropped down into the town Steven said 'I'm getting low on petrol, I'll get some at this garage.'

'Good,' said Margaret. 'I need the toilet.'

Steven pulled into the forecourt, and started to get some petrol, whilst Margaret went inside the garage shop. When he had finished filling his tank Steven joined Margaret inside, where she was choosing some sweets.

A door at the back of the shop opened and Frank Cobbert walked in. 'Hello Steven,' he said, 'I thought it was you I could see through the window, what are you doing here?'

Steven looked at Frank in astonishment. 'We're here for the weekend,' he said. 'Is this your garage?'

'That's right. Didn't you see our name on the board.'

'I'm afraid I didn't,' admitted Steven, 'I just looked at the brand of petrol.'

'Everyone does that,' laughed Frank, 'is this your wife?'

'Oh yes. Margaret this is Frank Cobbert one of the governors of Garage Trade.'

'Pleased to meet you,' said Frank. 'You're the one who does all the hard work, whilst your husband just swans off to meetings all day.'

'That's about the size of it,' smiled Margaret.

'Well I must say, you're both good at your jobs. Has Steven told you how he saved us from making a big mistake?'

'Yes,'

'As a matter of fact,' continued Frank, 'I've got a big decision of my own to make, and I was thinking about giving you a ring. But now you're here, perhaps you could spare me an hour or two.'

'I'm sorry Frank,' said Steven. 'I've promised the family a break from work. I could come back another day.'

'That's a shame,' said Frank. 'I've got to make my mind up by Tuesday. I don't suppose you could stay over to Monday morning and see me then?'

'No, I'm sorry, but I've an appointment at half past ten on Monday morning with a client I've already put off once.'

Frank sighed, 'Pity, I really would have liked your advice.'

'You could see Frank on Sunday afternoon,' chimed in Margaret. 'I could drop you off here, go somewhere with the kids, and pick you up later.'

'If your sure you don't mind,' said Steven doubtfully.

'I'm sure.'

'That's great,' cried Frank. 'I tell you what, I've got some complimentary tickets for Sea World, you could go there.'

'Great,' responded Margaret 'The kids would love that'.

'That's settled then,' said Frank. 'See you at two o'clock on Sunday.'

When they got back to the car Steven said, 'Thanks love.'

'That's alright,' responded Margaret. 'I though it was too good to be true that we were going to have no work for a whole weekend. By the way, I suppose it was a coincidence that we choose Frank's garage to get petrol?'

'Margaret!'

'Well, was it?'

'Not exactly,' admitted Steven. 'I knew he had a garage on Rye Valley Road, but I didn't know it was this one.'

Margaret gave him an unbelieving look.

'Honest,' he continued, 'and I certainly didn't know he wanted to see me. I wonder what it's all about?'

'You'll find out soon enough. Now then, let's get on with our holiday.'

On Sunday afternoon, Margaret deposited Steven at the garage, and drove off to the Sea World complex with the excited youngsters.

'Come on through into the office,' said Frank. 'Have you had a good time?'

'Yes thanks,' responded Steven.

'Good. I'd like you to meet my son Tom.'

A short pleasant faced young man stood up to shake Steven's hand. He was as dark as Frank was fair, but Steven could see the family resemblance in the set of the jaw and the smiling eyes.

'Pleased to meet you,' said Tom. 'I've heard quite a bit about you.'

'All good I hope,' laughed Steven

'Oh Yes. Especially how you spiked the guns of that stuck up prat Robin Richmond.'

'Now then,' warned Frank, 'no need for that.'

'Well he is,' said Tom, 'and there's no way I'm going to work for him.'

'Work for him?' echoed Steven in surprise.

'I'd better explain,' said Frank. 'I used to be the manager of a garage in the town which was owned by a big national group. Ten years ago, they decided to close it down, and two customers offered to put up half the money for me to start my own garage. It's gone from strength to strength, and now that Tom's joined me, I want to buy the other two out. I got our accountant to value the business and made them an offer. They didn't accept my first offer, but on the advice of the accountant I increased it, and they accepted. The problem is that Robin Richmond has heard about it from somewhere and has made an even higher offer, which the other two want to accept.'

'I see,' said Steven, 'and you can't match the offer.'

'As a matter of fact we can. Tom's prepared to take a second mortgage to buy their half of the business. But I'm not sure that I should let him. You see, it sticks in my craw that I've done all the work, and all they have done is taken half of the profits for nothing.'

'Except taking the risk of backing you when you started,' said Steven.

'I suppose so. The point is, should we increase our offer or not? You see, in one way, I've got them over a barrel.

There's a clause in the Articles of Association, which says that the shares can't be sold without the permission of a majority of the shareholders. As I own half the shares I can block any sale.'

'Equally, they've got you over a barrel,' said Steven. 'Because if you don't agree to the sale, presumably things will just carry on as they are now.'

'Exactly.'

'Lets have a look at the figures,' said Steven.

They spent the next hour going over the accounts. 'In my opinion,' said Steven, 'Robin's bid is a high one but it's not exorbitant.'

'So what do we do?' asked Frank.

'Let's look at your options,' said Steven. 'One, you could top Robin's bid and insist that it's your final offer. Two, you could do nothing and accept that your partners will continue to grow rich at your expense. Three, you could let your partners accept Robins offer. Finally, you could also accept Robins offer, and go away and do something entirely different.

'Well we're not working for Robin so three's out,' said Tom.

'And I'm not happy about two,' said Frank. 'It gets me upset every year end when I've got to pay over half of everything we make to those two.'

'So it's down to biting the bullet one way or the other,' said Steven. 'Is there any other business you want to get into?'

'Not really,' said Frank. 'I'm a bit old to start again.'

'And I've been in the garage business all my life,' said Tom. 'I've always wanted to follow in Dad's footsteps, and together we make a good pair. Don't we Dad?'

'Aye we do.'

'There you are then,' said Steven. 'There's nothing for it, but to swallow your pride, and match Robins offer. But make it very clear, that if they don't accept it, then that's it. There's no more.'

'Right. That's what we'll do,' cried Frank. 'Agreed Tom?' 'Aye.'

'Thanks for everything Steven,' said Frank. 'You set the situation out very clearly for us. Let us have a bill for a full days work, and add on the mileage. That should pay for your holiday.'

'Thanks very much, it certainly will,' replied Steven.

Promptly at 10:30 on Monday morning Steven pulled open the big double doors at Campbell's and waved to Mary, who was putting the kettle on in the corner of the warehouse. 'Right on time' she called, 'Alex is in the office. I'll be there in a minute.'

When Mary had brought in the tea and coffee, Steven went through the quotation with them. 'That seems OK by me,' said Alex. 'What do you think Mary?'

'Yes it looks all right, but where's the cost of the training? I told you I wanted a lot of support Steven.'

'That's covered by the commission I'm getting from Bernard,' responded Steven.

'But will that be enough?' persisted Mary.

'I'll give you all the help you need. Promise,' said Steven. 'Besides, if this installation doesn't go right, Margaret will have my guts for garters.'

'OK,' said Mary. 'Just as long as I can call on you when I need you.'

'That's settled then,' said Alex. 'When can you deliver Steven?'

'Next week, if that's all right with you.'

'Great. Next week it is then.'

As he climbed the rickety staircase to George's office on Tuesday morning, Steven wondered what Carol would be like. He tapped on the door, walked in, and stopped, dumbfounded.

The whole room had been cleaned, and had a light and airy look. The high drawing desk had been removed, and in its place a modern drawing board stood at the end of the room. George sat proudly at his desk wearing a smart V necked sweater and tie, and facing him, a small, plump, friendly faced woman of about forty, sat at another desk.

'Don't just stand there gawping,' bellowed George, 'come in.'

Steven pulled himself together and entered the office.

'Quite a change eh?' continued George, 'and all due to Carol here.' He waved his hand expansively at the other desk, and Carol stood up.

'You must be Steven,' she said in a pleasant South Yorkshire accent. 'I've heard all about you.'

'I always get worried when people say that to me,' laughed Steven, shaking the proffered hand. 'It makes me wonder what's been said.'

'Only good things, I can assure you,' continued Carol. 'Now then, you'll want a cup of tea. Milk, no sugar, isn't it?'

'That's right,' replied Steven slightly surprised.

'I told you,' said Carol, 'Uncle Percy told me all about you, including your shared liking for tea.'

'Ah yes, Percy. I was sorry to hear about his death.'

'Yes, I'll miss him. But he'd had a good innings, and he's in a better place now,' responded Carol. She turned away and busied herself making the tea, brushing a tear away as she did so.

There was an awkward pause, then Steven said, 'I see you still have that cartoon on the wall.'

'Oh yes,' replied George. 'Carol wouldn't let me take it down. Says it'll remind us of the mess I got in by quoting too low. It'll also remind us of Percy,' he added softly.

'Here's your tea Steven,' interrupted Carol briskly. 'Shall we get down to business?'

'Of course,' responded Steven, glad to be moving on to less delicate ground. 'What do you want to know?'

'Firstly, I want to look at the cash flow forecast you prepared, and then I want you to explain the costing system.'

'Certainly,' said Steven. 'I thought you might want to discuss the cash flow, so I've brought two extra copies.' He passed out the sheets of figures and they pored over them.

'Let me see if I've got this right,' said Carol at the end of the session. 'We need three thousand pounds to finance the Reynold's job, and we already have an overdraft of two thousand.'

'That's right,' replied Steven.

'But we could also do with some working capital, for equipment and such like,' continued Carol.

'Oh we could manage,' said George.

'George,' said Carol sternly, 'I've told you before. I am going to invest in this firm. And we're going to make it the best in the area. No more beaten up vans. No more scruffy offices. No more yard full of scrap. But good vehicles, clean offices, and good equipment.'

'All right, all right,' laughed George holding his hands up in mock defence. 'We do need some better equipment and vans, but it'll cost a packet.'

'How much?' demanded Carol.

George thought for a while, and then said slowly, 'If we get the vans on Hire Purchase, we'll only need the deposits, say fifteen hundred pounds. Add another fifteen hundred for the equipment and we need three thousand.'

'We'll buy the vans outright, second hand,' said Carol. 'And, knowing you, we'll double the cost of the equipment. All in all, twenty thousand should cover it.'

'Twenty thousand! That's too much,' said George. 'Steven, you talk some sense into her.'

As Steven opened his mouth to speak, Carol held up her hand. 'It's no good trying to dissuade me. It's Uncle Percy's money and it's what he would have wanted.'

'I know that,' agreed Steven, 'but twenty thousand is a lot of money. I think you ought to consider it very carefully before you do anything.'

'I appreciate that you're trying to help Steven, but I'm not the fool you take me for. Before he died, Uncle Percy had been planning to do just what I am doing now. He loved George like a son. He said he was a good craftsman, but hopeless with money. We'd calculated that the firm needed an injection of twenty thousand pounds to really make it work. His only stipulation was going to be that George took me on, instead of him. He was taken ill before he could tell you about it.' She paused and put a hanky to her eye. 'So you see, it's what he wanted, and I can't think of any better way to spend his money than to carry out his plans.'

George and Steven looked at each other across the desk. 'I've got to say Carol,' said Steven. 'I think you're taking a hell of a risk. But I can understand why you are doing it, and I admire you for it.'

George cleared his throat. 'I loved Percy as much as he loved me, and if that's what he wanted, that's what we'll do.' There was a pause, then he raised his voice defiantly. 'And we'll make it the best piping contractor in the country.'

'Well in Yorkshire anyway,' laughed Carol.

'If there's any way I can help......' said Steven.

'You can,' replied Carol. 'We must get this costing system working, so that I can keep an eye on what George is up to.'

'Right,' said Steven, 'let's get started.'

'I'll leave the pair of you to it,' said George, 'and I'll go and do what I'm good at—installing good quality pipework.'

When he'd gone, Steven looked at Carol seriously. 'I meant what I said, you're taking quite a risk you know.'

'It's not all that much of a risk. You see, I've prayed about it, and I cast a fleece.'

'Like Gideon in the bible?'

'I knew you'd understand. Percy said you were a Christian.'

'What was the fleece?'

'If the amount of money that you and George said we needed was less than twenty thousand, I would go ahead. You only asked for eight thousand between you, so my prayer was well answered.'

'But Gideon asked more than once.'

'So did I,' she laughed, and held her hand up to stop any further questions. 'I've put it in God's hands now, and I'm sure it'll work out. Now, about this system...........'

Steven arrived home tired, but happy. 'I think it's all going to work out very well,' he said over dinner. 'Carol has inherited Percy's way with figures, and I'm sure she'll keep George in check.

'Yes, there's nothing like a good woman behind you is there?' teased Margaret.

'No there isn't,' responded Steven, putting his hand on Margaret's, 'and I've got the best.'

'Talking about women supporting their husbands, I had lunch with Anne today.'

'Now you're not going to start that again.'

'Of course not. It's just that she's worried about Nigel. Something's up, but she can't put a finger on it.'

'Hmmm. Perhaps it's that McBride contract.'

'I suggested that, but she said it was more a personal thing, and changed the subject.'

'I wouldn't worry about it. They'll sort it out between themselves. And if they don't, its none of our business is it?'

'I suppose not,' said Margaret.

The youngsters were at youth club, so they had the evening to themselves. They sat in companionable silence, with Margaret doing a crossword, and Steven reading the paper. Suddenly Steven sat up, and said excitedly, 'The Chamber of Commerce are having a Charity Dinner Dance.'

'That's hardly world shattering news,' responded Margaret.

'But don't you see? We could have a table, and invite our clients. It would be good for customer relations.'

'Hmmm it might work. But who would we invite?'

'Well, there's Nigel and Anne, Alan and Isobel, Alex and Mary......'

'With us, that's a table for eight.'

'The tables are for twelve. We need another two couples.'

'How about Bob Russell and his wife?'

'I'm not sure how things are going to develop there,' said Steven 'and that goes for Bill Jones and Estelle.'

'Hmmm. I see what you mean. Well there's John and Helen, they've given us a lot of support.'

'That's a good idea, and I'll ask George and Carol. They're very nice people, you'd like them.'

'It's a long way to come,' objected Margaret, 'and where would they stay? They'd need two rooms, so we couldn't have them here.'

'True. But we could offer to put them up at that B&B place down the road. Just think, our own table at a Chamber of Commerce Dinner. Won't that be one in the eye for Claude!'

'Whatever happened to love and forgiveness?' said Margaret.

CHAPTER 14

When Steven and Margaret parked their car the next morning at Parkers, Steven noticed a brand new Morgan in Nigel's parking spot.

'I wonder who's that is,' said Steven, nodding his head in the direction of the gleaming new car.

'Perhaps its Nigel's,' responded Margaret.

'Don't be silly,' laughed Steven. 'He can't afford anything like that. It must be a visitor.'

'Morning Sheila,' said Steven as they made their way through reception, 'has Nigel got a visitor?'

'No' said Sheila.

'Well whose is the Morgan?'

'Oh that. It's Nigel's. Isn't it a beauty?'

Steven went white in the face, and strode angrily down the corridor. Margaret almost had to run to keep up with him. 'What's the matter?' she hissed when they got their room.

'What's the matter?' cried Steven then, dropping his voice in response to Margaret's hand gestures, continued, 'I didn't know about the car, that's what's the matter.'

'I don't see why you should know about it.'

'Because I have done a cash flow for the bank, which doesn't mention splashing out on a thirty thousand pound car. That's why.' He turned back and charged round to Nigel's office. He burst through the door without knocking, startling Nigel and Anne who were sitting at their desks.

'What's going on?' cried Steven.

'What do you mean?' replied Nigel defensively.

'I mean that expensive, gleaming monstrosity sitting in the car park.'

'Oh that.'

'Yes. That. Why didn't you tell me about it?'

'What's it got to do with you?'

'How are you going to pay for it?'

'By Hire Purchase of course.'

'And where did you get the deposit?'

'From the bank.'

'Did you tell Claude what the cheque was for?'

'Well.... No.'

'Exactly. How much are the repayments?'

Nigel squirmed, 'I'm not sure.'

'Not sure!'

'I'm going to get the paperwork later today. Really Steven. I resent this inquisition. It has nothing to do with you what I do with my firm's money.'

'It has everything to do with me when I prepare a cash flow for the bank, and I don't show the deposit or the repayments.'

'Steven. Steven. Calm down. Who gave the cash flow to the bank?'

'You did.'

'Exactly, and when I discussed it with him, I told him that this car was on order, and there may be a need for a deposit.'

'Did you? asked Steven sarcastically.

'I did,' confirmed Nigel, ignoring the sarcasm. 'What you don't understand, Steven, is that there's an eighteen month waiting list for these cars. You have to take them when they become available. They told me last week that mine was ready, and if I hadn't taken it, I'd have lost it. Don't worry. I could sell it tomorrow for two thousand more than I paid for it.'

'Hmmm,' snorted Steven. 'I still think I should have been told. Did you know about it?' he asked, looking at Anne.

'He told me yesterday afternoon,' she replied.

'And are you happy about it?'

'Lets put it this way; Nigel always needs a shove to get himself going. I've warned him, that if we don't get some orders soon, he'll lose that lovely car of his. So it's up to him to get the work. And I think he'll do it.'

'You see,' interrupted Nigel in a patronising tone, 'you accountants just don't understand what makes a top salesman tick.'

'No, we just have to find the money to pay the bills,' retorted Steven. 'Are there any more expensive items in the pipeline that I don't know about?'

Nigel looked him straight in the eye and said, 'None at all. Now then, would you like to come for a spin in her? She's fantastic—luxurious comfort with tremendous performance.'

He would have gone on, but Steven cut him short. 'No thank you, I've got work to do.'

When he got back to his room, he slumped into his chair and sat staring at the wall. 'What's happened?' hissed Margaret. 'I heard the first part through the wall, but then it went quiet.'

'He reckons Claude knows all about the car,' replied Steven wearily, 'but I don't believe him. We're going to have to get out of here. I can't work with someone who lies to me.'

'OK. We'll talk about it later' replied Margaret. 'You've had a phone call from a Jeremy Anderson. Who's he?'

Steven groaned. 'More trouble. You remember, he's the auditor at Russell and Scott's. I bet he wants to know what I've been saying to Bob.

'Now then old sport,' breezed Jeremy, when Steven rang him, 'how're things going?'

'Just at this moment, not very well,' replied Steven. 'I suppose you've heard about the problem at Russell's?'

'No. What's happened?'

'Oh. I thought Bob would have told you. I've fallen out with him over Barbara doing the accounts. To crown it all, I told him that everyone knew about him and Jennifer.'

'Ah. That was not very tactful. True—but not tactful.'

'I know. But there's nothing I can do about it now is there?'

'No there isn't. Anyway. Cheer up. I've actually rung to ask if you need any more work, and by the sound of it you do.'

'Too right I do. What've you got in mind?'

'A client of mine has got into a spot of bother with the VAT people and the Inland Revenue. He's a building contractor and his books are in a bit of a mess. I've recommended that he uses you to sort them out.'

'That's very good of you.'

'Think nothing of it old boy. Do you want the job?'

'Yes please. When can I start?'

'That's the ticket. How about tomorrow?'

'Fine. Where are they?'

'They've got a yard in the village of Hedgeley. They're called O'Connells. I'll meet you there at ten o'clock. OK?'

'OK. And thanks again.'

'That's all right. I told you I owed you one. And don't worry about Bob. He blows hot and cold. He'll probably ring you in a month or so to ask you to come in and sort Barbara out.'

'I hope so.'

'He will. Trust me.'

'Well?' enquired Margaret, 'that didn't sound like bad news.'

'It isn't. He wants me to start a new job for him tomorrow.'

'There you are then. Getting all het up about nothing.'

'I suppose so. We'd better get on with Garage Trade's month end figures. It looks as if I'm going to be busy again.'

As Steven approached Hedgeley the next morning, he came to a long, high wall made of concrete blocks, which had a battered sign above it saying, 'O'Connell—Building Contractor.' Steven drove in between two huge iron gates which had been swung back to reveal an immense, mud covered, yard. In front of a large, shed-like, workshop on the right hand side, stood various pieces of mechanical equipment and heavy lorries. To the left, there was a group of low buildings, with a portacabin standing slightly apart. Against the far wall in front of him were stacks of building materials. Steven braked and looked round in vain for Jeremy's car. He wound down his window, and called out to a tall burly workman walking across the yard, 'Excuse me. I've an appointment to see Mr O'Connell. Could you tell me where the offices are?'

Without a word, the man turned and pointed to the low buildings on the left. He then climbed into a lorry and started it up. Steven turned his car in the direction of the offices. As he drove gingerly through the quagmire, the huge lorry roared past him, showering the rear of his car with mud.

Steven parked his car on a concrete apron beyond the buildings and went through a door marked 'Office' into a short corridor. There were muddy boot marks on the lino floor, and dirty scuff marks on the walls. Filling the wall on his left was a large, high counter. Behind it, sat an equally large woman, with a computer on the shelf in front of her. Beyond her was an office with two or three girls sitting at their desks.

'Can I help you?' she demanded in a strong voice that matched her appearance.

'I've an appointment to see Mr O'Connell with Jeremy Anderson.'

The large lady turned in her chair, and bawled across the office, 'Kathy, that bloke's here to see Feargus.'

A slim, ginger haired, woman stood up from a desk by the window, and came towards Steven. She was about thirty-five, and was dressed in a shirt and jeans. As she got closer she smiled and said, 'I'm sorry, Feargus has had to go out, and Jeremy isn't here yet. Would you like a cup of tea or anything?'

'A cup of tea would be lovely,' replied Steven.

After asking a young girl in the corner to make two teas, Kathy lead the way back into the yard and across to the portacabin. There were no steps so they had to heave themselves into the cabin. 'One of these days I'll get a step made,' observed Kathy. 'Feargus has only just told me that you were coming, so I've not had time to put the heater on.' She bent over a calor gas heater and, after fiddling with it for a while, lit all three burners. 'There, that'll soon get it warmed up.'

Steven looked round the cold sparsely furnished cabin. There was a huge window at the far end, with shelf-like desks on either side of it. There were two battered office chairs in front of the desks, and two more directly in front of the door. There was a short narrow corridor to the right, which led to a closed door. On one wall was a print of a countryside scene, and on the other was a calendar, showing a full frontal nude, from which Steven hastily averted his gaze.

Kathy was watching him with a quizzical smile on her face, taking in his smart suit and shoes. 'Hardly the conditions you're used to, I imagine,' she said.

Steven thought of Calder Engineering, and said 'I've worked in similar conditions before, but I must admit, this takes some beating.' He flashed her a smile to show that he didn't mean any offence, and continued, 'I think I'll bring my wellies next time.'

'Oh there's no need to do that, we can fix you up from the store. You'll need them to go to the toilet.' Steven looked at her enquiringly. 'Its over there,' she said, and pointed at the workshop on the other side of the yard. 'That is, unless you want to use the ladies toilet in the office.'

'No thank you,' gulped Steven. 'I'll go over there. It'll be just like going down the yard when I was a kid.'

'We had an outside loo as well. Where did you live?'

'In Printer Street near the football ground.'

'Isn't it a small world? We lived in Joiner Street. Which school did you go to?'

'Briarfield.'

'Oh! I went to St Patrick's'

'The Mick's school,' said Steven automatically, then blustered, 'I'm sorry, I didn't mean to...........'

'That's all right,' laughed Kathy. 'You were the Proddy school. It's a long time ago now.' The two of them were still reminiscing about life in the streets of Rivingham, when Jeremy clambered in.

'Hello you two. Sorry I'm late. Have you introduced yourselves?'

'Oh yes,' replied Kathy, 'we were practically neighbours when we were kids.'

'Jolly good,' continued Jeremy. 'Where's Feargus?'

'He's had to go out, he won't be long.'

'Fair enough. Why don't you tell Steven what goes on here.'

'It would help if *you* would tell me first, what you are doing here,' responded Kathy with some asperity.

'You mean he hasn't told you?' gasped Jeremy.

'Does he ever tell me anything?' replied Kathy. 'He just said he had a meeting with you two, and would I cover for him while he went out.'

Jeremy looked uncomfortable. 'It's because of the VAT investigations. We couldn't give them all of the information they wanted, so we thought that we needed a better system.'

'But that's what Liz was brought in to do, wasn't she?'

Jeremy looked pained. 'I'm sure she's doing a good job on the computer, but she isn't qualified. She can't do Nominal Ledgers and Management Accounts.'

'And Steven can.'

'That's right.'

'Does he know all the ins and outs of our company?'

'Well no. Not yet. But he's very good at picking things up, aren't you Steven?'

'Err Yes. Especially where computers are concerned.'

'Who's going to explain to Liz that she's no longer going to do the job she came here to do?' asked Kathy.

'Oh but she is,' cried Jeremy. 'Steven's here to set up a system for Liz and yourself to follow. Not to do the accounts for ever.'

'That's right,' chimed in Steven, 'as my wife says, I'm always working myself out of a job.'

'Alright,' said Kathy, 'I'll believe you. But I'm not telling her. You can.'

'Fair enough,' responded Jeremy. 'Now, how about telling Steven what you do?'

'It's quite simple really,' said Kathy, turning to Steven. 'We dig holes and then we fill them in again.'

Steven laughed incredulously, 'You what?' he queried.

'We dig holes and fill them in again,' affirmed Kathy. 'We have the contract with the electricity board to dig all their trenches for them. Then they come along and lay their cables, and we fill the trenches in again.'

'Oh I see.'

'That's forty percent of our business, the rest is building houses and doing road resurfacing work and suchlike for the local councils.'

'And do you have job costing?'

'No, we've got nothing like that, and besides, it wouldn't be any use. We're paid by the foot. If the ground's easy we make money, if it's hard we don't. It's as simple as that.'

'She makes it sound simple, but of course it isn't,' interrupted Jeremy. 'Their turnover is three million a year, and its made up of a myriad of small contracts. They also sell materials for cash. It's a nightmare to audit, and the VAT man couldn't make head nor tail of it, hence the surcharge he's slapped on them.'

'So what do you want me to do?' asked Steven.

Jeremy was starting to answer, when a large lorry roared up and stopped outside the cabin with a squeal of brakes. Its engine continued to run as the cab door was slammed, and a large, fair-haired man, in scruffy working clothes, climbed effortlessly into the cabin.

'There you are Feargus,' chimed Jeremy, 'been out delivering a load of rubble as usual.'

'It was top soil this time,' replied the man, in a soft Irish brogue.

'I'd like you to meet Steven Barkley,' continued Jeremy, waving Steven forward.

Steven smiled, and said, 'We've already met. You gave me directions to the office.'

The big man shyly returned the smile, and shook the proffered hand with his large callused one. Feargus's light blue eyes were shrewd behind the smile, and Steven had a feeling of immense strength, which wasn't just physical.

'Right,' said Jeremy. 'I was just explaining to Steven what we would like him to do. Is it all right if I carry on?'

Feargus gave a little wave of his hand to signify his acceptance, and mumbling 'Back in a minute,' jumped out of the cabin door. They heard the lorry door slam and it roared off.

Steven looked with astonishment at Jeremy and Kathy, who both burst out laughing at his expression. 'You'll have to get used to that if you're going to work here,' laughed Kathy. 'He's never happier than when he's on site delivering materials, or driving a road roller.'

'But don't be fooled by his outward appearance,' chimed in Jeremy. 'He's a very shrewd operator. His only trouble is that he doesn't like paperwork of any description.'

'No, he leaves that all to me,' said Kathy. 'So tell me, what is Steven going to do for us?'

'Well, you're behind with the VAT returns, so we need to bring them up to date. Then I'd like him to work on producing a nominal ledger, so that we can cut down on the work we have to do at the year end.'

'Does that mean we'll save on your bill?'

'Eventually, yes.'

'Good. We'll do it then.'

'Thanks,' said Jeremy dryly.

'And how much will Steven cost us?'

'You'd better ask Steven that.'

'Oh, doesn't he work for you?'

'No. He's a self-employed consultant.'

'I'm not sure Feargus will like that. He's very suspicious of accountants you know. Look how long it took you to gain his confidence.'

'True,' admitted Jeremy. 'But I'm sure that Steven will win him over, just as I did.'

Steven, feeling uncomfortable at being discussed as if he wasn't there, interrupted them. 'If you like, I'll give you a fixed price for doing the VAT returns. After that we can agree a daily rate.'

'OK,' said Kathy, 'we'll do that. You've got one advantage already.'

'What's that?'

'You come from the right part of Rivingham! Come on, we'll go across and break the news to Liz.'

'I'll be off then,' said Jeremy.

'I thought you were going to tell Liz what was going on?' said Kathy in surprise.

'You're much better at that sort of thing than I am,' said Jeremy, flashing his winning smile. 'Besides, I've got another client to see in ten minutes. Toodle Pip.'

As Jeremy leapt out of the cabin, Steven and Kathy looked at each other. 'Ah well,' Kathy sighed, 'I suppose I'll have to do the dirty work as usual.'

'Is Liz so terrible?' asked Steven.

'She's all right once you get to know her,' replied Kathy. 'Feargus brought her in two months ago without telling me, but we get on very well.' She then grinned and, giving

Steven a sideways look, said, 'but most men are scared stiff of her.'

As they came into the office corridor the large woman behind the counter said 'Feargus has had to go out with another load of topsoil. He said he'll leave it to you to sort things out. What's going on?'

'Liz, I'd like you to meet Steven Barkley,' said Kathy.

Liz leant forward over the counter, and shook Steven's hand.

'I know you've been under pressure lately, so Steven's going to help us catch up with the VAT returns.'

Liz frowned. 'But that's my job,' she objected.

'I know, but if Steven gets them up to date first, then it gives you a straight line to start from, doesn't it?'

'I suppose so,' agreed Liz.

'And you've got you're work cut out getting the computer straight, haven't you?' said Kathy, sensing victory.

'Have you got computer problems?' asked Steven.

'Have I got problems?' echoed Liz. 'It's all a mess. And it doesn't help that it keeps on freezing for no earthly reason, and I lose all that days work.'

'That's what I mean,' interrupted Kathy. 'The VAT man's screaming for the returns, and with all you're computer problems, you haven't really got the time to sort them out have you?'

'No you're right. Steven can get them up to date, then I'll take them over again.'

'Great,' said Kathy. 'We'll get the printouts, and take them across to the cabin.'

'I'm not going out there,' said Liz firmly. 'You know what a struggle I have to get into that cabin. No. Mick's out so we'll use his office.'

'OK,' agreed Kathy, and led Steven through the door at the end of the corridor and into a small office. Liz soon appeared, puffing and blowing, and carrying two enormous print outs. She explained the system to Steven, who asked a lot of questions and made copious notes.

At the end of the session he said 'Thank you very much Liz. That was most helpful. I've got an appointment this afternoon, but I could start tomorrow morning if that's alright?' He looked at Kathy for confirmation, and she in turn looked at Liz. 'What do you think?' she said.

'I think he'll do,' affirmed Liz. 'He's asked all the right questions, and seems to have a better grasp of things than that fool of an audit clerk.'

Steven looked startled.

'She doesn't mean Jeremy,' explained Kathy, 'just the clerk who's doing the audit.'

'Oh. Right,' said Steven.

'That's settled then,' said Kathy. 'You can start tomorrow morning, and I'll have some wellies ready for you!'

When Steven arrived at Rivingham Cleaning that afternoon, Jean greeted him with a big beam and said 'Bill would like to see you straight away.'

'Do you know what he wants?' asked Steven.

'You'll see,' replied Jean mysteriously. 'I'll bring your cup of tea up.'

'Ah! My saviour!' cried Bill, as Steven entered his office, 'Come in. Come in.'

'What's all this about saviour?' asked Steven as he sat down.

'You've saved my marriage, that's all.'

For the first time Steven realised that Fiona wasn't in the room, and neither was her desk.

'What's happened? Have you sacked Fiona?'

'No. No. Nothing like that. We took your advice, and

we've split the company into two divisions, with Fiona based in a rented office in York. She's going to cover Yorkshire and Lancashire from there, and I'll do the North East from here. Neat Eh?'

'What does Estelle think about it?'

'She took some persuading, but when I pointed out that it was your idea, and that it was the only way to keep both our marriage and the firm intact, she agreed.'

'My idea?'

'Yes, you suggested reorganising things.'

'Oh yes, I remember. But I didn't think you'd go as far as you have done.'

Just then the door opened, and Jean brought two teas in. She placed them on the table, and left with a big smile on her face.

'What's she so happy about?' queried Steven.

'With Fiona moving to York, I've put Jean in charge of the office, and promised her a rise.'

'Whew. You certainly have reorganised. Can you afford it?'

Bill leant forward across the desk. 'Steven,' he said seriously, 'I don't care what it costs. Its worth anything in the world to save my marriage and my firm.'

'Fair enough. I'd better get down to Jean, and work out how we can give you the split of the figures between the divisions.'

'You do that. And Steven.'

'Yes?'

'Thanks a million.'

'All part of the service,' Steven responded lightly, but inside he felt a glow of satisfaction.

'There's been a phone call from Frank Cobbert, at Ryemouth,' greeted Margaret when he got home. 'The other directors have accepted his offer, and he's going to buy them out.'

'Great news.'

'Yes it is. He says it's all down to you, and he can't thank you enough.'

'Another happy client. If only all the days were like this one,' said Steven. 'I like helping people who appreciate me. Not working for people like Nigel, who couldn't give a damn about me.'

'Yes, but we still need the Nigel's of this world to pay the bills,' warned Margaret, 'so don't you do anything silly.'

CHAPTER 15

Steven put on an old suit and drove out to Hedgeley. It was a lovely morning and he enjoyed the drive through the countryside. As he passed through Netherton he caught a glimpse of the rear of a Morgan sticking out of a garage, and thought it strange that there were two of them in the area.

He parked his car in O'Connell's yard and entered the office. 'Ah, there you are,' boomed Liz, 'we thought you weren't coming.'

Steven looked at his watch, 'Its only ten to nine,' he muttered.

'We start at eight. You'll have to get up early in the morning if you're going to work here.'

'Errr. Right,' responded Steven, nonplussed.

'Don't take any notice of her,' laughed Kathy as she came across the office, 'she's just winding you up.'

Liz gave Steven wicked grin, and turned back to her computer.

'The heater's on,' continued Kathy, as she lead the way to the cabin, 'and I'll get Orla to make you a cup of tea.'

She opened the door to the cabin and they were met by a warm, fumy fug. The office was littered with computer print outs, and sitting at one of the desks was a stout, middle aged man, with a moustache.

Kathy introduced them. 'This is Bert Townsend,' she said, 'he's doing the interim audit. Bert, this is Steven Barkley who is going to help us with the management accounts and things.'

The two men shook hands and Steven instinctively liked Bert.

Kathy pointed in the corner. 'I've put a pair of welly boots there for you. They're size nines, I hope that's OK?'

'Just right for me,' replied Bert.

'I take size seven,' said Steven, ' but I'm sure I'll manage. Thanks very much.'

'Not at all. I think you've got everything you need in here, but if you've any problems give me shout.' She opened the door and jumped down from the cabin. She leant back in and called, 'I've asked Seamus to make you a step, and he says he'll have it ready later today.'

The door slammed shut, and Steven turned to Bert with a smile, 'Has everyone here got an Irish name?' he asked.

'Just about,' responded Bert, 'you should see the wages, they're a nightmare. There's loads of Finnegans, Donovans and O'Malleys. And they're always changing. They say that the men stay for less than six months, so they don't get caught for tax. But how can I check if someone's left, or just changed his name?'

'Quite a problem,' sympathised Steven.

'As for the VAT!'

'What about the VAT?' asked Steven in alarm.

'Nothing balances. The computer doesn't tie up with the day books, and the cash sales don't tie up with anything.'

'Oh. I'm supposed to bring it up to date.'

'So I hear. Well, the best of luck. The VAT man went away to have a nervous breakdown after his visit.'

Steven looked worried, but Bert laughed. 'I'm only kidding. He did give up though. Said he couldn't spend any more time on it, and slapped a penalty on them. It's a lot better since the dragon arrived.'

'The dragon?'

'You must have met Liz.'

'Oh her!'

'The men are all terrified of her. She orders them about like nobody's business. You see, she pays the wages, so she's got the whip hand. If they don't produce all the delivery notes and receipts, their wages mysteriously go wrong. I drink at the same club as a lot of them, and they're always complaining about her.'

'She does seem to be a strong character,' mused Steven.

'Strong character? You just wait until you've crossed her,' said Bert.

The rest of the morning passed uneventfully as both men concentrated on their work. They were interrupted at eleven thirty by Orla, a slim young girl with long raven coloured hair, who said in a soft Irish brogue, 'I'm goin' to the shops for some bait. Does either of yous want anythin'

'No thanks,' said Bert, 'I've got to go out.'

'A ham sandwich and a cake would be nice,' said Steven, and gave her some money.

'She's pretty,' remarked Steven, after she had gone.

'Aye she is,' responded Bert, 'she's Feargus's daughter.'

'His daughter?' echoed Steven in surprise.

'She's his eldest. By all accounts there's another five back in Ireland, who'll come over and join her when they're old enough.'

'Don't they live here?'

'No. Feargus's wife and family are still in Ireland. He visits them every so often, but he spends most of his time either working, or in the Irish club.'

'Where does he sleep then?'

Bert gave him a grin, and jerked his head towards the closed door at the end of the cabin. 'In there,' he said.

'You're joking!'

'I'm not. You ask Kathy.'

'How do you know so much?'

'I told you. I meet a lot of them socially,' said Bert, and resumed his work.

'I think I'd better go to the loo,' said Steven, pulling on the large wellington boots, 'where is it?'

Bert pointed out of the window. 'It's at the back of the workshop. Seamus will show you were it is.'

'Seamus?

'Yes, he's the foreman. His office is at the front of the workshop. You can't miss him.'

Steven opened the cabin door and stretched out his left leg to step down. The wellington slipped off his leg, hit the soil, and bent over. His foot, continuing its downward path, hit the side of the boot, throwing Steven off balance. He gave a yell and fell ignominiously onto the dirty doorstep.

Bert rushed over as Steven struggled to his feet, pulling his left foot out of the wellington as he did so.

As Steven dejectedly brushed down his suit with his hands, Bert started to laugh. He quickly stopped when Steven gave him a glare, and then said, 'I'm sorry. I shouldn't have laughed. But you looked so pathetic standing there, with only one wellie on, and mud on your bottom.'

Steven smiled ruefully, 'I suppose I do look a sight. It's a good job I put on an old suit. Well, I need the loo more than ever now.' He leaned out of the cabin, picked up the boot, and put it on again. This time he held on to the doorjamb as he gingerly put first one foot, then the other, down to the ground. He limped across the yard to the workshop, to be greeted by a little leprechaun of a man, with a ruddy face and twinkling blue eyes.

'I see you had a bit of bother,' he remarked with a grin.

'You can say that again,' said Steven, not returning the grin.

'I'm sorry about that. I promised Kathy I'd make you a step. And I'll do so straight away, so I will.'

'Thanks,' said Steven slightly mollified.

'You'll be wanting the toilet. It's through the back there.'

As Steven started to walk towards it, a large Doberman leaped out the shadows at him, barking fiercely. Steven jumped back in terror, but the dog stopped in mid air and fell to the ground, restrained by a strong metal chain.

Seamus came up behind Steven. 'Don't worry about him,' he said. 'His barks worse than his bite. He's a big softy really. Aren't you Cuddles?' He went down on his haunches, and put his face close to the dog's menacing mouth. The dog stopped growling, and licked the little man's face with obvious affection. 'There you are you see, soft as putty. You can stroke him if you like.'

Steven put out a hand towards the dog, but it stopped licking Seamus's face and gave a low growl.

'I think I'll give it a miss,' said Steven, withdrawing his hand.

'Fair enough. I think you gave him a bit of a shock. Next time I'll introduce you properly.'

'Thanks,' said Steven, and carried on to the rear of the workshop. There was a doorway through which Steven could dimly see a urinal, with another open door to the right, which led into a small, filthy, cubby-hole containing a toilet. Steven used the urinal, and beat a hasty retreat. He passed the dog, which gave him a low warning growl, and Seamus, who cried after him, 'I'll have the step done this afternoon so I will.'

There was no sign of Bert when he got back to the cabin, but his sandwich and a cake together with a large mug of tea were on the desk with his change.

After his lunch Steven made his way across to the office. Over the counter he could see Liz, with a flushed expression on her face, grimly inputting invoices to the computer for all she was worth.

'Errmmh. I wonder if you could spare me a few minutes?' asked Steven.

'No I can't,' snapped Liz, not looking up, 'can't you see I'm busy?'

'Its just a couple of queries.'

'I don't care how many there are. This bloody computer went down on me just before lunch, and I've got to re-input all these invoices.'

'Oh. I see,' said Steven weakly.

Liz continued to input, and there was an awkward pause. Finally she said 'Kathy'll be back in a minute, she'll help you.'

'Oh. Right,' said Steven and beat a hasty retreat.

When Steven returned to the cabin, he found that Bert was back at his desk. 'Have a good lunch?' he asked.

'Fine,' grunted Bert without lifting his head.

'Good,' said Steven and, taking the hint, settled down to his work.

After about ten minutes, there was a knock on the cabin door. Steven opened it, and looked down to see a grinning Seamus standing at the foot of two wooden steps. 'What about these?' he cried proudly.

Steven looked at the steps doubtfully.

'Try them,' called Seamus, and Steven obediently did so. 'Solid as a rock,' pronounced Seamus with satisfaction. 'I made them out of old pallets. Do you think they'll do the trick?' he asked, looking at Steven anxiously.

'Certainly,' Steven assured him, 'just what the doctor ordered.'

'Fine. Fine,' beamed Seamus. 'I'll get back then.'

Steven went up the steps into the cabin and said to Bert 'We've got some steps, do you want to see them?'

Bert didn't look up but grunted, 'No thanks.'

A few minutes later there was a commotion at the door, and Kathy came in carrying a pair of wellingtons. 'I see that Seamus has made some steps,' she said.

'Yes, aren't they great?' replied Steven.

'Not if you've got something in your hand, and the door opens towards you,' retorted Kathy. 'I dropped these boots trying to get it open. Still, we'll get used to it I suppose. I've brought you some smaller wellies. They'll keep you upright.'

'Why? Have you heard about my fall?'

'Heard about it? The whole world's heard about it, haven't they Bert?'

Bert looked up shamefaced. 'Well, I did tell one or two people about it.'

'One or two? All the workforce is talking about it.'

'There were a lot of them in the pub,' admitted Bert, giving Steven an embarrassed look.

'Thanks a lot,' said Steven, noticing for the first time the smell of alcohol, and stale tobacco smoke.

'Sorry,' mumbled Bert, and turned back to his work.

'Anyway, we can't have a top notch consultant falling all over in the yard can we?' said Kathy. 'So I've brought you a pair of size sevens.'

'Thanks very much,' said Steven.

'It's the least we can do. Now about those queries, Liz has nearly caught up, and she says she can see you in about half an hour, is that all right?'

'Fine.'

At first, Liz answered Steven's queries grudgingly, but,

by the end of the session, she had mellowed. 'Good,' said Steven, 'that's got the first quarter balanced. I can see what I'm doing now, so I'll be able to balance the rest of the year more easily.'

'So we'll see you on Monday?'

'I'm afraid not. I've got a computer to set up.'

'Tuesday then.'

'It'll depend on how Monday goes.'

Liz looked at him in exasperation then bawled across the office, 'Kathy. Steven says he can't come back until the middle of next week.'

Kathy got up from her chair and came across to them with a serious expression on her face. 'Can't you come any earlier?' she asked. 'The VAT man has only given us till the end of the month to get things sorted out, otherwise he'll slap another penalty on us.'

'The problem is, that I've promised to set a computer up next week,' said Steven. 'What I'll have to do is work the two jobs together, if you don't mind me just coming and going without an appointment.'

'No, we don't mind,' said Kathy

'What time do you finish at night?'

Liz snorted, 'We're supposed to finish at four, but its usually five or later before Kathy and I get away.'

'Fine,' said Steven, ' I'll come in on Tuesday afternoon and carry on. OK?'

'It'll have to be,' said Liz.

'Thanks very much,' said Kathy.

When he got back to the cabin, Bert had gone. 'That's funny' thought Steven. 'He didn't say he was finishing early.'

After dinner Margaret said, 'I've rung everybody about the Dinner Dance, and they'll all be delighted to come.'

'You haven't asked Nigel and Anne have you?'

'Of course I have.'

'After Wednesday's episode I wasn't sure I wanted them to come.'

'Stuff and nonsense. Just because you're jealous of Nigel's new car.'

'I'm not jealous.'

'Of course you are. Come on. Admit it.'

'All right. I suppose I am a little bit jealous, but I'm more concerned that he didn't tell me about it before hand.'

'Perhaps he's frightened of you.'

'Nigel. Frightened of me? Whatever for?'

'Because you make him face up to the facts, and he doesn't want to.'

'Hmmm. You may be right. Ah well, we'll enjoy ourselves in spite of him. Have you asked George and Carol?'

'I talked to Carol, and she sounded very keen. She was going to ask George, but I think they'll come.'

'If Carol wants to, I'm sure they will.'

'Why do you say that? She sounded very nice over the phone.'

'Oh she is. But she knows what she wants, and she'll get it. Where are they staying?'

'That's the funny thing. I offered them the boarding house, but she said not to bother, and she'd book them in at the hotel.'

'Staying the night at the Blue Bell eh. That'll set them back a bit. Things must be looking up.'

'Hmmm,' said Margaret thoughtfully, 'I wonder?'

'What?'

'Oh nothing. Have you booked the table?'

'No. I'll get on to it straight away.'

On Monday morning Steven drove out to Dacre to collect the computer for Campbell's. He was greeted by Doris, who sent him straight through to Bernard's office. The computer was sitting on the desk, and the floor was covered in boxes of all shapes and sizes.

'Just in time,' greeted Bernard. 'I've loaded all the software, but I've left the computer connected up so that you'll know which cable fits which part.'

'Oh, I didn't realise I'd have to put it together. For the demonstration I just carried it in out of it's box.'

'Ah, that was our machine. You've got to show the customer that he's getting a brand new piece of kit, and not a second hand model.'

'I suppose so,' said Steven, 'but I've never put a computer together before.'

'Oh there's nothing to it. I'll show you how it's done as we're dismantling it.'

'Will you be in this afternoon if I need any help?' asked Steven.

'Of course I will, don't worry.'

After they had disconnected the equipment and put it into its boxes, they loaded Steven's car. 'You're going to have to get an estate car,' observed Bernard, as he squeezed the last box onto the front passenger seat.

'Let's see how things go first,' muttered Steven, and set off. Instead of going straight to Campbell's, he drove home. He carried all the boxes into the dining room, and when Margaret arrived home for lunch, the room was littered with them. Steven was pouring over a manual.

'What on earth's going on?' Margaret demanded.

'Bernard insisted on boxing everything up. So, before I

went round to Campbell's, I decided to make sure I could put it all together.'

'And can you?'

'Not quite. I'm not sure where this printer cable fits, and I've got a spare power lead.'

'Well you'd better give Bernard a ring.'

'I suppose so. But he's already shown me once. He'll think I'm a right fool.'

'That's better than being a right fool in front of Alex and Mary isn't it?'

'OK. I'll ring him straight away.'

'Dacre Electric's,' answered the familiar voice of Doris.

'Hello Doris, this is Steven, can I speak to Bernard please.'

'He's not in.'

'Not in! But he promised he would be.'

'He's gone to the wholesalers. He said to tell you that he'd be back at two o'clock.'

'Two o'clock,' shouted Steven, 'that's no good to me. I need to speak to him now.'

'There's no need to shout at me,' said Doris tartly.

'I'm sorry,' said Steven, 'but I have to speak to him urgently. I've got a computer in bits here, and I don't know where to fit everything.'

'Well you could try him at the wholesalers, he might be still there.'

'Good idea, give me the number.'

Doris gave him the number and rang off.

'He's gone out,' Steven cried to Margaret, 'and he promised me he would be in.'

'All right. All right,' said Margaret soothingly.

'It's not all right,' shouted Steven, 'I need to get this damned computer together and round to Campbell's. They're waiting for it.'

'Don't take it out on me,' snapped Margaret. 'I told you not to get involved with him, but you ignored me. I'm going to make lunch.'

Steven glowered after her for a moment, and then rang the wholesalers. To his relief Bernard was still there and was soon brought to the phone.

'Hello Steven,' he said breezily, 'what's up?'

'What's up?' Steven yelled. 'You're supposed to be standing by to give me back up.'

'No I'm not.'

'Yes you are.'

'Steven. Calm down. What exactly did I say to you?'

'You said you'd be in if I needed you.'

'No I didn't. I said I would be in *this afternoon* if you needed me, didn't I?'

'But I need you now.'

'I can tell that, but that's not what we arranged.'

'OK. OK. That's not what we arranged. But I'm stuck. I've got pieces of equipment all over the dining room, and I need your help.'

'That's better. I'm just down the road from you. I'll be round in five minutes.'

Steven put the phone down and walked slowly into the kitchen.

'Well?' demanded Margaret.

'He's just down the road,' said Steven in a subdued voice. 'He'll be here in five minutes.'

'And why wasn't he there when you needed him?'

Steven shuffled his feet. 'It was a misunderstanding,' he admitted. 'He actually said that he would be there this afternoon if I needed him. But, because he was still at the shop when I left, I thought he would be there all day.'

'So, are you going to apologise?'

'Yes, I'm sorry. I'm just so worried that it'll go wrong.'

'You should have thought of that before.'

'All right,' snapped Steven 'there's no need to go on about it.'

'Steven,' warned Margaret.

'OK. I'm sorry. I'll go and read the manual while I'm waiting for Bernard.'

Bernard was as good as his word, and arrived within five minutes. After Steven had introduced him to Margaret, he led him into the dining room.

'Now then, what's the problem?' Bernard asked,

'It's the link from the computer to the printer,' explained Steven, 'I'm not sure where it fits, and I've got a power lead left over.'

'Let's have a look,' said Bernard. 'See? You can't really go wrong. It'll only fit this port here.'

Steven looked shamefaced, 'Oh yes, I see now.'

'Where were you trying to put it?'

Steven pointed to another socket at the back of the computer.

'No wonder you were having problems,' laughed Bernard, 'that's the serial port not the parallel port.'

'Err right,' said Steven. 'Then there's this cable.'

Bernard looked at the back of the computer and said 'You haven't got a power lead to the screen.'

'I thought this lead was for that,' said Steven, pointing to a one that ran from the computer to the back of the screen.

'No, that only sends the signal from the computer to the screen. It still needs its own power lead,' said Bernard, in a tone that implied that any fool should know that.

'Oh. Right,' said Steven chastened. 'Thanks very much.'

'All part of the service,' said Bernard breezily. 'Now then, shall I help you to pack it all up again?'

'No thank you' said Steven hastily. 'It'll help me to understand it better if I do it myself. That's why I brought it home in the first place.'

'Well, if you're sure,' said Bernard doubtfully, 'I'll get back to the shop.'

'I'm sure,' said Steven, 'and thanks again. I'm sorry I lost my rag.'

'Oh don't mention it. We all do that sometimes. Anyway I'll be in the shop this afternoon as promised. OK?'

'OK.'

'I hope you don't expect me to help you pack it all away,' said Margaret, when Bernard had gone.

'I'm not going to pack it away,' replied Steven. 'I'm going to take it round in as few bits as possible, so that I don't have any problems putting it together.'

'But I thought Bernard....'

'Bernard didn't want them thinking it was second hand, that's all,' interrupted Steven, 'but Alex won't query that with me supplying it.'

'OK. On your head be it.'

With some difficulty, Steven loaded the computer and printer into the car and drove to Campbell's.

'There you are,' greeted Mary, 'we thought you'd got lost.'

'Slight technical problem,' muttered Steven. 'Do you think Alex could give me a hand?'

The two of them carefully manoeuvred the computer out of the car and into the office and then Steven brought the printer in.

'I thought we were getting a new computer?' said Mary. 'You are.'

'Well why isn't it all in boxes?'

'Because I put it together first at home, and thought it would be easier if I brought it round all ready to go.'

'Fair enough,' commented Alex.

'Well, seeing its you....' said Mary.

'I'll bring the packaging round tomorrow,' said Steven.

'Oh there's no need for that,' said Alex.

But Steven, with a quick look at Mary's doubtful expression, said 'No problem, its just cluttering up our dining room anyway.'

Alex turned back to his work, and Mary watched as Steven connected all the parts together, and switched the machine on.

Some words flashed onto the screen, and then disappeared, leaving it blank.

'What was that?' asked Mary.

'Oh, just technical details of the computer,' said Steven. 'Don't worry about it. Come on, let's get started.'

'Remember you promised me an idiots guide,' warned Mary.

'I remember,' said Steven. 'I'll make some notes as we go along.'

Mary took her place in front of the screen and, following Steven's directions, started to input the customer's details. After she had input three customers, Steven said, 'Right, I'm just going to the loo. See if you can follow these instructions.'

When he came back, Mary was sitting in front of the screen looking very frustrated. 'What's the matter?' he asked.

'Your instructions are useless, that's what,' cried Mary.

'What do you mean?'

'What's this word 'return' mean?'

'It means press that key there.'

'But that key has 'enter' written on it.'

Understanding dawned on Steven. 'I'm sorry,' he said, 'it's a term we use with computers. It comes from the early days, when they had electric typewriter keyboards, and they used the carriage return key on it to signify the end of an entry.'

'Well that's no help to me. I use a manual typewriter.'

'Right. I'll change it.'

'I told you I'd be useless.'

'No you're not. Come on. We'll go through it again. Step by step. And I'll write everything in plain English this time.'

At the end of an hour Steven said, 'You're doing very well. Is it all right if I leave you now? I've got another client who needs some figures doing urgently.'

'But what happens if I get a problem?' cried Mary.

'You'll be alright,' soothed Steven. 'All you have to do is to continue to put the customers in. When you've finished you can close down and switch the computer off.'

'How do I do that? Have you written it down?'

'No, I haven't,' admitted Steven. 'I'll do it now.'

'In English mind you, and then I'll try it out before you go,' warned Mary.

'OK.' Laughed Steven, 'in English.'

He quickly wrote out the instructions and, after Mary had pronounced her approval of them, left for O'Connells at three o'clock.

CHAPTER 16

On the way to Hedgeley Steven once again saw the tail end of a Morgan sticking out of a garage in Netherton. 'I must tell Nigel he's not the only one in the district with a Morgan,' he thought. 'That'll sicken him off!'

'Hello,' said Liz in surprise, 'we didn't expect you until tomorrow.'

'I've got an hour to spare, so I thought I'd pop in, is that all right?'

'Of course it is,' she replied and bawled across the room, 'Kathy, Steven's here, have you got the key for the cabin?'

Kathy came across the room with the key in her hand. 'I thought you weren't coming till tomorrow,' she observed.

'I said I'd fit you in when I could. I've got a spare hour, so I thought I'd come in. Is there a problem?'

'No, not really. It's just that Liz and I had planned to leave on time tonight to do some shopping.'

'Oh, does that mean that the place will be locked up?'

'The offices will be, but the yard will be open, and Seamus is usually here till the last wagon comes in.'

'What about Bert?'

The two women looked at each other, and Kathy said, 'He's had to go home.'

'Is he not well?'

'You could say that,' snorted Liz.

Steven was going to pursue the subject, but a warning look from Kathy made him change his mind. 'I'll get on then ' he said. To his surprise, when he got to the cabin the steps were on their side, and partly underneath it. He replaced them under the door, let himself in, and got on with his work.

After half an hour Kathy came in. 'I've brought you a cup of tea,' she said. 'We're packing up now. When you want to go, just lock the cabin and take the key across to Seamus.'

'Right-ho,' answered Steven.

Kathy hesitated, 'About Bert,' she said.

'Yes?' said Steven encouragingly.

There was a pause. 'How well do you know Jeremy?' she asked.

'Not very well,' admitted Steven.

'But he trusts you,' persisted Kathy.

'I think so,' replied Steven, in a puzzled tone.

'That's what I thought. You see, we have a problem with Bert, and we don't know what to do about it.'

'He seemed a nice chap to me,' remarked Steven.

'Oh he is, that's part of the problem,' said Kathy, and paused again.

'Look,' said Steven. 'Why don't you tell me what's bothering you, and if I can help, I will.'

'Thanks,' said Kathy, flashing him a smile. 'Its like this. When he first started, like you, we thought he was a nice man. And he is. There was no problem for the first week. In the second week, we noticed that we didn't see much of him on an afternoon, but didn't think too much about it. But last week.........He has his lunch in the pub that the men use, and they started making comments about how much drink he could put away in a session. He started going home early, and on Friday he was gone by two o'clock. The last straw came this afternoon. He didn't come back from lunch till two thirty, and he was reeling. Seamus saw him fall off the steps and went over and picked him up. To cut a long story short, we sent him home with one of our drivers.'

'Hmmm,' said Steven. 'I see your problem.'

'Yes, and it's made worse by the fact that he's such a nice man.'

'What do you want me to do about it?'

'We wondered if you could have a word with Jeremy. It's not just that the man needs help, but we're paying for a full day's work, and we're not getting it. Our audit fee will be astronomical, and Feargus'll go through the roof.'

'Well it's a bit difficult, but I'll ring him tonight when I get home.'

'Thanks, I can get a good nights sleep now.'

'Have you been worrying that much?' asked Steven in surprise.

'Oh that's just me,' she laughed. 'I worry about everything. And he's such a nice man, I don't want to get him into trouble.'

'You've done the right thing,' Steven assured her, 'and I'm sure Jeremy will do his best to help Bert.'

'Thanks again,' said Kathy. 'Goodnight.'

Steven settled down to his work and gradually every one but Seamus and Cuddles went home. He looked at his watch. 'Half past six, time to go.' he thought and put his papers into his briefcase. He got his coat on, put the lights out, opened the door outwards and went down the cabin steps............................

Steven eased himself on the office chair and rubbed his hands to keep out the cold. 'That was when I made my mistake,' thought Steven, 'I should have gone home, then I wouldn't be sitting here waiting to be rescued.

Every time Steven looked out of the window there was Cuddles, still on guard, not moving a muscle.

After what seemed an eternity, Steven heard the gates open and a car drove into the yard. The lights at the workshop went on and a voice called 'Cuddles! Cuddles! Where are you? Come here!'

Steven shouted with all his might, 'Help! Help! Seamus, is that you?'

'Who's there?'

'Its me. Steven. Can you call Cuddles off.'

'Saints preserve us! Cuddles. Come here. Come here at once.'

There was silence for a minute, and then Seamus said, 'You can come out now.'

Steven gingerly opened the door to see the little man standing with Cuddles on a chain. At the sight of him, the dog started barking fiercely again, but Seamus said 'Stop that Cuddles,' and jerked on the dog's chain. 'I'm sorry about that,' he continued. 'No one told me you were here, so I let Cuddles out to patrol the yard and went home.'

'But my light was on,' protested Steven.

'To be sure, but I thought it was Feargus come back early. The dog knows him you see, so he doesn't bother him. '

Seamus bent down and picked up Steven's briefcase. 'Is this yours?'

'Yes.'

'It's a bit worse for wear,' observed Seamus, as he handed the mud-covered case over. Steven shuddered when he noticed the teeth marks on the base of the case, and thought how close he'd come to serious injury.

'It's a good job I decided to check to make sure there was no damage in the gale,' observed Seamus, 'can I get you a drink or something?'

'No thanks. I just want to go home.'

'Fair enough, I'll let you out.'

'Where on earth have you been,' demanded Margaret when he got home, 'I've been worried sick about you.'

'It's a long story' replied Steven wearily, 'I'll tell you about it later, right now I just want a hot shower and something to eat.'

Later in the evening Steven rang Jeremy at his home. 'Now then old sport,' responded Jeremy cheerily, 'what can I do you for?'

'It's a bit difficult,' Steven began. 'It's about Bert.'

'Oh,' said Jeremy, all heartiness going from his voice.

'I think he's got a bit of a drink problem. He had to be sent home from O'Connells this afternoon, and Kathy had a word with me about it. She didn't know what to do, so I said I'd give you a ring. I hope you don't mind.'

'Mind? Of course not. But I can't understand it, I used to work with Bert when I was an articled clerk. He was very good to me, and taught me a lot. We lost touch when I moved on after I qualified, but he came to see me a couple of months ago. He said he was out of work, and could I give him a job. I knew how good he was, so I took him on.'

'He is good,' said Steven, 'in the morning.'

'Quite.'

'What are you going to do?'

'What I should have done in the first place. I'll ring an old chum of mine who used to employ Bert and find out the background. Then I'll have a word with him.'

'Best of luck, and if there's anything I can do, let me know. I like Bert.'

'Yes, we all do. Well, thanks again Steven. I'll let you know what happens.'

The next morning, Steven set off for Campbell's with a boot full of empty boxes.

'Hello Mary, how's it going?' he greeted as he walked in to the office.

'All right, I suppose,' responded Mary coolly.

'Steven,' said Alex. 'You did say this was a new machine, didn't you?'

'Of course it is,' replied Steven in surprise.

'It's just that there's one or two scratches on the side.'

'Oh, I probably did that when I brought it. Let's have a look.'

'They don't look like new marks,' commented Mary, as she turned the computer for Steven to look at them.

'Hmmm. They don't,' agreed Steven.

'And who are Casey Packaging?' continued Mary.

'I haven't the faintest idea,' replied Steven. 'Why?'

'Because that's the name that flashes on the screen when you switch it on,' retorted Mary.

'What are you saying?' asked Steven in alarm.

'We're saying,' said Alex quietly, 'that this is not the new computer we paid for.'

'But Bernard said it was,' cried Steven. 'It was all boxed up and everything.'

'Where are the boxes?'

'In the car, I'll get them.'

'They look new enough,' said Alex doubtfully, as Steven put the boxes down on the floor.

'Lets have a good look at them,' said Mary.

'There's no address labels,' said Alex.

'No. But you can see where they've been,' said Steven.

'Why would anyone want to tear them off?' asked Mary suspiciously.

'Probably because they had Dacre Electric's on them,' said Steven.

Mary snorted, and started shaking all the packing out of the boxes. The others joined in, but all they produced was a pile of polystyrene and plastic wrapping.

'Wait a minute. What's this?' asked Steven, as he peered into an empty box. He reached in and pulled out a piece of paper that had been caught in the flaps at the bottom. He opened it out, and then looked at the others in dismay. 'It's a delivery note from Bingham computers,' he said slowly, 'made out to Casey Packaging.'

'There you are,' cried Mary, turning to Alex. 'I told you it was second hand.'

Steven looked from one to the other in growing panic. 'I hope you didn't think I knew about this?' he cried.

'We did wonder last night,' admitted Mary.

'But you're actions this morning prove that you didn't,' said Alex, and Mary nodded her head in agreement.

'Thank goodness for that,' sighed Steven. 'I'd better get on to Bernard straight away.'

'Just let's think about it for a minute,' said Alex. 'What are you going to say to him?'

'I'm not sure, ' admitted Steven. 'Tell him he's sold us a second hand machine I suppose.'

'And what if he denies it?'

'I'll show him the proof.'

'You can't do that over the phone.'

'No....'

There was a pause, then Mary said, 'I think we ought to get him here, and tell him what we think of him.'

'You're right,' said Alex. 'Steven, give him a ring and get him to come here this morning.'

'But how can I do that?' queried Steven.

'Tell him anything you like. Tell him there's something wrong with the machine. Say what you want, but get him here.'

'All right, I'll try,' said Steven. He thought for a moment, and then picked up the phone. 'Bernard,' he said, when Doris put him through, ' I'm at Campbell's and I've got a bit of a problem I can't sort out. Can you come over straight away and give me a hand?'

'What sort of problem?'

'It doesn't seem to want to run up properly. It flashes on the first screen and then nothing.'

'How many times have you tried it?'

'Well Mary's tried it a few times, and I've tried it twice,' lied Steven. 'I can't quite read the message that keeps flashing up. I'll have a go at freezing it on the screen so that I can read it properly.'

'No don't do that,' cried Bernard. 'Switch the machine off and I'll be over straight away.'

Bernard arrived in half an hour.

'That was quick Bernard,' said Steven. 'You must have broken all the speed limits to get here so fast.'

'Well you did say it was urgent,' mumbled the big man.

'Yes it is. I'd like you to meet my clients,' Steven said, and added, 'who are also my friends.'

Bernard shot him a cautious look as he shook hands with Alex and Mary. 'Right,' he said, with a false show of cheerfulness, 'let's have a look at the problem shall we?' He moved over to the desk followed by the rest of the group. 'Errr. If you don't mind, I'd like to have a look at it by myself first.'

'Right-ho,' said Mary, 'would anyone like a coffee?'

'Tea please,' said Steven.

'I know that silly,' said Mary, 'Bernard would you like one?'

'That's very kind of you, yes please.'

Bernard turned back to the computer and switched it on. It immediately sprang to life and as usual flashed past the first screen then showed the correct program.

'That seems OK,' said Bernard, puzzled.

'Yes it does, doesn't it?' said Steven. 'Let me have a go.'

Bernard switched off the computer and Steven took his place in front of it. He switched on the machine, and as the first screen appeared, he quickly pressed the 'pause' key. The first screen stayed full of writing, with the words 'Licensed to Casey Packaging' across the top.

'What did you do that for?' burst out Bernard, gazing in horror at the details on the screen.

'Because we asked him to,' said Mary as she walked through the door. 'Have a coffee, you'll need it.'

Bernard's face went puce, then white, and he slumped in his chair.

'Right,' said Steven. 'I think I, and my friends, deserve an explanation.'

'I'm sorry,' said Bernard wearily. 'I was in a bit of a hole, and didn't know how to get out of it. Then you came along.'

'All green and wet behind the ears I suppose,' said Steven.

'Something like that,' admitted Bernard.

'Who are Casey Packaging?' asked Mary.

'Were,' corrected Bernard. 'They went bust just over a month ago, and I'd just installed this computer. Their cheque bounced, so I went round to see what was going on. I arrived at the same time as the receivers, so I grabbed the machine and legged it. They weren't best pleased, but

I told them it was still my property until paid for, and they could sue me.' He chuckled at the memory. 'I'd just got back when I got your phone call. You were like manna from heaven.'

'Quite,' said Steven.

Bernard's face resumed its troubled expression. 'There's nothing wrong with the computer you know.'

'Just that it's second hand, and we've paid full price for it.' chimed in Mary.

'I've actually given you a good discount,' said Bernard.

'I should think so too,' retorted Mary.

'You could have told me it was second hand,' said Steven angrily. 'You've put me in an impossible position.'

'Yes, I can see that,' admitted Bernard. 'But how was I to know they were your friends?'

'Well they are, so you can take your flaming computer away,' cried Steven.

'Just a minute,' said Alex. 'Have you paid for the machine Bernard?'

'Yes I have,' said Bernard.

'And Binghams won't take it back?'

'That's right. They're no help at all.'

'What's the delivery on a new one?'

'Three months. That's why I gave you this one,' said Bernard, desperately trying to justify himself.

'OK. This is what we'll do,' said Alex. 'We'll take it off your hands for cost plus 10%. On condition that you pay Steven his commission.'

'But that'll take all my margin,' protested Bernard.

'Take it or leave it,' warned Alex.

'All right,' said Bernard. 'Cost plus 10% it is.'

'Right,' said Alex. 'You can send us a revised bill, with a copy of Binghams invoice attached, and we'll pay it by return, less Steven's commission.'

'You don't trust me much, do you?' said Bernard.

'Do you blame me?'

'No, I suppose not,' answered Bernard. 'But believe me, I've never done anything like this before.'

'Well you won't do anything like it again, will you?' chimed in Mary. 'It was your own fault you know,' she said, as Bernard stood up to go. 'If you'd provided it all boxed up, and newly packed, we wouldn't have thought anything about it. But when Steven brought it in all in pieces.......'

Bernard stopped and glared at Steven. 'You mean you didn't repack it?' he roared.

'No,' said Steven.

'You....., You....,' cried Bernard, lost for words. Then he burst into laughter. 'Serves me right,' he chuckled. 'I should have known.' He left the room, shaking his head and muttering. 'Wet behind the ears. Wet behind the ears.'

'Why did you do that?' demanded Mary.

'I felt sorry for the man,' admitted Alex. 'We've had problems of our own with customers going bust on us. I just thought it would suit both parties to come to some sort of a deal.'

'Both parties? What's in it for us?'

'Firstly, we get a computer that's almost new for a knock down price. Next, we don't have to wait three months for a replacement and finally, if Bernard gets his invoice in straight away, we can get it allowed against tax for this year. I think that's a pretty good outcome.'

'Well, when you put it that way.....'

'I do. But Steven, you've got to learn to be less trusting of people if you're going to stay out of trouble.'

'Point taken,' said Steven.

They spent the rest of the morning sorting out Mary's queries and then Steven drove to O'Connells. As he drove into the yard, he shivered as he thought about the events of the previous night.

'Hello,' boomed Liz, 'we thought you wouldn't be coming back after last night.'

'So you've heard?' replied Steven.

'There's not many secrets in this place,' laughed Kathy as she joined them. 'But seriously, are you all right?'

'Yes thanks. No harm done.'

'No thanks to that hound,' chimed in Liz. 'We've told Seamus it's a dangerous beast, but he won't have it. Well, he'll have to do something about it now.'

'You won't have it put down?' asked Steven in alarm.

'Oh no, its too good a guard dog for that,' said Kathy. 'But he'll have to be more careful about letting it out in future. You could have been killed.'

'Well, as I say,' said Steven, 'no harm done. Is Bert in the cabin?'

'No he hasn't turned up this morning,' said Liz. 'Maybe he heard about the hound!'

'Maybe,' said Steven as he took the key for the cabin and left.

After a short while, Kathy appeared with a cup of tea. 'I thought you might like this,' she said. 'With all the fuss I don't suppose you got to talk to Jeremy last night.'

'As a matter of fact, I did, and he was very grateful.'

'But what's going to happen to Bert?'

'I don't know, but you've done the right thing, so stop worrying.'

'I can't, he is such a nice man when he's sober.'

'Hopefully Jeremy can get it sorted out. He's promised to let me know what happens, and I'll make sure you know too.'

'Thanks.'

'Don't mention it. Now I've got one or two queries, do you think Liz is free?'

'Yes, and if she isn't, she'll stop what she's doing for you.'

'Oh. Right. I'll come across then.'

Liz greeted him effusively. 'Of course I've got time. I'll just finish putting these invoices in, and then I'm all yours.'

Steven sat beside her at the desk as she rattled away at the keyboard. 'Have you had any more problems with it freezing?' he asked.

'About twice a week on average,' she responded, carrying on with her work. 'The maintenance man is baffled. I've had a new screen, new keyboard, new innards, its practically a new machine.'

A workman came in with a piece of paper and some money in his hand.

'Cash sale,' he grunted.

'Give it here,' snapped Liz, and leant forward to take the money from him. From his side view Steven saw the keyboard disappear under her ample bosom. When Liz had finished talking to the workman she turned back to the screen. 'I don't believe it,' she screamed, 'it's done it again. Kathy, get that maintenance man on the blower straight away.'

'Errm,' said Steven diffidently. 'I think I know what's causing the problem.'

'You what?' cried Liz.

'Errm.'

'Spit it out man.'

'Its when you lean forward.'

'You what?'

'Its when you lean forward to get something from the counter, you press down on the keyboard.'

'But I take my hands off the keyboard.'

'It's not your hands that's the problem.'

Liz looked at him puzzled for a minute, and then leant forward. Realisation dawned. 'Its my Boobs,' she shouted. 'Its my bloody boobs!' and she gave Steven a big hug.

The whole office turned to look in amazement at a red faced Steven, and a laughing Liz. 'Come and look,' cried Liz. All the girls gathered round as Liz demonstrated time and again, how her bosom squashed the keyboard as she leant forward.

After the pandemonium had died down, Kathy said 'That's all very well, but how are we going to stop it happening in the future?'

'I'll just have to have my boobs cut off,' laughed Liz.

'I don't think that'll be necessary,' smiled Steven. 'But you'll either have to reduce the height of the desk, or put you keyboard somewhere else.'

The door opened and Jeremy came in.

'Steven's sorted the problem with the computer,' cried Liz. 'It's my boobs!'

'Pardon?' asked Jeremy in amazement.

'I'll tell you about it later,' laughed Steven. 'Is it me you want, or Kathy?'

'Both of you actually,' said Jeremy.

'Right,' said Steven, with a quick look at Jeremy's strained expression, 'we'll go over to the cabin shall we?'

'It's about Bert,' started Jeremy when they got to the cabin.

'I hope I haven't got him into trouble,' interrupted Kathy.

'No, you haven't got him into trouble,' Jeremy assured

her, 'but he is in trouble nevertheless. It seems that two years ago his wife left him for another man, and he hit the bottle. It got gradually worse, until the last firm he worked for started getting complaints from the clients. They asked him to find another job rather than sacking him.'

'So he came to you,' said Steven.

'Yes, and because they wanted to give him a chance, the last firm gave him a reasonable reference. With hindsight, I can see that there were some hidden warnings, but because I already knew him, I ignored them.'

'What's going to happen now?' asked Steven.

Jeremy sighed, 'I don't know. I saw him this morning and we had a long talk. He's very ashamed of what he's done, and pleaded for another chance, but can I afford to take the risk?'

'He really needs some expert help,' said Kathy. 'With the men being on their own over here with nothing to do but drink, we've had one or two problems ourselves in the past. We found that the best thing is to get them to Alcoholics Anonymous. I'll let you have the address if you like.'

'Does it work?' asked Steven.

'Generally it does. You see, most of the men here come from the same part of Ireland, so they know each other's problems, and help each other. But make no mistake, he'll need a lot of help and support to beat this.'

'Hmmm......' said Jeremy doubtfully, 'I'll think about it. Anyway, I came round to say thank you to you both for telling me about it. We'll obviously pull Bert off the job, and send someone else round.'

'Oh there's no need for that!' cried Kathy, 'Just tell him that he hasn't got to go to the pub at lunchtime, and I'll put Liz on to see that he doesn't!'

'And it might help if he could work over in the office,'

said Steven. 'It's a bit lonely over here on your own you know.'

'OK. We'll see what we can do,' said Kathy.

'That's very good of you,' said Jeremy.

'Well, as I've said before,' said Kathy, 'he's a nice man and he deserves a break.'

'Right,' said Jeremy thoughtfully.

Margaret met Steven with a face like thunder. 'What have you been up to at Campbell's,' she demanded.

'What do you mean?' asked Steven, taken aback by her outburst.

'I've just had Mary on the phone. She says to tell you that Bernard has been round with his revised invoice, and they'll pay you tomorrow.'

'Oh! That's good.'

'Is it? When I asked Mary what had happened, she said that they'd saved your bacon. She told me all about Bernard trying to sell them a second hand machine, and how we nearly lost them as friends.'

'How do you make that out?'

'Because Mary said they wondered last night what you were up to. If they hadn't been so understanding, we could have been in serious trouble, and damaged our friendship as well.'

'Oh I don't know about that.'

'Well I do. In future you will not do any work for friends. It's not worth it.'

'But Margaret.....'

'Steven,' warned Margaret.

'All right. No more work for friends.'

'Good. And you can forget working with Bernard again.'

'But it's the first time he's done anything like that.'

'So I hear. But who's to say he won't do something similar in future?'

'You're probably right,' admitted Steven.

'I know I am,' said Margaret.

CHAPTER 17

The phone rang as Steven was getting his breakfast the next morning.

'Steven? It's Nigel here. Where've you been? We haven't seen you in ages.'

'I've been busy with some new jobs.'

'Well forget them and get over here.'

'I can't, I've got appointments.'

'Break them,' cried Nigel, his voice getting higher. 'This is an emergency.'

'OK. OK.' said Steven soothingly, 'keep your hair on. I'll come over straight away.'

'Who was that?' asked Margaret.

'It's Nigel. He needs to see me urgently. I'll go and see him on the way to Campbell's. Give them a ring will you, and tell them I'll be a bit late.'

'Steven!'

'I know. I know. They're our friends. But Nigel sounds desperate. I'll be as quick as I can.'

'Ah Steven,' greeted Nigel, 'thanks for coming. Read that.' He handed Steven a short letter from the bank, which Steven quickly skimmed through.

When he had finished, he looked up at Nigel with a puzzled expression on his face. 'All this says, is that a new manager has been appointed instead of Claude. What's wrong with that?'

'And that he wants to come and talk our facilities over with us.'

'So?'

'So? Steven. Don't you realise what this means? I could pull the wool over that fool Keighley-Smythe's eyes, but I won't be able to do it to someone new. I'm ruined!'

'Don't be silly. What does Anne think about it?'

'She's gone to an aunt's funeral in South Wales, and won't be back till tomorrow.'

'Look, it can't be that bad. Why don't you give this new chap a ring and arrange a meeting next week. I'll come in tomorrow to update the cash flow, and then you can get it over with. Its always best to grasp the nettle you know.'

'If you say so,' responded Nigel.

'I do say so. Now then, I'll be off. By the way, did you know you're not the only one with a Morgan in the area?'

'No I didn't, and at the moment Steven, that's the last thing on my mind.'

'Quite. I'll see you tomorrow. Can you update those sales figures for me?'

'Yes Yes. Of course,' answered Nigel.

'I gather Margaret's not best pleased with you at the moment,' said Mary, with a wicked smile on her face.

'No,' admitted Steven. 'She thinks I nearly lost you as friends. I didn't, did I?'

'It was quite close,' admitted Alex. 'But we decided to give you a chance to explain yourself, and we're glad we did.'

'I see,' said Steven slowly.

'That's all over now,' said Mary. 'But we're expecting extra special service from you.'

'Oh you'll get it,' said Steven. 'Margaret'll see to that.'

'Good,' said Mary. 'Now I've got all the customer details loaded, what do you want me to do next?'

'Before we get into that,' interrupted Alex. 'How much

commission do we owe you? Then I can send Bernard his cheque.'

'I agreed ten per cent,' said Steven. 'But that'll take all of Bernard's margin, so I'll settle for five.'

'You'll do no such thing,' burst out Mary. 'If you agreed ten percent, that's what you'll get.'

'And don't worry too much about Bernard,' said Alex kindly. 'If I know his type, he'll have negotiated an additional discount somehow. He won't be out of pocket, mark my words.'

'If that's the way you want it,' said Steven.

'It is,' said Mary. 'Now then , what about my invoices?'

'Move over,' said Steven, 'and I'll show you.'

'Don't forget the idiot's guide,' warned Mary.

'I won't,' promised Steven, 'and I'll also show you how to back up your data.'

'Why should I want to do that?'

'In case something goes wrong, and you need to restore it.'

'Restore it?'

'Yes. Put back any work that the computer has lost.'

'Steven,' warned Mary, 'you're frightening me!'

'There's no need to be frightened. It's just a precaution.'

'If you say so,' said Mary.

They worked together until after lunch, and then Steven said, 'I'll move on now if you don't mind. You're still on for Saturday's dinner dance, aren't you?'

'I don't know,' said Mary, casting a glance at Alex.

'Hmmm. In the light of what's happened.........,' responded Alex.

Steven looked at them horrified. 'You don't mean.......?'

They both burst out laughing. 'Mary's just winding you up,' said Alex. 'Of course we'll be there.'

Relieved, Steven left for O'Connells.

'There you are,' greeted Liz with a welcoming smile.

'How's the computer?' teased Steven.

'Smashing. No problems at all. Thanks to you.'

'Just doing my job,' smiled Steven, giving a mock salute.

'Ah, but that was above and beyond the call of duty,' said Kathy, as she came across the room carrying a parcel, 'so we've bought you this.'

Steven unwrapped the parcel to reveal a shiny new brief case. 'Oh you shouldn't have,' he gasped.

'It was the least we could do, what with the dog an' all,' said Kathy.

'We're docking it from Seamus's wages,' chimed in Liz, with a smile, which showed she didn't mean it.

'I'm overwhelmed,' said Steven.

'Well don't get too carried away,' said Kathy, 'the VAT man's been on again about the returns.'

'I should be finished by Friday,' responded Steven. 'I'll get on with it straight away.'

'It's no good,' thought Steven, later in the afternoon, 'I've got to go to the toilet.' He put on his size seven wellington boots, and made his way gingerly across the yard. Seamus saw him coming, and stepped out of his office.

'How are you today?' he asked solicitously.

'Fine thanks,' replied Steven. 'Is Cuddles around?'

'No. I've built him a kennel round the side, so you can get to the toilet without going past him.'

'That's very good of you.'

'Not at all. Do you want to see him?'

'Err no thanks.'

'Aw come on. He's all chained up and he won't hurt you.'

'OK. If you think it'll be all right.'

'Of course it will,' beamed the little man, and scurried off round the corner.

Steven cautiously followed him.

'Here he is,' cried Seamus, with his arms round the hound. 'He's a big softy at heart, aren't you Cuddles?'

The dog wagged its tail furiously as it licked Seamus's face. Suddenly it saw Steven, and in a trice its demeanour changed. It jumped from Seamus's grasp barking loudly. It bounded towards Steven, who took one look at its slavering jaws, and bolted back round the corner. He ran into Seamus's office and slammed the door, expecting at any moment to hear the crash of the hound against it.

'Steven,' cried Seamus, 'where are you?'

'I'm in your office,' called Steven.

'What on earth for?'

'So that Cuddles can't get at me of course.'

'He can't do that. Come on out.'

Steven cautiously opened the door, and looked round it. There was no sign of the dog. 'Where is he?' he asked.

'Round the corner of course. I told you, he's chained up.'

'But he came for me.'

'I'm sorry about that. But it was only to the length of his chain.'

'It seemed a pretty long chain to me.'

'It is a bit long,' admitted Seamus, 'but that's to allow him space to move about.'

'A bit too much space if you ask me.'

'Ah there, there. I think you've got off on the wrong foot.'

'You're telling me,'

'Will you come round now, and make friends?'

'No. I'm afraid not Seamus. Enough is enough. I think both Cuddles and I know where we stand, and we'll leave it at that.'

Seamus sighed, 'I suppose you're right, but it's a pity. He can be such a friendly dog.'

'I'll take your word for it. By the way, how did he get such a stupid name?'

Seamus bridled. 'Its not a stupid name. He can be very affectionate. Actually it was Kathy. When she first saw him as a puppy, she said he was lovely and cuddly, and it stuck.'

'I bet she doesn't give him many cuddles now,' observed Steven, heading for the toilet.

'He's very affectionate,' Seamus called after him. 'He's just highly strung that's all.'

Steven waved to acknowledge the comment, but declined to answer. It was obvious that nothing would change Seamus's opinion of his beloved dog.

Steven's heart sank as he came through the door and saw Margaret's expression. 'What's happened now?' he asked wearily.

'Mary's been on the phone, the computer's broken down.'

'Oh no!' groaned Steven.

'Oh yes!' replied Margaret. 'They're waiting for you now. I rang you at O'Connells, but you'd left.'

'I didn't want to meet that dog again,' said Steven. 'I'll give Campbells a ring and find out what the problem is.'

'Steven,' cried Mary, 'can you come over straight away? We've got a message on the screen, and the computer won't do anything.'

'What does it say?'

'Error 235.'

'Is that all?'

'That's all.'

'I'll come over now.'

Steven jumped into his car and drove over to Campbells, cursing the evening rush hour traffic as he did so.

'There it is,' said Mary pointing to the screen.

Steven looked dumbly at the message.

'What does it mean?' asked Alex.

'I've no idea,' admitted Steven. 'Have you got the manual?' Mary passed the thick book over, and Steven started to pour over it. 'What were you doing when it happened?' he asked.

'I'd nearly finished inputting those invoices,' Mary responded.

'And had you taken a back up?'

'Not since lunchtime when we did one together. Will you be long?' she continued. 'It's just that I've got Women's Fellowship tonight, and Alex has got a lodge meeting.'

'OK. I'll take the machine and the manual home with me, and see if I can sort it out. If I can, I'll re-input the invoices for you.'

'Are you sure?'

'It's the least I can do.'

'Right-ho, if you're sure.'

'I'm sure.'

'What on earth......?' exclaimed Margaret, as Steven carried the computer in.

'You told me to give them good service,' replied Steven, 'and that's what I'm doing.'

'Can you sort it out?'

'I don't know, but I'm going to try.'

'You don't need me do you? It's Women's Fellowship tonight.'

'I know, Mary's already told me.'

'Good. I'll be off then.'

'What about my dinner?'

'It's chicken broth. If you ask her nicely, Katy might warm it up for you.'

'Thanks a lot!' said Steven.

'It's your own fault,' responded Mary. 'See you later.'

Steven went into the living room where the children were watching television. 'Katy,' he said, 'Can you warm my dinner up for me while I get this computer in?'

'Why me?' demanded Katy. 'Why can't Jason do it?'

'Because I need him to carry some things in for me.'

'But I'm watching Top of the Pops! It's nearly finished,' cried Jason.

'It won't take a minute,' snapped Steven. 'Now come on the pair of you, or I'll switch that Tele off.'

'Aw Dad!' they both moaned, as they reluctantly left their seats to do his bidding.

Steven set up the computer, and poured over the manual whilst he ate his broth. He found a section on trouble shooting, but all it said against Error 235 was 'Power failure.' 'That's funny,' muttered Steven to himself, 'Mary didn't mention anything about the power going down. I'll give it a try.'

He switched the computer on and it started up perfectly, but when he tried to go into the last invoice that Mary had put in, it came up with the message 'File corrupt.'

'Oh no,' groaned Steven, 'that means I'll have to restore and input all the invoices again.'

He got Mary's back up discs out, and restored the data as it had been at lunchtime. Then he started to re-input the invoices. He just got started when Margaret arrived home. 'You're early,' he said looking at the clock.

'Yes. I decided to skip coffee and come home to see if you needed any help.'

'Thanks. I could do with some. If you'll read the details off the invoices I'll key them in. It'll be much quicker.'

They settled down to work, and Jason popped his head round the door. 'Does anyone want a cup of tea?' he asked.

'We'd love one thanks,' said his mother.

'Didn't offer me one before,' muttered Steven softly.

'Perhaps you didn't treat him right,' said Margaret.

The next interruption was Katy. 'We're going to bed now. I've set the breakfast table. Sorry about my reaction earlier Dad, but you've got to admit, you were a bit over the top.'

Steven's jaw dropped. 'All I did was ask you to warm my dinner up,' he protested.

'More like ordered,' retorted Katy.

'Yeah,' chimed in Jason, 'and ordering me to carry in the equipment when I wanted to finish watching Top of the Pops.'

'All right, All right,' said Margaret, 'you're Dad was under a lot of pressure.'

'Well there was no need to take it out on us,' said Katy.

'That's enough,' said Margaret. 'We told you when this started that there would be problems.'

'Yes, but you didn't tell us it would make Dad all nasty,' cried Katy and ran out of the room. Jason gave them a glare and followed her.

'Now look what you've done,' said Margaret.

'Me? I haven't said a word—you've done all the talking.'

'Did you shout at them?'

'Well, I may have snapped a bit.'

'That means you did. Go upstairs and apologise.'

'Why? It was their fault. They wouldn't help me.'

'They would've done if you'd asked them properly. I know you're under stress, but there's no need to pass it on to your family.'

Steven sighed. 'You're right. It's just that I've promised O'Connells to have their VAT return done by Friday, and Nigel wants his cash flow tomorrow. So I could have done without Campbells computer breaking down. And it's funny, because I'm on a commission, I feel even more responsible than usual on a job.'

'That's because you've moved from being an independent consultant, to a supplier.'

'You're right. I'll not do that again!'

'You'd better not! Now then, are you going up to say goodnight to the kids?'

'Yes all right,' said Steven and kissed her on the cheek.

'That's the first time this week,' said Margaret.

'It isn't, is it?'

'Yes.'

'I'm sorry. I'll make it up to you, I promise.'

'Go and make it up to the kids first.'

'OK.'

The next morning Steven was waiting for Alex and Mary when they arrived at their warehouse.

'You're an early bird,' greeted Mary.

'I've got another appointment this morning, but I thought I'd deliver your computer first,' replied Steven. 'I've re-input all your invoices, so you should be OK now.'

'You shouldn't have,' said Mary. 'What time did you finish last night?'

'Eleven-thirty.'

'You're making me feel guilty now.'

'There's no need. I told you I'd look after you, and I will,' said Steven as he assembled the computer, 'By the way, do you have any problems with your power supply?'

'No,' responded Alex. 'Mind you, we don't use much power. Why do you ask?'

'Because Error 235 refers to a power failure.'

'We didn't notice anything,' said Alex.

Steven shrugged his shoulders and said, 'Ah well. It's all right now. I suggest you take a back up at lunchtime, just in case.'

'What would've happened if we hadn't had that back up?' asked Mary curiously.

Steven looked embarrassed. 'You'd have lost all your customers details,' he muttered.

'You what? All that work?'

'Yes,' admitted Steven. 'That's why I suggest you take constant backups.'

'Oh I will.'

'Do you mind if I don't come in again today? It's just that I've got a couple of rush jobs on, and I could do with the extra time.'

'No. That's fine,' said Mary. 'I've got a lot of invoicing to catch up on, so we'll see you tomorrow.'

Nigel was waiting for Steven as he walked into reception, 'Where have you been?' he cried.

'I had to return a computer to a client,' said Steven, ' and it's only nine o'clock.'

'I've been here since eight,' stormed Nigel. 'I've told you before, you need to get your priorities right.'

'I did,' muttered Steven as he followed Nigel down the corridor.

'What was that?'

'Oh nothing. When does Anne get back?'

'I'm picking her up from the station at eleven o'clock, so we need to get on.'

'Fair enough. Have you done those sales figures?'

'Yes. They're pretty much in line with last times.'

'Has the McBrides contract come in yet?'

'No.'

After Nigel had given him the sales figures, Steven went into his own room and started revising the forecast. About half past eleven he heard Nigel and Anne's voices as they came down the corridor and entered their room. Gradually he became aware that their voices were getting louder and louder. He began to pick out odd words, such as 'Bank manager. Forecast. McBrides.' Then he heard the door slam, and Nigel's footsteps down the hall.

A few moments later Anne came into Steven's room.

'Hello Anne,' he said, 'sorry to hear about your Aunt.'

'Thanks,'

'Were you very close?'

'She was my favourite, and the last of the family. I'll miss our weekly telephone calls.'

'Still, at least you kept in touch.'

'Ye..sss,' replied Anne, obviously preoccupied. 'When will you be finished with the figures?'

'I'm almost done. Nigel hasn't changed much, so it's just a case of updating them and putting in the car repayments. By the way, did Nigel tell you he's not the only one with a Morgan in the area.'

'Really?'

'Yes. I often see one at Netherton when I pass through on the way to Hedgeley.'

'Interesting.'

'Yes. Isn't it? Do you want me to show the effect if you don't get the McBrides contract?'

'But we're not going to get it.'

'You what?'

'We're not going to get it,' Anne repeated. 'That's why Nigel's so upset about the bank manager coming tomorrow.'

'Tomorrow? But I thought it was going to be next week.'

'The manager's away next week, on a course or something, so he's coming tomorrow morning.'

'So that's why he's in a state.'

'Yes.' There was a pause, then Anne said. 'Where did you say that other Morgan was?'

'At Netherton. It's usually parked in a garage, but you can see its boot sticking out. Why?'

'Oh nothing.' She seemed to make her mind up about something, and said, 'I've got to go out. Leave the figures on my desk will you.'

'I can come back if you'd like.'

'No. We may be some time.'

'OK. I'll see you on Saturday then.'

'Saturday?'

'The dinner dance.'

'Oh yes. I'd forgotten about that.'

'Seven o'clock in the cocktail bar.'

'Fine. See you there.'

Steven was just tidying up when the phone went. 'Is that you Steven?' demanded a taught female voice.

'Yes,' answered Steven.

'It's Mary.'

'Oh, Mary. I didn't recognise your voice. Is anything wrong?'

'That bloody message has come up again, pardon my language.'

'Oh no.' groaned Steven.

'What are you going to do about it?'

'I'll come over straight away.'

'I think you'd better.'

Steven sat with his head in his hands for a moment, then he picked up the phone and rang Bernard. He explained the problem, and asked for his advice. 'That's a difficult one,' said Bernard, 'I'll ring Bingham's and see what they suggest.'

'OK. I'll get over to Campbells and you can ring me there.'

When he walked into the office at Campbells, a grim faced Alex greeted him. 'What's going on Steven?'

'I don't know,' admitted Steven. 'Have you taken a back up?'

'I was just about to do so, when the message came up,' wailed Mary. 'I've put in over a hundred invoices this morning. Have I lost them?'

'I'm afraid so.'

The phone rang. 'It's for you,' said Alex, 'it's Bernard.'

'I've rung Binghams, and they say that there must be a power surge somewhere,' said Bernard. 'Have they got a photocopier or any machinery linked to the same circuit?'

'Not that I can see.'

'Well check it out. All they can suggest is that you put a clean line in.'

'A clean line?'

'Yes, one that goes straight back to the mains.'

'I see, and what will that do?'

'It'll make sure that there's no interference on the circuit. If that doesn't do the trick, they'll have to buy a UPS.'

'What's that?"

'It's a box which sits between the computer and the mains and makes sure that there's an uninterrupted power supply.'

'Oh I see. And are they very expensive?'

'About a thousand pounds.'

'A thousand pounds!'

'Yes. I'll see if I can get one cheaper, but that's what Binghams quoted.'

'Oh!'

'It mightn't come to that. Check out the present supply first, and let me know how you get on.'

Steven slowly put the phone down.

'What was that all about?' asked Mary.

'They're convinced that it's the electricity. Have you got a photocopier?'

'No.' replied Alex.

'Any machinery at all?' asked Steven.

'We told you this morning,' said Mary in an exasperated tone, 'we haven't got anything.'

'Well I'm stumped,' admitted Steven.

'What was all that about clean lines, and a thousand pounds?'

'It's about making sure you've got an uninterrupted power supply to the computer,' said Steven.

'It seems to me,' said Alex thoughtfully, 'that they want us to throw money at it, with no guarantee of solving the problem.'

'It looks a bit like that,' admitted Steven. 'I'll restore the data again and you re-input the invoices, taking a back up every hour. That way, if the problem occurs again, we'll not have so much to catch up.'

'If you say so,' said Mary.

'Alex, would you mind getting a quote for a clean line from your electrician?'

'OK. If you think it's worth it.'

'Well it might be quite an easy job, and there's no point in spoiling the ship for a half pence of tar is there?'

'I suppose not,' replied Alex, 'as long as it is just a half pence of tar and not a thousand pounds.'

'Here's the phone number I'll be at this afternoon. Any more problems, give me a ring, and I'll ring you tonight. OK?'

'OK.'

'Feargus is in the cabin,' said Liz when Steven asked for the key, 'so it's open.'

'Is it still all right for me to work in there?'

'Of course it is.'

There was no sign of Feargus when Steven got to the cabin, so he settled down to work. As he did so, a man in a smart suit came through from the other part of the cabin. With a shock, Steven realised that it was Feargus.

'I didn't recognised you,' he blurted out.

The big man gave him a slow smile and said softly, 'I'm off to see the bank manager with Jeremy. You've got to look the part you know.' With a wave of his hand he left the cabin, and Steven saw him driving out in a Jaguar. 'I wonder,' he thought, 'if dressing in working clothes is also looking the part.'

Kathy, bringing him a cup of tea, interrupted his reverie.

'I've just seen Feargus all dressed up,' he commented.

'Yes, he can look smart when he wants to,' smiled Kathy.

'Which way does he prefer to dress?' asked Steven.

'I don't know. It depends on what he's doing.'

'That's what I thought. He dresses for the part doesn't he?'

'You're right,' answered Kathy in surprise, 'You should see him when he's going home on holiday. Quite the dapper man about town.' Then changing the subject she said, 'how are you getting on with the VAT returns?'

'I've finished the first two quarters, and I'm nearly finished the third.'

'Oh that's great.'

'I've got the forms ready. Who shall I get to sign them?'

'Me, I suppose.'

'It has to be a Director or Company Secretary,' warned Steven.

'That's right, I'm the Company Secretary.'

'That's OK then.'

'No it's not,' retorted Kathy.

'What do you mean?'

'I mean that it's not OK being the Company Secretary,' she cried, and tears welled into her eyes.

'What's the matter?' asked Steven in alarm.

Kathy took a handkerchief out of her pocket, dabbed her eyes. She sat down and looked at him carefully. 'You're not an auditor are you.' It was more a statement than a question

'You know I'm not.'

'No. What I mean is, you haven't got to report things to the authorities?'

'Well, I would have problems with my Institute if I did anything wrong. But no, I don't have to report things to the authorities.'

Kathy sighed. 'You see, they're all Irishmen here.'

'I've gathered that,' said Steven dryly.

'You don't understand. They are all proper Irishmen, with Irish passports.'

'So?'

Kathy sighed again. 'I won't go into details, but there are things going on that, shall we say, are not quite legal.'

'What do mean? Are they gun running or something?'

Kathy looked startled. 'Oh no, nothing like that. Let's just say that all the cash isn't accounted for.'

'I see,' said Steven thoughtfully. 'But what has this got to do with them being Irish?'

Kathy looked at him scornfully. 'I told you. They've got Irish passports. At the first hint of trouble they'll be off across the Irish Sea, and we won't see them again.'

'Surely not.'

'Oh yes! Three months ago we had a VAT inspector here, and Feargus decided to take a long holiday at home. He didn't come back until the VAT man had given up.'

'I see,' said Steven again.

'Do you? Who do you think'll be left carrying the can when they all shoot off back to Ireland. Little Molly Muggins.'

'Hmmm. And I suppose you're not Irish.'

'No I'm not. Neither have I got an Irish husband like Liz.'

'Quite. But you can always claim that you were just a clerk carrying out orders.'

'Not if I'm Company Secretary,' said Kathy, and burst into tears.

Steven looked at her helplessly. 'Have you been worrying about this long?' he asked.

'Since the VAT inspector came,' sobbed Kathy. 'I can't sleep at nights thinking about it. What if I go to prison? What'll happen to my kids?'

'There, there, I'm sure it won't come to that. You'd probably just be fined.'

'But how would I pay the fine?' wailed Kathy, 'we'd lose our house.'

'Well, there's nothing for it but to resign as Secretary.'

'Can I do that?' asked Kathy.

'Of course you can.'

'But where would that leave Feargus?'

'He'd have to appoint someone else.'

'But who?'

'That's not your problem. Look, I'll ring a solicitor I know, and he'll go through it with you. He'll be in a better position to advise you, because he's covered by client confidentiality.'

Kathy looked doubtful. 'I'm not sure. What if Feargus finds out what I've been saying?'

'It's up to you. It's your only way out. Think of your husband and kids.'

Kathy looked at him as if he had hit her, and then straightened herself up and said, 'Right. I'll do it.'

'Good girl,' said Steven, 'you're doing the right thing.' He picked up the phone and rang Bob Russell.

'Hello Steven,' said Bob, 'long time no speak.'

'Yes,' agreed Steven, ignoring the thought that the long time wasn't his fault, 'I've got a friend here who needs a bit of advice fairly urgently.'

'Is it a personal matter?'

'No. She's a Company Secretary and wants to resign.'

'That's a bit unusual isn't it?'

'It's an unusual situation, believe me. She'll explain it all when she sees you.'

'I'm intrigued. I could see her at half past four this afternoon if that's any help.'

Steven cupped his hand over the handset and said to Kathy, 'Half past four tonight. OK?'

Kathy looked startled for a moment, and then nodded her head. 'Half past four,' confirmed Steven. 'Her name's Kathleen Duffy.'

'Right,' said Bob, 'will you be coming with her?'

'No I don't think so.'

'Fair enough. By the way, Barbara's doing quite well on the accounts, but she has one or two queries. Could you pop in one day next week and give her a hand?'

'Certainly,' replied Steven, thinking about Jeremy's prophetic words. 'Bye.'

'You certainly move fast,' said Kathy.

'Well it needed sorting out,' said Steven. 'We can't have a pretty girl like you not sleeping at night, can we?'

Later in the afternoon the phone rang. 'It's a woman called Mary on the line' said Liz, 'shall I put her through?'

'Yes please,' said Steven, quaking in his shoes.

'Hello, is that you Steven?' asked Mary.

'Ye...ss' answered Steven.

'You don't need to be so frightened,' laughed Mary. 'I've just rung to tell you that we got a clean line put in about half an hour ago, and everything's working fine.'

'That was quick.'

'Well, we thought about what you said, and decided, for what it costs, we might as well have it done.'

'That's great, but keep on taking the back ups.'

'Oh I will, don't worry,'

'Right. I'll be round tomorrow morning.'

'Fine.'

'On my way home I saw Anne's Triumph Stag at the house where the Morgan lives,' said Steven to Margaret that night.

'What Morgan?'

'You know, the one that I saw parked at a house in Netherton.'

'You never told me about it.'

'Haven't I? Well I told Anne that there was another Morgan in the area.'

'You what?'

'I told Anne about the second Morgan.'

'How do you know it's a second Morgan?'

'Because it was parked in a garage in Netherton. Nigel doesn't live there.'

'Was is the same colour?'

'I could only see the back end of it, but it could have been.'

'Hmmm,' said Margaret thoughtfully. 'Where did you think you saw Nigel's Range Rover that time?'

'At Netherton,' said Steven. 'You don't think...........'

'I do. I think you've dropped Nigel right in it!'

Steven looked horrified for a moment, then chuckled, 'Serves him right for buying such a distinctive car! And I thought he'd be put out because there was another one in the area!'

'He'll be put out all right when Anne gets through with him,' said Margaret.

CHAPTER 18

Steven was just getting out of his car outside Campbells when there was a blast of a horn. A large cement mixer lorry rushed past him at speed, just missing the edge of the half open door.

'I was nearly knocked down by a cement mixer lorry out there,' he said when he got inside.

'We've had a couple of near scrapes ourselves,' said Alex. 'There's a plant out the back and the drivers are on bonus, so they drive like mad men. I'll have to have a word with Sam the manager.'

'Never mind, 'said Mary, 'I'll make you a nice cup of tea, and then we can get on. I stayed back till seven o'clock last night and got all the invoices entered. And no sign of Error 235!'

'Great,' said Steven. 'We'll get on to posting the cash this morning.'

They worked for about an hour, then Steven said, 'Right. Let's take a back up.'

'Surely we don't need to now,' protested Mary. 'The clean line's solved the problem.'

'Probably,' agreed Steven, 'but I'd still like you to take regular back ups, just in case.'

'All right,' said Mary, 'if you say so.'

They worked steadily through the morning, taking regular back ups. Just before twelve Steven said, 'If you don't mind Mary, I'll move on now. I'll be at the same place as yesterday if you need me.'

'Right-ho,' said Mary, 'but I'm sure I'll be all right now.'

As Steven walked to his car he heard a whooshing noise and a clattering. He looked round, and saw a cloud of steam and dust rising from the top of the cement mixing plant, which towered over Campbell's premises. He was about to drive off when he saw Mary running across the road towards him, gesticulating madly. He wound down his window, and felt his heart sink as Mary blurted out, 'It's done it again!' Her eyes filled with tears as she said despairingly, 'The bloody thing's done it again.'

'Damn,' said Steven, as he turned off his engine, and slowly walked back into the office.

'What are we going to do now?' wailed Mary. 'All that work!'

'Have you taken a back up?' asked Steven.

'Five minutes ago.'

'Good. At least we haven't lost much.'

'That's not the point Steven,' shouted Mary. 'We can't use the computer if it keeps on breaking down on us.'

'All right, all right,' said Alex, walking over and putting his arms around her, 'we'll get it sorted.'

'I'm not touching it again until you do,' sobbed Mary.

'No ones asking you to,' said Alex gently. 'Look, why don't you go and get us a sandwich or something, while Steven and I try to sort out what to do next.'

'All right,' said Mary drying her eyes. 'What would you like Steven?'

'Ham and peas pudding would be lovely, but I don't really deserve it.'

'Don't be silly,' said Mary,' we know it's not your fault, it's the bloody machine. There I've sworn again. I don't normally, but it's so frustrating.'

'I know,' said Steven,' it's driving me to swearing as well.'

'So I've noticed,' smiled Mary. 'I'll go and get the sandwiches.'

When she'd gone Steven and Alex looked at each other. Steven held his hands out in a helpless gesture. 'I'm stumped,' he admitted. 'It's got to be the electricity supply, but why is it happening?'

'It's funny you know, but it happened about this time yesterday,' said Alex.

Steven suddenly thought about noise that he'd heard as he'd gone to his car. 'I wonder if it's got anything to do with the cement plant out the back?' he mused.

'Why should it?' asked Alex.

'Because there was a funny noise coming from it when I went to my car. Do you think you could ask them what they were doing?'

'If you want, but I think you're clutching at straws.'

'Please,' begged Steven.

'OK,' said Alex reluctantly, 'but you can speak to them.' He dialled a number and then said, 'Sam? It's Alex here from next door. We're having some problems with our computer, and I wondered if you could have a word with our consultant?'

He passed the phone over to Steven who said 'Hello Sam. We're having a problem with the power supply. Have you any difficulties?'

'No,' answered Sam,' none at all.'

'Oh!' said Steven disappointedly. 'When I was outside just now there was a big whooshing noise and a cloud of dust, what was that?'

'Oh that was when we cleaned the plant down. You see, bits of cement get stuck in the chutes, so we have to flush them through with boiling hot water.'

'And how often do you do that?'

'Normally twice a day. Twelve o'clock when we break for lunch, and four o'clock when we close down.'

'And does that take a lot of electricity?' asked Steven excitedly.

'A fair bit,' admitted Sam. 'We have to do it at full force you see.'

'Thank you. Thank you very much Sam.'

'Not at all.'

Steven put the phone down and turned to Alex in triumph. 'There's the culprit! The mixer plant uses a lot of power at twelve o'clock and four o'clock every day, and it must cause the electricity supply to surge.'

'But what about last night? Mary had no problems.'

'The plant was shut down by then.'

'Not when she started.'

'When did she start?'

'As soon as the electrician had finished.'

'What time was that?'

'About four o'clock.'

'Can we get the exact time?'

'Yes, I've got his time sheet here.' Alex picked up a piece of paper from his desk and said slowly, 'It says five past four.'

'That's why you didn't have a problem last night!' cried Steven in triumph. 'Your power supply was disconnected whilst the electrician worked on it.'

Mary walking in with the sandwiches interrupted them.

'We've solved it!' cried Steven. 'It's the mixer plant next door.'

'You what?'

'It's the mixer plant,' confirmed Alex. 'They use a lot of electricity at twelve o'clock and four o'clock every day.,

'That's all very well,' said Mary, 'but where does that leave us?'

Steven looked non-plussed, and the excitement drained away. 'There's always a UPS system,' he said.

'At a thousand pounds? Come on Steven, be realistic,' said Mary scornfully.

'The only other alternative is to switch the computer off twice a day.' said Steven.

'Hmmm. That might work,' agreed Alex.

'Or throw the whole thing out!' said Mary.

'You can't do that!' exclaimed Steven in horror.

'Oh can't we?' responded Mary, 'you just watch us!'

'I think we'll have to think about it for a while,' interrupted Alex. 'I'll have another word with Sam, and see what can be done.'

'OK,' accepted Steven, 'if you want to talk it over further, you know where I am.'

'Yes we do,' said Alex, 'and don't worry Steven, we're not blaming you.'

'No, but Margaret will!'

'Feargus wants to see you,' said Liz, as Steven walked into O'Connells, 'he's in the cabin.'

'Do you know what it's about?' asked Steven.

Liz was non-committal. 'You'll find out,' she said, and turned back to her work.

There was no sign of Kathy, so Steven made his way to the cabin. Feargus was sitting at one of the tables looking at some papers.

'You wanted to see me?' said Steven.

'Yes. I hear you've been giving Kathy advice.'

Steven gulped. 'Errr Yes.'

'Hmmm. I had no idea she was getting herself into such

a state. Anyway we've got it all sorted out, and she's away to the solicitors now.'

'That's great,' said Steven, with a sigh of relief.

'Glad you think so. Now, about you. You seem to like giving advice to all and sundry, even when it's not your business.'

Steven gulped again, 'I just like helping people,' he said.

'Well, just remember who's paying the bills,' Feargus said sternly. 'In future, come to me with any problems.'

'Right.'

'OK. I'm off to site now. I hear Liz wants you to help her with the accounts.'

'Does she?' asked Steven in surprise.

'Yes, and I've agreed. But don't forget who's boss.'

'Oh I won't.'

Kathy was all smiles when she came in later that afternoon.

'I hear it's all been sorted out,' said Steven.

'Yes,' Kathy replied, 'thanks to you.'

'Think nothing of it. Who's going to be the new Company Secretary?'

Kathy smiled. 'Seamus.'

'Seamus!'

'Seamus,' she confirmed.

'But he's got nothing to do with the admin.'

'Exactly. He'll just sign the forms that we put in front of him. It was Feargus's idea. Neat isn't it?'

'But is that allowed?'

'According to your solicitor friend it's a bit unusual, but he could find no law against it.'

'Does Seamus know what he's letting himself in for?'

Kathy frowned a bit and then said, 'I think so. I had a good talk to him, and so did the solicitor. The thing is you see, he has no dependants or property to worry about, so he's quite happy.'

'Well I never,' said Steven shaking his head in disbelief.

'I bet you've never had a job like this before'

'You can say that again,' said Steven.

'It's not my fault!' shouted Steven, in reply to Margaret's inquisition as the family ate their dinner. 'I can't be responsible for the power supply.'

'No. But you should never have taken the job on in the first place. I told you not to,' replied Margaret in equally loud tones.

'But we need all the work we can get.'

'But not from our friends. I wish I'd never agreed to you going on your own. Any more problems like this, and I'm getting out.'

The ringing phone interrupted them. 'I'll get it,' said Jason and darted into the hallway. 'Its for you Dad,' he called out. 'Some woman called Anne.'

Steven exchanged looks with Margaret and they both went to the phone.

'Steven,' burst out Anne, without the usual pleasantries, 'is it all right if I come round to see you?'

'When?'

'Now.'

Steven glanced at Margaret enquiringly who nodded her head.

'Give us half an hour. The kids and Margaret will be in, so we'll have to sit in the dining room.'

'That won't bother me, in fact I'd like Margaret to be there.'

'I wonder what that's all about,' Steven mused as he put the phone down.

'I can guess,' said Margaret dryly. 'Come on, help me with the dishes.'

Anne arrived promptly in half an hour. 'Thanks for seeing me at such short notice,' she said. 'A lot's been happening, and I thought I'd bring you up to date, seeing that it involves you.' She paused, and looked at Steven across the dining table. 'That Morgan you saw was Nigel's,' she stated.

'We'd worked that out,' admitted Steven.

'He's been seeing that tramp Maxine for all this time,' said Anne, her lips trembling. 'He's set her up in a house and has been visiting her when he was supposed to be on sales visits.' Her voice broke into a wail, 'How could he?' she cried, and burst into tears.

Margaret moved round the table and put her arm round her.

'The problem is, I still love him!' cried Anne and her sobs got louder.

Steven looked on helplessly and said, 'Shall I get you a cup of tea or something?'

Anne nodded her affirmative, and Steven gladly escaped into the kitchen. He'd just put the kettle on, when Jason and Katy crept into the room. 'What's happening Dad?' hissed Jason.

'Anne's having problems with her marriage,' whispered Steven 'we'll tell you about it later.'

The children nodded and, responding to Steven's shooing movements, returned to the living room.

Anne had composed herself when Steven returned. 'I'm sorry about that,' she said. 'It's just that I've had to bottle it up all day, and it all came out.'

'We don't mind,' said Margaret. 'What are friends for?'

'Thanks. Where was I? Oh yes. I went to Netherton

yesterday afternoon and confronted the pair of them. You should have seen their faces when I knocked at the door! To cut a long story short, we had a stand up fight and then I left, telling Nigel he had to choose between her and me. To my surprise, he came round this morning, begging forgiveness. I suppose you'll think me a fool, but I agreed to take him back as long as he stopped seeing that trollop.'

She paused and looked enquiringly at Margaret, as if seeking reassurance that she'd done the right thing.

Margaret nodded her head gently, so Anne continued. 'We saw the new bank manager this morning, who was not best pleased with the cash flow situation. In fact, he threatened to close us down unless we injected a substantial amount of cash. Nigel hasn't got any cash. The house is mortgaged to the hilt, and in any case, it's in my name.'

She paused again and a smile crossed her lips, 'That was my trump card. My Auntie died last week and left me her house, worth about forty thousand pounds. As you know Steven, that's more than enough to meet our current shortfall and give us some working capital.'

Steven nodded in agreement.

'But surely,' Margaret burst out, 'you're not going to give him all that money?'

'Not quite. We're going to increase the share capital, and I'm going to have a fifty- percent shareholding. I'm also going to become joint managing director. That way I can keep an eye on things, and make sure that he gets out selling.'

'Has Nigel agreed?' asked Steven.

'He's got no option,' said Anne triumphantly. 'It's either that, or close the firm down and he loses everything.' A shadow crossed her face. 'He *is* a good salesman you know, when he's motivated properly.'

'And you can do that?' queried Steven.

'I don't know,' admitted Anne, her face twisted with doubt. 'But what else can I do to save my marriage?' She paused again and then said softly, 'I still love him you see.'

'Well he doesn't deserve you,' said Margaret, 'but we women do some daft things for our men folk at times, don't we Steven?'

'Err yes' agreed Steven, then, to change the subject, asked Anne, 'you said that all this affected us.'

'Yes. That's why I came round. If I'm going to be more involved in the day to day running of the company, and Nigel's out selling, we need someone to run the accounts and admin. I'd like you to join us as financial director.'

Steven looked stunned. 'This is a bit sudden,' he said, and looked across at Margaret for help.

'It's very good of you Anne, but I think we need to think about it.' said Margaret.

'Oh I understand that,' agreed Anne. 'But if we're going to pull the business round, we need to get started straight away. If you're not going to take it, I'll have to get an advert in the paper next week.'

'Give us the weekend,' said Margaret.

'Fine. You can name your own salary Steven. You know better than anyone what we can afford.'

'Thanks,' said Steven, still shell-shocked.

'I'll be off then,' said Anne.

'Will you still be coming to the dance?' asked Margaret.

'Of course,' replied Anne. 'Mind you, I don't think Claude Keighley-Smythe will be there.'

'Oh? Why not?' queried Steven.

'Because he's not exactly flavour of the month with the bank,' smiled Anne. 'Jim, that's our new manager, says he's lent too much money to dodgy customers just on their word, instead of basing it on hard facts and figures. He's being relocated to one of the mining villages in Durham. Apparently that's the equivalent of outer Mongolia in banking circles!' She laughed, and then said, 'Thanks for seeing me. It's cheered me up getting it off my chest. See you tomorrow night. And I'd love to have you with us Steven.'

To their surprise, when Steven and Margaret went into the living room, Jason jumped up and turned the television off.

'What's happening?' demanded Katy.

'Anne and Nigel are having some problems with their marriage, that's all.' said Steven.

'Had they been arguing like you and mum?' queried Jason.

'What do you mean?' asked Steven in surprise.

'Have they been shouting at each other, like you two?' asked Katy almost in tears.

'Yes,' chimed in Jason, 'has she left him, like Mum's going to?'

Margaret looked at them in horror. 'Who said I was going to leave?'

'You did,' cried Katy.

'I didn't.' denied Margaret.

'You did,' continued Katy, starting to cry. 'You said that if there was any more trouble, you'd get out.'

Margaret looked helplessly from Jason's twisted face to Katy's crumpled form crying in the chair. 'Come here, silly,' she said, holding her arms out, 'I'm not going to leave your dad. I just meant that I would stop working for him. That's all.'

Katy rushed to her arms, sobbing her heart out. 'But everyone that Dad talks about is having trouble with their marriage.'

'Not everyone,' protested Steven.

'Well it seems like it to us,' retorted Jason. 'And then you two start fighting, and we think that we're next.'

Steven and Margaret looked at each other guiltily. Steven put one arm round his son, and the other round Margaret and Katy. The four of them stood in a huddle in the middle of the floor. 'Listen to me you two,' he said fiercely. 'This family is the most important thing in the world to me, and nothing, absolutely nothing, is going to come between me and you.'

'Amen to that,' said Margaret, and gave him a kiss.

'Anyway,' continued Steven, 'I may not be working for myself much longer, Anne has offered me a job.'

'But I thought you liked being a consultant,' said Katy, drying her eyes.

'I do. But it has it's ups and downs,' said Steven, 'and anyway it might make me less bad tempered.'

'I'm not so sure about that,' laughed Margaret. 'We've got the weekend to think about it, so lets leave it for the moment. Who's for milky cocoa and shortbread's?'

'What do you think?' asked Steven, when the children had gone to bed.

'What about?' replied Margaret.

'Anne's offer of course.'

'Oh that! I was thinking about the kids worrying about us falling out.'

'So was I. That's why I think I should take up Anne's offer.'

'How would that help?'

'Well, I wouldn't have to worry about where the next job was coming from.'

'True.'

'Or how I'm going to pay us this month. I'll be able to be off sick instead of worrying about who'll do the work.'

'But you've never been sick.'

'I know, but I could be.'

'Steven, you're talking nonsense,' Margaret said. 'Are we broke?'

'No.'

'Have you got plenty of work?'

'Just at the moment I have.'

'Steven,' said Margaret, 'stop being so pessimistic. It's not like you.'

'I know. It's just that the situation at Campbells has upset me. They could end up by throwing the computer out, and it'll all be my fault.'

'Earlier on you were saying it wasn't your fault.'

'I know, but I'm sure they'll be thinking of suing me, or at least demanding their money back.'

Margaret looked at him in horror. 'Can they do that?'

'Yes.'

'But you told me it was the power supply.'

'I'm pretty certain it is. But how do I prove it?'

'I don't know. But you'd better find a way quick.'

'There you are. Getting upset again. That's the difficulty of working together. We both get involved in the problems, and we never get away from work.'

'I only get worried when it's our friends.' said Margaret with some asperity.

'I know. But can't you understand? Most of my clients become my friends, so their worries become my worries. And it gets me down when I can't help them.'

Margaret's face softened. 'But you do help them. That's why you set up on your own in the first place. I think you should think about it a bit more.'

'You're right as usual,' said Steven quietly. 'I'll leave it till Sunday before I make a decision.'

CHAPTER 19

Steven and Margaret deliberately arrived early for the reception, and the cocktail bar was quite empty when they walked in. In a corner of the room they saw George and Carol talking to Claude Keighley-Smythe.

'I thought Anne said Claude wouldn't be here,' muttered Steven. 'We'd better go and rescue them.'

He led the way across the room. 'Hello Steven,' boomed George, whilst they were still some way off, 'what can I get you?'

'It's my shout,' said Steven getting closer,' but first let me introduce you to Margaret.'

'Pleased to meet you at last,' boomed George, ' and this is Carol.'

Carol smiled and shook Margaret's hand.

'Have you met Claude, Margaret?' enquired George, in a less friendly tone.

'Oh yes,' replied Margaret as she reluctantly took Claude's proffered hand. 'I'd heard you weren't coming tonight,' she continued.

'Who told you that?' said Claude. Margaret just shrugged her shoulders, so he continued, 'I was just telling George, that I have another function to go to, but I thought I'd pop in to the reception first, and meet some of my customers.'

'But I hear you're moving on?' said Steven.

'Yes. Yes. I'm afraid so,' said Claude. 'If you'll excuse me there's someone over there I'd like to see.' With a brief nod to the group, he rushed across to a couple who had just entered the room.

'That's got rid of him,' remarked Steven. 'Now then, what are we having to drink?'

'Before you do that,' said Margaret, 'do I gather that congratulations are in order?'

Carol smiled, and held out her left hand on which was an engagement ring. George, with a slightly embarrassed smile, said, 'Err yes. We got engaged yesterday. This weekend is a sort of celebration.'

'Fantastic!' said Steven, 'this calls for champagne.'

'No. No.' laughed Carol, 'we don't want a lot of fuss.'

'OK. If you say so,' said Steven, 'but at least let me get you a drink.'

As he was waiting at the bar to be served, Jeremy joined him. 'Now then old sport, what are you having?'

'Hello Jeremy. Thanks very much, but I'm in the chair tonight. Got my own clients to look after.'

'I see. Well I owe you one, and so does Bert.'

'What's happened about him?'

'Well, thanks to you and Kathy, I decided to give him another chance. I got in touch with Alcoholics Anonymous, and they recommended a clinic where he could get some help. He'll be in for at least a couple of weeks, and then he'll come back to work.'

'It's very good of you to help him.'

'It's the least I could do after all the help he gave me as an articled clerk. But you didn't owe him anything, and yet you helped him. You make a habit of helping people, and it's really appreciated, believe me.'

A tap on Steven's shoulder interrupted them. It was his friend John, who grinned a greeting, and said, 'Margaret sent me. The rest of your guests have arrived, so you need some more drinks.'

'I've got mine,' said Jeremy, 'so I'll be off. I might have

another job for you Steven. Give me a ring next week.'
With a wave of his hand he left them.

'Client of yours?' asked John as they waited for the
barmaid to get their order.

'Not exactly. He's a Chartered Accountant and he's
introduced me to one or two clients.'

'I see. Business good then?'

'I think so.'

'You think so. What sort of answer is that?'

'We're just at a bit of a crossroads at the minute, I'll tell
you about it later.' He paid for the drinks and, with John's
help, carried them back to their party.

'I presume Margaret has made the introductions?' said
Steven after he had served the drinks. They all nodded their
agreement so he continued, ' and have Carol and George
given you their news?'

Everybody looked at Carol and George who looked
slightly embarrassed. 'Steven!' hissed Margaret. 'They
didn't want a fuss.'

'I know, but its not every day one's clients get engaged,'
said Steven, ignoring Margaret's black looks.

'Engaged! How lovely,' said Helen.

'Yes,' chimed in Mary, 'lets see the ring.'

As Carol shyly held out her hand, the ladies clustered
round her, and Isobel barked, 'Very nice. Well done.'

The men took it in turns to shake George's hand. The
last to do so was Nigel. 'Congratulations,' he said grudgingly.
'Do you work together?'

'We do as a matter of fact,' said George, beaming all
over his face.

'Mistake. Big mistake,' glowered Nigel. 'Worst thing I
ever did.'

'It's not always the case, is it Alex?' interrupted Steven,
as George's face started to fall.

'No, of course not,' said Alex. 'You have you're ups and downs of course, but all in all it's great.'

'Yes,' chimed in Alan with a laugh. 'The only problem is, that your wife knows where you're supposed to be, so you can't get up to mischief!'

They all laughed with him, except Nigel, who supped his drink morosely.

Dinner was called, and as they moved towards the dining room, Steven noticed Claude slinking away towards the entrance. Nigel also noticed Claude's movements. 'There he goes,' he sneered, 'off to nurse his broken ego.'

'He's got another function to go to,' said Steven.

'Another function my foot,' snarled Nigel. 'He just couldn't face the fact that he's finished. He's gatecrashed the reception, so that he could pretend that he was still important. Pathetic isn't it.'

Steven felt a pang of pity, as he watched the hunched figure go through the swing doors and into the street.

The conversation flowed freely during dinner with the exception that Nigel, who was drinking copious amounts of wine, hardly ever joined in. As the sweet was being served, he suddenly said in a loud tone, 'Now then, Mister Clever Consultant. Are you going to tell everyone about the mess you've got us into?'

There was a deathly hush, and Steven flushed.

'Nigel,' said Anne sharply. 'It's got nothing to do with Steven.'

'Oh hasn't it? sneered Nigel. 'What about his cash flow that shows that we're going bust. Explain that Mister Smart Face.'

'It was based on the sales figures you gave me,' said Steven in a quiet voice.

'No it wasn't. You didn't include the McBrides contract.'

'Because Anne told me you weren't going to get it.'

'And you believed her before me,' sneered Nigel.

'Yes,' replied Steven angrily, 'every time.'

'I suppose it's got nothing to do with the fact that she's giving you a directorship, and kicking me out?'

'Nigel! That's enough!' said Anne jumping up. 'Come on. We're going home.'

'All right. All right. I'm going. It makes me sick just to look at his smug face.' He staggered to his feet and turning to Anne, said, 'And don't think you'll be able to jump into his bed as quickly as you jumped into mine.'

Anne slapped his face with all the force she could muster. Nigel went sprawling to the ground, knocking his chair over with a crash as he did so. The whole room went quiet, as people craned their necks to see what was going on.

George, who had been sitting next to Anne, helped Nigel to his feet, and the rest of the diners in the room tactfully resumed their meals. Anne grabbed Nigel by the arm and started to pull him towards the entrance. Steven stood up to follow her, but Margaret laid a restraining hand on his arm. 'I'll go,' she said softly. She caught up with Anne and took Nigel's other arm as they made their way unsteadily towards the exit.

As he resumed his seat Steven said, 'sorry about that folks, as you can gather, they're going through rather a sticky patch.'

Everybody murmured polite nothings, and resumed their sweets. 'More wine anybody?' asked Steven, desperately trying to lift the mood of the table.

'Yes please,' said John. 'It's a very nice wine, did you choose it yourself?'

Steven shot John a grateful look, and started a discussion

about the merits and demerits of various wines. The others joined in, and soon the conversation was flowing freely again. Anne appeared at the doorway, and made her way across to the table. The men started to stand up, but she made a gesture for them to stay seated.

Steven looked to see if Nigel was following, but Anne said, 'We've called a taxi, and Margaret's keeping an eye on Nigel.' She bit her lip, and they could see that she was close to tears. 'I just want to say how sorry I am for what's happened,' she said. 'As you'll have gathered, we're having rather a hard time at the moment, but that doesn't excuse Nigel's behaviour.'

'It's just one of those things,' said Steven. 'Forget it.'

'I can't forget it, and I won't. I just want to make it clear to everyone that none of this is Steven's fault. He's helped us a lot over the last six months, and without him we wouldn't have survived till now.' Tears welled into her eyes. 'I'm sorry,' she said brokenly, and hurried out of the room.

'I think I'd better go and see what's happening,' said Steven.

'I wouldn't,' said Alan, 'I think you'd better leave them to Margaret.'

The others nodded in agreement, so Steven subsided into his chair. A waitress came up to clear the table. 'Coffee?' she asked, 'or does anyone want tea?'

'He does,' said the women with one voice, and pointed to Steven. Then they all burst out laughing.

'Does he get tea at your place as well?' Carol asked Mary.

'Get it? He demands it!' replied Mary.

Once again the ice was broken as they vied with each other to tell tales about Steven's love of tea. Margaret came back in the middle of it and joined in happily with the banter.

Steven muttered quietly in Margaret's ear, 'Are you OK?'

'Yes,' she replied quietly, 'we'll talk about it later.'

The band was a good one, and soon everyone was on the floor dancing.

'How were Nigel and Anne?' asked Steven, as he and Margaret glided round the floor to a quickstep.

'All right,' said Margaret.

'Come on, what's happened?'

'Nothing. I told you, we'll talk later.'

'If that's what you want,' said Steven. 'I wonder what those two think about it all,' he said, nodding in the direction of George and Carol, who were oblivious of anyone else on the floor.

'Oh they're in love. Anyone can see that,' replied Margaret. 'They'll do all right.' Steven nodded in agreement, but, because he was concentrating on manoeuvring through a gap in the crowd of dancers, he didn't see the troubled expression which crossed Margaret's face.

'We'll be going soon,' said Alan, during a gap between dances. He bent forward to talk into Steven's ear. 'It's none of my business, but what did Nigel mean about a directorship?'

'It's a bit complicated,' replied Steven. 'But, to cut a long story short, Anne's putting money into the firm, and wants me to join them.'

'And will you?'

'I'm not sure,' admitted Steven.

'It's your decision of course,' said Alan. 'All I'll say is that you're a damn good consultant, and it would be pity to loose you. As far as Garage Trade are concerned, I've been told by the Governors to offer you the job of Treasurer.'

'That's very good of them.'

'No more than you deserve. I was going to see you next week, but seeing that you are obviously at a turning point, I thought you needed all the facts before you made up your mind.'

'Got over Nigel's comments yet?' asked John, as they made their way towards the toilets.

'Just about,' replied Steven.

'Good. The rest of your clients seem to think highly of you.'

'Do they?'

'Oh yes. You come highly recommended. We're thinking of computerising our accounts, and I'd like you to give us a hand.'

Steven stopped in his tracks. 'John, I don't know what to say.'

'What do you mean?'

'I'd love to help you of course, but Margaret doesn't want me to take on any more jobs for friends.'

'Why ever not?'

'Because when things go wrong, the situation gets complicated by the personal relationships.'

'Well Alex and Mary seem perfectly happy with the advice you gave them.'

'Have they said so?'

'Oh yes. They're going to get rid of the computer, but they say it's not your fault.'

'What! They haven't told me that.'

John looked embarrassed. 'I'm sorry, I shouldn't have said anything. I think in view of what happened with Nigel, they thought you'd had enough bad news for one night.'

'You're right,' said Steven, as they resumed their progress towards the toilets, 'this night is not turning out like I expected at all!'

Alex and Mary were taking a breather when Steven returned to the table, so he sat next to them. 'Have you made you're mind up about the computer?' he asked.

Mary looked troubled and glanced at Alex to answer. 'Yes we have,' he answered, 'we're going to take it out.'

'But why?' asked Steven, 'we know what the problem is now.'

'I know, but you see, we can't do anything about it. I had a word with Sam, and we tested the power supply next time he cleaned the chutes. Sure enough there was a surge.'

'There you are then,' said Steven.

'It's not as easy as that,' sighed Alex, 'It appears that sometimes they have a special mix so they have to have an extra cleaning session. That means that Sam can't guarantee the times when the plant will flush the chute.'

'Well we can get a UPS,' said Steven.

'It's not just that,' said Mary. 'I've been doing some invoices, and to be frank, it's not saving me a lot of time.'

'But we could work on that,' said Steven.

'No Steven,' said Alex gently. 'It's not on.'

'But there's no need for you to worry,' said Mary. 'We've taken it home, and the kids think it's great for space invaders. And Alex is going to do his church manager's minutes on it, aren't you?'

'Yes, that's right,' agreed Alex. He looked at Steven's crestfallen face and said, 'It's not your fault Steven, you did the best you could.'

'Yes, but it wasn't good enough.'

'Don't be silly,' said Mary. 'None of us knew about the power supply problem, and you've proposed a solution which will work. But we don't want to spend any more money on it.'

'I suppose you're right,' agreed Steven.

'Of course we are. Come on, give me a dance, and cheer up!'

'What a night!' sighed Steven as he put his slippers on and relaxed into his armchair.

'You can say that again!' said Margaret, as she slumped opposite him, 'my feet are killing me.'

'Everybody seemed to enjoy it,' continued Steven. 'Apart from Anne and Nigel of course.'

A frown crossed Margaret's face, 'Ye...ss,' she said.

'What's the matter? Come on, out with it.'

Margaret straightened herself up in her chair, and looked directly at Steven. 'Nigel says you and Anne are having an affair,' she said quietly.

'You what!' cried Steven.

'You heard. Nigel says you are having an affair with Anne.'

'That's preposterous.'

'Is it?'

'You know it is.'

'How do I know?'

'Because I love *you*.' Steven crossed the room and sat on the arm of her chair. 'How can you believe such a twisted liar like him?'

'I just don't know. She's very attractive, and I know you like tall slim women.'

'Of course I do. I'm married to one. But I swear, there is nothing going on between us. Nigel's only trying to get his own back because of Maxine.'

'Your probably right,' admitted Margaret with a sigh.

'You know I'm right,' said Steven. He put his arms around her and gave her a loving kiss which, after some hesitation, she returned. 'Well tonight's settled one thing,' he continued.

'What's that?'

'There's no way I'm going to work for Anne and Nigel.'

'I think you're right,' smiled Margaret.

'So I'd better start looking for another job.'

'Why?' asked Margaret in surprise.

'Because being a consultant is putting too much strain on our marriage.'

'Don't be daft.'

'I'm not being daft. Do you know what Alex and Mary are going to do with their computer? Take it home and play space invaders on it.'

'I know. Mary told me.'

'Oh!'

'And she also told me it wasn't your fault, and that I hadn't to blame you.'

'Oh!'

'And then John told me that I've forbidden you to work for him.'

'I only said...'

'I know what you said, and it's right. But you could have found a more tactful way of doing it.'

'I'm sorry.'

'So you should be,' laughed Margaret.

'Alan says the Governors want me to become the Treasurer,' said Steven.

'There you are then.'

'Where am I?'

'Staying as a consultant, silly.'

'Do you mean that?'

'Of course I do,' said Margaret laughing up at him. 'Where else would we get such good experience?'